ADVANCE PRAISE FOR THE ESMERALDA GOODBYE

Corey Lynn Fayman's THE ESMERALDA GOODBYE is a finely crafted coming-of-age story. Lovers of classic crime fiction will recognize the homage in the title—Raymond Chandler's PLAY-BACK was set in Esmeralda, a thinly disguised version of La Jolla, CA. Through Fayman's historical lens, a Who's Who of 20th century figures and one young police officer discover there's meanness and mayhem aplenty in their 1950s seaside paradise.

    ALAN RUSSELL, number one bestselling author of BURN-ING MAN

Fans of James Ellroy rejoice! The Esmeralda Goodbye is a startling and shocking snapshot of an era, with gritty prose that grabs you by the throat.

    DAVID PUTNAM, author of the bestselling Bruno Johnson series

Jake Stirling, a naive cop with a haunted past, is put to the test in Corey Fayman's latest page-turning thriller, THE ESMER-ALDA GOODBYE. Worthy of Raymond Chandler, who figures centrally in the novel, Fayman deftly balances a noir whodunnit with a keen portrayal of the social and political environment of the 1950s as Hollywood celebrities, the FBI, and the criminal underworld converge in the exclusive beach town of La Jolla, a toxic combination that results in murder.

ONA RUSSELL, Award-winning author of the Sarah Kaufman historical mystery series and host of Lithub's AUTHORS IN THE TENT.

ALSO BY COREY LYNN FAYMAN

Also by Corey Lynn Fayman:

Black's Beach Shuffle

"A terrific start to this series." *Mysterious Reviews*

"Swift, compelling chapters that are rife with interesting characters."
La Jolla Village News

Border Field Blues

"A powerful new voice on the crime-fiction scene, Corey Lynn
Fayman delivers a potent dose of sex, drugs, and rock 'n' roll."
ForeWord Reviews

"A rollicking and fast-paced crime novel." *San Francisco Book Reviews*

Desert City Diva

"Fans of wisecracking California crime solvers will enjoy this
working- class PI with a poet's soul." *Booklist*

"Offbeat characters and popular musical lore distinguish this
decidedly unusual tale." *Publishers Weekly*

Ballast Point Breakdown

"A crisp, fast-paced fourth in series P.I. mystery with contemporary
tones readers won't be able to put down. Highly recommended."
Chanticleer Reviews

"This standalone installment will satisfy both newcomers and series
fans with a fascinating mystery and colorful cast." *Booklife*

Gillespie Field Groove

"Lovers of a good mystery story and music will enjoy this book which is as musically educational as it is thrilling." *Booklife (Editor's Pick)*

"Gillespie Field Groove hits all the right notes. Music fans and general mystery readers alike will enjoy this story's irresistible beat." *Blue Ink Review (starred review)*

THE ESMERALDA GOODBYE

THE ESMERALDA GOODBYE

COREY LYNN FAYMAN

KONSTELLATION
PRESS

Published by Konstellation Press, San Diego

www.konstellationpress.com

Editor: Lisa Mathews

Cover design: Corey Lynn Fayman

ISBN: 979-8-9868432-5-4

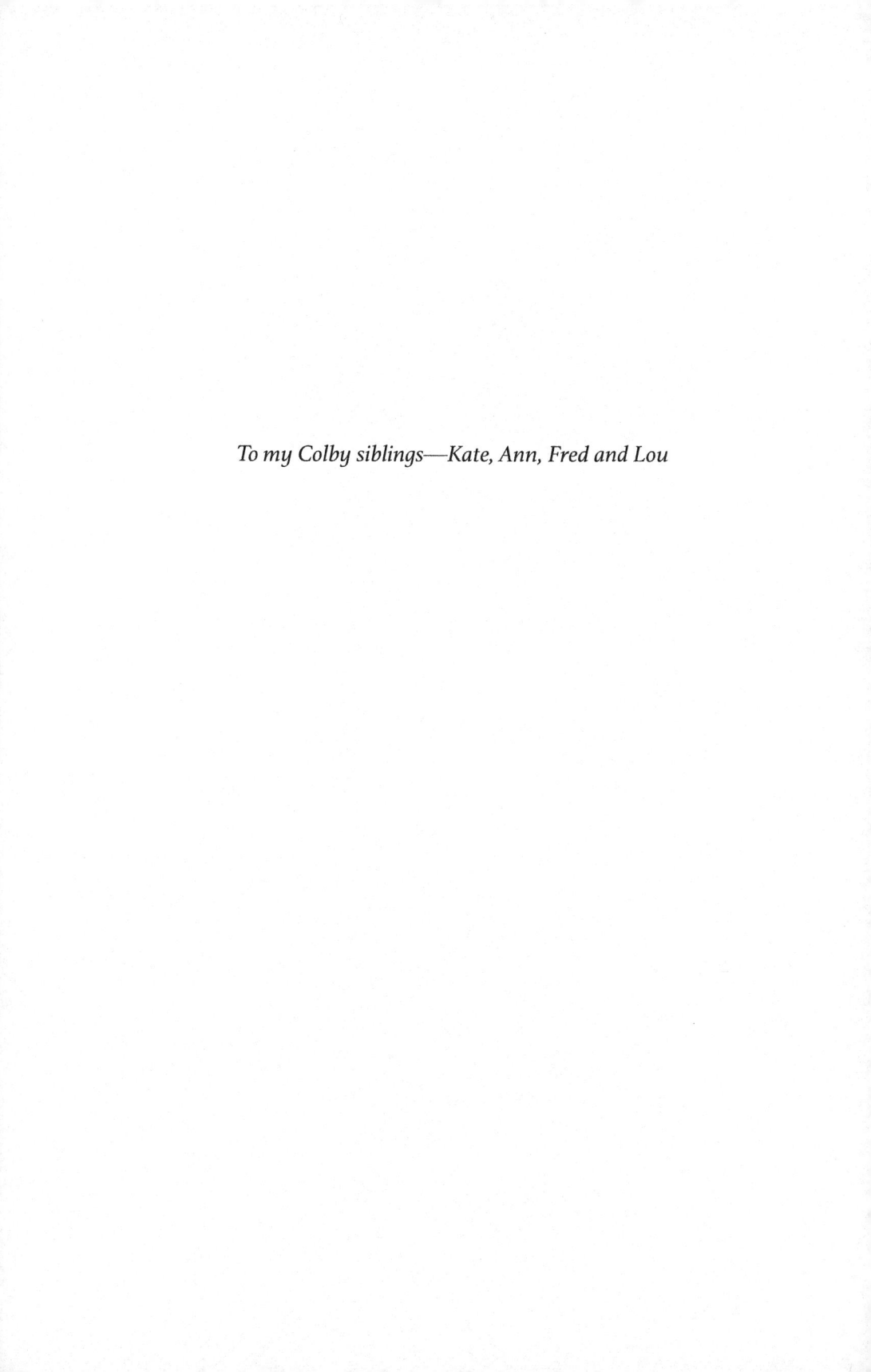

To my Colby siblings—Kate, Ann, Fred and Lou

1

O fficer Jake Stirling parked his patrol car near the sharp curve on Camino de la Costa, glanced at the house across the street and wondered if the man inside had killed himself yet. He opened the car door and climbed out. Waves crashed on the rocky shore below, where skeletal silhouettes of abandoned artillery batteries loomed against the purpling sky, remnants of a U.S. Navy training facility from the Second World War. The roar and rumble of those guns had been a regular feature of Jake's life when he was a kid; practice rounds fired by Navy recruits soon shipped out to sea. The guns had gone silent after the bombing of Hiroshima ten years ago. The Japanese invasion of La Jolla, California had never arrived.

He crossed the street and walked up the steps to the front door of the house. The lights were on inside, but the curtains were drawn. He knocked and then took a step back and to one side like he'd learned in his training. Rookies often drew the La Jolla beat their first year. It was quieter than other parts of the city. But a drunk with a gun was dangerous, even if he lived in a nice house by the sea. The door opened.

"Good evening, Mrs. Denton," Jake said, recognizing the woman in the doorway. Mabel Denton and her family lived in the colored section of town. She cleaned and cooked for rich people. Her husband ran a window-cleaning business. Solid citizens. Their son Willie went to school with Jake's brother, Danny.

"Jake," she said. "What are you doing here?"

"Is this Mr. Chandler's house?"

"Yes. I work for Mr. Chandler sometimes. What is it?"

"Mr. Chandler called the station," Jake said. Mrs. Denton looked unconcerned, but she always seemed imperturbable, like Jake's mother. Women with quiet strength, who'd raised young children while their husbands went off to war. "He said he was going to shoot himself."

Mrs. Denton frowned.

"Oh, dear," she said. "I guess you'd better talk to him. Come in."

Jake crossed the threshold and followed her down the hallway.

"I left Mr. Chandler in the study ten minutes ago," she said. "I took him some tea. He seemed very tired. So sad. His wife died a few months ago."

They arrived at the study. It was a leathery room with a heavy wood desk and a reddish-brown easy chair in front of the fireplace. The chair was empty.

"He took the phone," said Mrs. Denton, indicating a cable that ran from the wall, along the carpet and out another doorway. She raised her voice. "Mr. Chandler? Where are you? There's someone here to see you."

No one answered. Jake felt the back of his neck tingle.

"Mr. Chandler," he yelled. "This is Jake Stirling of the San Diego Police. Captain Lennox asked me to look in on you."

A loud bang from the back of the house made them both flinch. Jake unsnapped his holster, put his hand on the butt of his gun.

"Mr. Chandler," he said, tracking the phone line down the dark hallway. "This is Officer Jake Stirling of the San Diego Police Department. Captain Lennox wanted me to check on you. Are you hurt?"

He reached a closed door at the end of the hallway. A dim swath of light leaked out from beneath it. Something rustled on the other side of the door.

"Mr. Chandler, are you okay?" Jake said. "If you're injured, if you're alive, please say something."

"Cissy," a voice said from behind the door.

"That was his wife," Mrs. Denton whispered. "Her name was Cissy."

Jake nodded.

"What's on the other side of this door?" he said.

"It's the bathroom," she said.

"I'm sorry to hear about your wife, Mr. Chandler," Jake said, addressing the man behind the door. "Just put the gun down and let's talk about it."

There was no answer.

"Mr. Chandler?"

"I'm doing it," the voice said from behind the door. "I'm doing it now."

Mrs. Denton shouted, "No, no."

Jake shoved the door open. In the dim light he saw a man lying in a claw-foot tub, dressed impeccably in coat and tie, white shirt, and dark slacks. A steel revolver glinted in the man's hand as he turned the barrel toward his mouth.

"Stop!" Jake screamed, leaping toward the tub. A deafening blast assaulted his ears as he fell on the man and a blizzard of wood chips exploded around him. He ripped the gun from the man's hands, stood up and stepped away from the tub. He broke the gun open, emptied the cylinder and put the bullets in his pocket. The gun was an ancient revolver, rusty and loose. It was a wonder the thing hadn't fallen apart. The man in the tub began to weep.

"I'm a damn coward," he burbled through tears. "I couldn't do it."

"Are you injured, sir?" Jake said. "Are you hurt?"

"I'm a fake," the man said. "A namby-pambly milksop."

A light went on in the hall. Mabel Denton stood outside the door.

"Is he okay?" she said.

Jake nodded. He felt his heart thump, waves pounding against the shore of his ribcage. He couldn't speak.

"Mr. Chandler?" said Mrs. Denton, addressing the man in the tub. He didn't respond.

"Let's get him out of there," Jake said, his voice returning somehow. Mrs. Denton stepped into the bathroom. The man in the tub continued to sob.

"Oh, Mr. Chandler," Mrs. Denton said, leaning down to address him. "What have you done to yourself?"

"I want to be with Cissy," the man in the tub said.

"I know, I know. She was a lovely person. But she wouldn't want you to act like this. It's undignified."

"Go away," the man said. He turned on his side and folded in on himself. "Leave me alone. I'm going to sleep."

"Not in the bathtub, Mr. Chandler. Let's get you to bed."

Mrs. Denton tugged at the man's sleeve. He shook her off.

"Leave me alone. Go away. I'm a yellow coward."

Mrs. Denton looked over at Jake.

"He drinks too much," she said. "It's been worse since his wife died. I don't know what to do."

"We can't leave him there," Jake said, thinking of his own father, who used to sit at the kitchen table every night with a six-pack of Schlitz, scratching in his notebook and staring out the window, the beer, and his father, gone by the time Jake and his siblings woke up the next morning. John Stirling got drunk every night for six months straight, until the night he drove his car to Windansea Beach and walked into the ocean. He'd been gone for three years.

"Mr. Chandler," Jake said. "I need you to get out of the tub. We need to make sure you're not injured."

Chandler opened his eyes and lifted his head, giving Jake the once over.

"You're a cop," he said, resting his head against the rim of the tub.

"Yes, sir. Jake Stirling of the San Diego Police. Captain Lennox sent me."

"Lennox?"

"Captain Lennox, sir. He said you called him."

"Lennox is a bastard. I'm onto him, you know. He's a fucking crook."

"Watch your language, Mr. Chandler!" said Mrs. Denton. "You know Mrs. Chandler wouldn't want you to talk that way."

"Cissy's dead," said Chandler. "I can say whatever I want without her damned Victorian fussing."

Chandler went still, as if focused on something behind his eyes.

"Cissy," he said, slumping back into the tub.

Mrs. Denton looked over at Jake.

"What should I do?" she said.

Jake rubbed his forehead then pulled the handcuffs from his belt.

"You can't do that, Jake," she said as he leaned down and clamped the cuffs to Chandler's wrists.

"Why not?"

"He's a writer. Raymond Chandler. He's famous."

"I don't care who he is. I'm following protocol. Attempted suicide is a crime in this state."

"Is he going to jail?"

Jake stood up.

"They'll check him into the psych ward at the hospital for a few days."

"He didn't mean what he said about Captain Lennox. He drinks too much. He's grieving."

Jake sighed and put his hands on his hips.

"I need to get back to my car and call this in. You stay here and keep Mr. Chandler company. I have to follow the rules."

Mabel nodded, acquiescing. Jake walked back down the hallway. He exited the house, crossed the street, reached in his car for the radio mic and put in a call. The operator squawked back at him. Jake requested an ambulance, gave the address. The operator confirmed. He placed the mic back in its cradle, leaned both arms on the roof of the car and took a deep breath.

An exhilaration surged through him like rushing water. This was why he'd become a cop. To serve and protect. He'd put his life on the line and saved a man from killing himself. He hoped Captain Lennox would take note. Jake Stirling hadn't screwed up. He'd handled the situation.

Except ... he'd gone pretty hard at Mr. Chandler, jumping into the tub and taking the gun away. Maybe too hard. Chandler could have been hurt. Some expensive bathroom fixtures might have been broken. The whole incident seemed a blur now, a noisy violence in his head. Mabel Denton had said her employer was famous and Mr. Chandler could afford domestic help, which meant he was wealthy. Rich people didn't like having their lives interrupted by policemen, especially a wet-behind-the-ears rookie who pulled them over for speeding or running a light, who showed up at the front door with complaints from the neighbors. The wealthier denizens of La Jolla treated cops like they were servants.

The gun. Where was the gun? He checked his pockets for the bullets he'd emptied from the cylinder. They were still there, but he couldn't remember what he'd done with the old revolver. He must have left it somewhere in the house, putting it down absentmindedly while he talked to Mabel Denton. He'd catch hell if the captain showed up and found the weapon still in the house. Captain Wade Lennox was the toughest cop in the city, a war hero who'd single-handedly taken down two Japanese machine-gun nests on Iwo Jima, who'd saved Jake's father after the two of them were ambushed by the city's biggest mobsters. Wade Lennox had walked away from every fight he'd been in, leaving his enemies defeated or dead. People said he'd be chief of police someday. In the meantime, his job was to make new recruits miserable.

The moon had started to rise. A solitary surfer sat out on the water, a dim and familiar silhouette. The silhouette waved. Jake raised his hand in reflex then turned and headed back to the house. He needed to retrieve Mr. Chandler's revolver before the captain or anyone else arrived on the scene. He wanted his incident report to be perfect, tied up with a bow. It wasn't just Captain Lennox. The whole police department had its eyes on him. The whole town. Because of Jake's father and the man on the surfboard. Because of the thread they'd unraveled together.

Jake pulled on his earlobe as he crossed the street, wondering how long the ringing would last. He thought of the day when the Navy's training guns had shut down, when their thumping gave way to silence, and peace descended on his little town like a resonant fog. His family had been happier then. Everyone had been happier.

2

Jake seated himself at the counter of Gene's Waffle Shop in downtown La Jolla, three blocks from the police substation. It was eight in the morning, and he'd just finished an overnight shift. He ordered his usual—bacon and eggs, a side of biscuits and gravy. Other people's breakfast was his dinner. A man entered the restaurant and took a seat next to him.

"Good morning, Jake," he said.

"Good morning, Mr. Miller."

"Starting your day or just finishing?" Miller said, noting Jake's uniform.

"I worked graveyard last night," Jake said.

"Anyone from the arthritis gang give you trouble?"

"No, sir. Pretty quiet last night. Not a peep."

"You've been on this beat a while. Shouldn't they have moved you to a more exciting part of the city by now?"

Jake shrugged. He'd been working the La Jolla beat a year and a half now. Captain Lennox had apologized to him last December, saying something about cutbacks and hiring freezes, but Jake wasn't unhappy with his assignment. It was boring sometimes, but it kept him close to his family, supporting his mother, watching little sister Lucy grow up, and keeping teen-aged brother Danny in line.

"Your dad worked the La Jolla beat his first year," Miller said. "Before he became a detective. I met him at one of Candace DuBarry's beach parties. Your dad had to break things up and send everyone home. He was a good man. He'd be proud to see you in uniform."

"Thank you," Jake said, staring into his coffee as he stirred in cream and sugar. He didn't like it when people talked about his father. He didn't like people telling him what his father would think, not even Mr. Miller, who was a decent old guy who spent his days playing tennis, spearfishing, and diving for lobsters, his nights drinking at the Whaling Bar with the local wags, impressing visitors from back east with his permanent tan.

The waitress brought Jake's order and poured a cup of coffee for Mr. Miller as he glanced over the front page of the San Diego Union. Miller had been a reporter once, covering the harbor beat. At some point he'd collected the stories he wrote for the paper, put them in a book, sold the book to a publisher and made a million dollars. *I Cover the Waterfront*. That was the name of the book. Someone made a movie based on the book. Someone wrote a song about it too, the song they used for the theme of that old Jack Webb radio show, *Johnny Madero, Pier 23*. Jake had never read the book. He didn't read much. Not like Danny. Danny read everything.

"What do you think of this bomb, Millie?" Miller said, addressing the waitress.

"What bomb?"

"Says here in the paper the Navy tested an atom bomb off our coast last year. Blew it up under water."

"I wasn't living here then," Millie said. Mr. Miller continued to read from the paper.

"Operation Wigwam they called it," he said. "Top secret.

Some of the scientists from the oceanographic institute were involved. Says here they're studying the uptake of atomic radiation in mackerel. You might want to check your tuna fish sandwiches for radiation."

"Really?"

"I'm joking. I think. Here's a quote from Dr. Revelle. *The atomic bomb is going to be a wonderful oceanographic tool.* Hmm. I wonder what Caleb Shapiro thinks about that."

"I don't like hearing about bombs," said the waitress.

"Absolutely right, Millie," said Miller, rustling through the newspaper. "It's not a proper topic for breakfast. Let's see. Racing season starts soon. You ever go, Jake?"

"I don't gamble," Jake said.

"Good for you," Miller said. "It's a dirty business. The racetracks are all run by gangsters."

"I didn't know that," Millie said. She was a pleasant-looking young woman, a little older than Jake, with a relaxed confidence he found attractive. She'd moved to La Jolla to wait out her divorce. That's what she'd told Jake, anyway.

"Oh sure, Millie," said Miller. "Gangsters launder their money through racetracks. Our politicians know it, but none of them do anything. Too many pockets getting the grease."

"I won twenty dollars at Santa Anita one time," Millie replied. "Before I moved here. I like watching the horses. And looking for movie stars."

"You ever see any?"

"I saw Elizabeth Taylor there last year. She's so beautiful. John Wayne came into a restaurant where I used to work, with his family. He looked kind of old. Did you know he wears a toupee?"

Max Miller chuckled.

"Ah, Millie. It's always disappointing when you peek behind the curtain."

"What do you mean?"

"Nothing. It doesn't matter. The Hollywood hordes will

descend upon us soon, with racing season and the Playhouse both starting up. The Texas oilmen will rustle up their fancy rancho and the town will get noisy, like it does every summer."

"I like a little noise," said Millie. "I like having people in town."

"You're young, Millie," said Miller. "Young people like noise and excitement and parties."

"You get invited to a lot of parties, don't you, Mr. Miller?"

"Oh yes, I'm a shiny trinket for the blue bloods to display, like one of those extravagant pieces of jewelry they haul out for the Jewel Ball every year. Everyone likes to have a writer or two at their soirées, someone exotic to class up the occasion. Not too many though, just enough to keep things from becoming a total bore."

"It sounds like fun to me," Millie said.

"I'd rather go fishing most of the time," said Miller. "But an old hack like me can't resist free booze and canapes. You never get over your hungry days. Ever since Ray Chandler debarked for merry old England, my wife and I are on everyone's list for these kinds of things."

"Chandler?" Jake said. "Is he that writer who lives on Camino de la Costa, near the old gun batteries?"

"The very same, Jake. He sold the house, though. Dear Ray has departed our shores for the promised land of his childhood. He never did warm up to our little village and once Cissy was gone, things took a turn for the worse."

"Who's Cissy?" said Millie.

"His wife," Jake said. "Mr. Chandler tried to kill himself after she died."

"Oh!" said Millie. "That's so sad."

Mr. Miller glanced at Millie, then swiveled his head toward Jake, a glint in his eye.

"Our young policeman was there, Millie. He may not have realized it at the time, but Jake saved the life of a great writer. It was in the newspaper."

"It was?" Millie said, turning her attention to Jake. "When did this happen?"

"Last year," Jake said, looking down at his coffee. "April, I think. It wasn't me in the newspaper, though. Just a little article about Mr. Chandler calling the police and saying he was going to kill himself."

"Jake here showed up and grabbed the gun right out of Ray's hand," said Miller.

Jake turned back to Mr. Miller. "How'd you know that?" he said.

Miller smiled. "This is my town, Jake. I know everyone. Including the local crime reporters."

"I didn't talk to any newspaper reporters."

"A certain police captain might've bragged on you. Off the record."

Jake stopped eating for a moment, placed his silverware back on the plate. He couldn't believe Captain Lennox had said anything good about him to newspaper reporters. To anyone. Lennox had rarely given Jake any sort of encouragement, not even an 'attaboy'.

"That's right, Millie," Miller continued. "Jake here saved my friend Ray. Almost got himself killed when that old gun went off. Ray got to live another day, win another award, make another pile of money, then tootle off to the old country to get his knob polished by the landed gentry, the ungrateful bastard."

Millie laughed. "You're funny, Mr. Miller," she said, then left her spot behind the counter to check on the customers sitting in the booths. Jake watched her in the mirror on the wall behind the counter. Millie glanced back at him and smiled.

"Nice girl," Miller said, catching their look. "You should ask her out sometime."

Jake looked down at his coffee. He felt his skin flush. He and Millie had been dating for a month. They were trying to keep it a secret until Millie's divorce came through.

"I'm glad Mr. Chandler's feeling better," he said, picking up his fork and scratching at his hashed potatoes. "Did Captain Lennox really talk about me?"

"That's what I heard," Miller said. "Though knowing Wade as I do, I'd lay odds it was mostly to make himself look good. Crediting himself for hiring you."

"Mr. Chandler didn't like Captain Lennox," Jake said.

"Ray doesn't like anybody, Jake. I wouldn't worry about it."

"He called him a crook."

"You don't think your boss is a crook, do you Jake?"

Jake shook his head. "No. Of course not."

"Well, when Ray's in his cups he's liable to say anything. The man sees corruption in everyone and everything. He's a misanthrope through and through."

"What's that mean? Misanthrope?"

"It's a disease writers get. When they peek behind the curtain too many times."

Jake creased his brow and stared at his plate. He couldn't understand Mr. Miller sometimes. The high school English teachers had talked a lot about writers using symbols and metaphors, but Jake always had a hard time with it. He didn't understand why they needed to make things so complicated. People should just say what they mean. Or not say anything.

"Well," Miller said, filling the silence that had fallen between them. "It's probably a good thing Ray's gone back to England. For him and for us. His personality was always more suited to rainy climes than sunny ones."

"Yeah, I guess."

"As far as your boss goes, I wouldn't worry. Your dad knew him. He never told you Lennox was a crook, did he?"

"No. He always said Wade, I mean Captain Lennox, was a hero. He saved my dad's life."

"Well, there you go. Who are you going to believe—your dad or a jaded old pulp writer?"

Jake nodded. "I didn't believe Mr. Chandler," he said. "I just wondered why he said it."

"He was probably working on a novel. Making stuff up."

"Yeah, I guess," Jake said. He pushed his plate away from the edge of the counter, pulled two dollars out of his pocket and slid the bills under his coffee cup. Fifty cents would be a generous tip, but he didn't want to cheat Millie. He stood up and reached for his hat on the counter.

"Good to talk to you Jake," Miller said.

"You too, Mr. Miller."

"How's your mother?"

Everyone knew Jake's mother from her job at the Mayfair grocery store. People asked about her all the time.

"She's doing fine," Jake said.

"Well, say hi to her for me."

"I will."

Jake put his hat on and turned toward the door.

"Say, Jake," said Mr. Miller. "Maybe you can help me?"

"What is it?"

"I got a letter from Ray about a week ago. He asked about that gun you took away from him. That old Webley. He'd like to get it back."

"He didn't claim it before he left town?"

"No. I guess not," said Miller. "Is there some way he can get it sent to his address in England?"

Jake shrugged. "It should be in evidence storage. Downtown. You'd have to talk to the clerks. I don't know if they can send something like that to England. You might need to claim it in person and send it yourself."

"Yeah, that's what I thought."

"He should just buy a new gun if he needs one. That thing was falling apart."

Miller nodded, acknowledging Jake's point.

"That's what I told him," he said. "Ray says the gun has sentimental value. He said he killed Germans with it."

3

Grace Stirling surveyed the dining room table. Roast beef, mashed potatoes, and green beans. Bread and butter. Apple pie for dessert. The rest of the week's meals might come out of boxes and cans, but on Sundays she tried to do something special. It was the one day of the week she felt she had some control over her life and her family. Her children had drifted away from her, becoming separate planets, but Sundays were still the center of a shared solar system, when elliptical orbits intersected at the dinner table.

She tried not to think of how much she'd spent on the roast, how she'd have to scrimp elsewhere. Her children deserved a nice dinner as much as rich families did, maybe more. Sunday dinner had become a magical adhesive that held the family together after John's passing, after Jake had moved out of the house and started working as a policeman. It was an anchor of hope and domestic dignity. She would survive. Her children would thrive. They would overcome the difficulties of their father's faithless act. Once the children were safe and secure, she could look to her own happiness. Mr. Hartwell, from church, had asked her out on a date last week. She'd demurred, but he'd promised he'd ask again. She might not decline the next time.

"Dinner's ready," she called to the back of the house.

Jake walked into the dining room. Lucy trailed behind him, carrying a plush toy, a blue and white octopus. Lucy's room was filled with sea creatures—dried sand dollars and starfish, plastic and plush versions of crabs, seahorses, turtles, and various fish. Jake had brought the octopus earlier, wrapped in gift paper. He'd missed Lucy's birthday last week.

"Something smells good," Jake said, sounding just like his father.

"Roast beef," Grace said. "Sam at the market picked it out for me. Where's Danny?"

"In his room. He's reading."

Grace sighed. Danny always had his nose in a book. He was the least sociable of her three children, the most withdrawn and rebellious, the one who got in trouble at school. The school administrators had put him in a special homeroom this year, a classroom for kids who were disruptive or just didn't fit in—kids who argued with teachers, read comic books, kids who wouldn't stop doodling or playing drums on their desks.

"Danny!" Grace called. "Dinner's ready."

There was no answer. Lucy propped her octopus on the edge of the table and sat down. Jake took his place at the head of the table. Grace raised her voice.

"Daniel Stirling, get in here now!"

She started towards the back of the house just as Danny walked into the room, reading. He took a seat at the table across from Lucy, his nose in his book the whole time. Danny's agility while reading astounded Grace, like a high-wire circus act. Her children were brilliant and confounding, each one remarkable in different ways.

"Danny," she said. "It's time to put down the book."

"Just a minute," he said.

"Now!" Grace insisted. Danny raised his hand as if to push his mother's voice away.

"Danny!" Jake said, becoming the boss. "Do what your mother says."

Danny dropped his hand, dog-eared a page, and closed the book. He looked over at Jake.

"She's your mother too," he said.

"Of course," Jake said. "But you're the one who's not showing respect."

"Now, boys," said Grace. "Let's not fight."

"She's all ours Mommy," Lucy chimed in.

"Yes, Lucy," said Grace. "You're all special to me. Now, who wants to say grace?"

"I do, I do," Lucy said. Her mother nodded. They all bowed their heads. Lucy cleared her throat and began.

"Thank you, God, for this roast beast. And for our Mommy who cooks it. Thank you for our father who is in heaven. Blessed are we who do hunger and thirst. And thank you for my octopus. Her name is Veronica. Amen."

"Amen," said the others.

"That was very nice, Lucy," Grace said. "Now put your octopus under your seat and pass your plate to Jake so he can give you some of this lovely roast beef."

The table fell silent for a moment as everyone passed their plates to Jake. He put two slices on each plate, the smaller well-done bits for Lucy and the larger, bloody middle cuts for Danny and himself. Grace split the difference, taking the pinkish cuts in between. They passed the potatoes and beans.

"You may begin," Grace said. Her children attacked their food with exuberance. Grace didn't mind the enthusiasm, but she insisted on proper etiquette, like Emily Post.

"Lucy, chew with your mouth shut ... Danny, hold your fork properly ... Jake, elbows off the table."

Once table manners had been addressed, they could begin a proper conversation. It had always been important to Grace that everyone get a chance to speak, that they share their lives and thoughts at the dinner table. It was something she and John had cared about equally, until the last six months of John's life when her husband lost interest in his family, went silent, and began drinking too much. Grace wanted her children to be adept at conversation, to be able to discuss things politely while dining, and not just shovel in food.

"Jake," she said, starting with her oldest, "Do you have any news you'd like to share?"

"What?" Jake said. "Oh, yeah. I got a promotion."

"What's a promotion?" Lucy asked.

"It's when you move up to a bigger job."

"Like when I go to fifth grade next year?"

"Yeah. Kind of like that. You get paid more."

"How much do you make?" Danny asked.

"Shush, Danny," said Grace.

"What?"

"It's not polite to ask someone how much money they make."

"That's stupid."

"It's okay, Mom," Jake said. "I'm a certified patrolman now, a union man. I make three hundred and fifty dollars a month. That's more than four thousand a year."

"Wow!" Lucy said. "That's a lot of money."

"Not really," Danny said. "Mr. Shapiro makes eight thousand dollars a year at the Ocean Institute. And he's not even a scientist. Miss DuBarry makes seventy thousand a year. She doesn't do anything."

"Miss DuBarry is rich," Jake said. "She comes from old money. How do you know all this anyway?"

"Rachel told me about her dad. Willie told me about Miss DuBarry."

"And how would Willie Denton know how much Miss DuBarry makes?"

"He saw her tax return when he was cleaning windows at

her house. Working for his dad. He said it's hard not to look at things in people's houses sometimes."

"I'm sure it is," said Grace. "But Willie needs to keep his eyes to himself."

"And he shouldn't go around telling people how much money other people make," Jake said.

"Why not?" said Danny.

"The wrong people will hear about it," Jake said. "Con men. Crooks."

"That's dumb. It's not like people don't know the DuBarrys are rich."

"Now, boys," said Grace. "Let's drop the subject. We should be happy for Jake. He makes more than I do. He can buy his own roast beef."

"Yay for roast beast!" crowed Lucy.

They all laughed. Grace felt relieved to have changed the subject. It bothered her when the children talked about money, especially other people's money. A lot of the kids they went to school with came from wealthy families. She didn't want her children to covet what those families had. She coveted it herself sometimes. It was difficult not to. She turned her attention back to the table.

"Danny, what book is that you're reading? I can't see the title."

"Oh, nothing," Danny said, looking disconcerted. His eyes darkened when he glanced at the paperback book on the table, as if he'd forgotten it was there. He grabbed the book and slipped it into his back pocket. Grace knew the look. It was just like the one Jake had given her after she'd found the girlie magazine under his bed, back when he was in high school. Grace put out her hand.

"Let me see the book," she said.

"Give her the book, Danny," Jake said.

Danny glared at his older brother a moment, then reached in his back pocket, pulled out the book and handed it to his mother. She glanced at the front cover and wrinkled her nose.

"The Killer Inside Me," she said. "That doesn't sound particularly edifying."

"It's about a sheriff who sleeps with prostitutes and murders people," said Danny. "It's all from his point of view."

"It sounds hideous." Grace frowned.

"Why do you want to read something like that?" Jake said.

"I think it's interesting. Getting inside the criminal mind."

"It's disgusting, that's what it is," Jake said. "What gives this guy the right to write stuff like that?"

"The Constitution of the United States," said Danny. "That's what."

Jake rolled his eyes.

"Books like that are disgusting," he said. "They undermine the fabric of society. People need to respect authority. Watch Dragnet if you want to learn about law enforcement."

"That show is dumb."

"It's what cops really do. They don't go around murdering people."

"How do you know?"

"Well," Grace said, raising her voice to intercede. "One thing I do know. This is not a subject for dinnertime discussion. I will have a look at your book, Danny. You and I can talk about it later."

"Mom?" Lucy said.

"Yes?"

"What's a prostitute?"

⁓

AFTER DINNER, Danny retreated to his room while Lucy sat with her new octopus and watched Disneyland on the Philco. Grace washed dishes in the kitchen. Jake dried. After they'd finished, he pulled a five dollar bill out of his pocket and handed it to his mother.

"What's this?" said Grace.

"A little extra," Jake said. "To help out."

Grace took the bill.

"Thank you. That's wonderful news about your promotion," she said. "I know your ... I'm proud of you."

She'd almost told Jake his father would have been proud. It was true, but that wound was still painful for Jake. He couldn't remember the good man his father had been, only the miserable man he'd become, the man who'd abandoned his own family. She wanted to hug her son, damp his pain with a motherly embrace, but he was too old for that now, resistant to maternal affection. Jake worried about weakness, about not being strong enough. There was a remoteness in him, like his father, a moat around his interior castle. Another woman might find a way in. A woman stronger than Grace. A woman who could soften the blow of what Grace planned to say.

"Lucy likes her new octopus," she said, redirecting her thoughts for the moment. "Where did you find it?"

"At the Cave Shop." Jake chuckled. "I think she'd prefer a real octopus though."

Grace looked at him quizzically.

"Last week," Jake continued. "When I took them to Cove Beach. Todd DuBarry was there. Snorkeling. He'd speared an octopus. Lucy couldn't stop looking at it."

"You talked to Todd?"

Jake nodded.

"How is he doing?" Grace asked. Jake shrugged. A dark look crossed his face. Grace waited. Jake wasn't good at holding back truth.

"Danny was kind of a jerk about Todd," he said. "He called him a pervert. He grabbed Lucy and tried to drag her away."

Grace sighed. She tilted her head and rubbed her temple, wondering if the pain would ever go away.

"I'll talk to Danny," she said. "It wasn't Todd's fault, what happened to your father."

"I know. I apologized for Danny's behavior."

Grace nodded. Jake always did the right thing. In some ways, life would be even harder for him than Danny. Now was as good a time as any to tell him about her decision, the changes she wanted to make. She pointed to a shoebox on the kitchen counter.

"That's for you," she said. "I've been cleaning out your father's old things."

Jake walked over, picked up the shoebox and pulled off the lid.

"Is this Dad's old badge?" he asked. His mother nodded.

"And his medals," she said. "I thought you should have them. He was a good cop, Jake. All his friends on the force told me that. I know you'll be a good policeman too."

"I hope so," Jake said, flipping through a notebook he'd found in the box. "What's this?"

"Those are his case notes," Grace said. "About the *Creeper*."

"These should be stored in the evidence room, along with the case files."

"It's a copy," Grace said. "Every night, when your father got home, he'd take everything he'd written down in his case notebook and write it in that one. He said it was important, if he lost the other one or something happened to him. That all his notes would be safe."

Jake leafed through the notebook, trying to decipher his father's handwriting.

Grace cleared her throat. "There's something I've been thinking about. I wanted to talk with you before I tell Danny and Lucy. It's about your father."

Jake paused, looked up from the notebook. Grace steeled herself, found her courage.

"I want to start the legal process," she said. "To make it official. To have John declared dead. He's gone. We need to move on."

Jake tilted his head and stared at the floor. Grace tried to read the emotions flickering over his face, divining his thoughts, but she knew it was pointless. People often mistook Jake for dull-witted, but they had it wrong. He was deliberate. He worked over his thoughts until he felt sure of what he wanted to say.

"What happened to your father," Grace said. "It wasn't Todd DuBarry's fault. And it wasn't yours either."

Jake lifted his head and turned to look at her.

"Dad's gone," he said. A flat tone. Controlled. "I know that. I know he's not coming back."

4

Jake sat on the bed of his second-story apartment, studying the notebook his mother had given him two weeks ago. It was his father's old case notebook, a duplicate of the original that was stored with the rest of the case files in the police department's evidence building downtown. Jake had the night off, but he'd caught the graveyard shift all week and found he could only sleep during the day. He'd been to the movies with Millie and walked her home afterwards. Their date ended earlier than he'd wanted it to. Millie had to open the Waffle Shop the next morning. She needed her beauty sleep. There was nothing on TV except a test signal. He had a long evening ahead of him with nothing to do.

John Stirling's detective badge lay on the night table next to the bed. Jake hadn't yet decided what to do with his father's badge and medals, torn between displaying them in a memorial box or hiding them in a drawer. The medals provided shiny evidence of his father's professional achievements, but the notebook contained items of more compelling interest to Jake, a glimpse inside his father's mind, especially in the twenty pages of notes on the *Creeper* investigation, the case Detective John Stirling had never closed, the case that had ruined him.

Everyone in the San Diego Police Department agreed that John Stirling had been a top-notch detective—smart, dedicated, and fair. They also agreed that he'd lost his way, drowned himself in alcohol and resentment after the town he lived in turned against him, after his investigation uncovered sordid doings among La Jolla's moneyed class, shining an unwelcome light on unspoken arrangements.

Repercussions from the investigation included at least three divorces and more than one lawsuit. Jake had played a key part in the cataclysm. He'd followed his conscience, told the truth, but in doing so had destroyed his closest friendship and brought disaster down on his own family. As he reviewed the pages of his father's notebook, it felt like a talisman, a mysterious key that might unlock secrets of the great calamity.

The *Creeper* was the department's unofficial name for the mysterious prowler who'd set the town on edge the summer after Jake's high school graduation. Someone leaked the name to the press and local newspapers soon flashed it in their headlines. The *Creeper* had never injured anyone or stolen anything of great value, but his actions were unsettling, especially for a populace that took pride in never locking their doors. A mist of paranoia slipped into the town's consciousness like a morning fog sweeping in from the sea.

The *Creeper* struck late at night and in the early hours of morning before daylight. The first reports seemed almost hallucinatory, stories from wealthy matrons who'd returned to their homes to find pieces of furniture rearranged, doors left open, clear indications that someone had been in the house. Nothing of value went missing, not at first. Later victims noted personal knickknacks or pieces of jewelry that had disappeared from their houses—insignificant trinkets they could barely believe anyone would want to steal. The crimes seemed more disconcerting than dangerous, but they put everyone on edge, worried about an escalation. The *Creeper* had a preternatural gift for striking when no one was around, as if he knew everyone's schedule. Finally, an arrest was made. Everyone breathed a sigh of relief. Then came the news that the young man they'd arrested was the town's high school hero—Todd DuBarry, Jake's best friend and heir to the New Haven DuBarry fortune. Touchdown Todd. TD.

Late one summer night a police officer on patrol had spotted a shadowy figure leaving the Bruning mansion on Mt. Soledad. When confronted by the officer, the suspect claimed he was only out for a late-night walk. Todd DuBarry was eighteen years old at the time, just out of high school. His All-American reputation might have given the patrolman a reason to let him go if the patrolman hadn't asked Todd to empty his pockets first. In Todd's front pants pocket was a woman's watch, crusted with diamonds. When Todd refused to provide a credible explanation for having the timepiece, the cop felt sure he'd captured the *Creeper*.

What the police didn't know at the time, but Jake did, was that Todd DuBarry had a box full of other people's jewelry stashed in the back of his closet in the family mansion of glass-encased modernism that sat alone on the cliffs between Cove Beach and the Shores. Todd had shown the collection to Jake while they were in high school and sworn him to secrecy. But the day after Todd's arrest, Jake broke his vow. He told his father about the stash of items he'd seen in Todd's hiding place. A warrant was served, the DuBarry's house searched, the stash confiscated. Todd was officially charged. The *Creeper* had been caught. The DuBarrys hired a lawyer.

From the very start, though, John Stirling found the evidence against Todd perplexing. None of the items in Todd's collection matched the items claimed as missing in the *Creeper* reports. None of the victims identified Todd's items as belonging to them. Todd, under advice of the lawyer his family had hired, refused to give any information on how he had come by them. None of the items could be matched to the burglary reports. Frustrated, John Stirling interrogated his own son, hoping to dislodge some pertinent information about Todd's mysterious treasure. And Jake had provided the answer. His father questioned some of the victims again. And others, who provided reluctant alibis for the young man. Todd was released. All hell broke loose.

Gigolo. The first time Jake heard the word was after Todd was released, when Grace Stirling said it to Jake's father at the kitchen table one night after all the kids were in bed. *You mean to tell me Todd DuBarry's a gigolo?* Jake's father confirmed her question with an affirmative grunt. It was Danny who told Jake what the word meant. Before long the whole town began whispering the g-word—at restaurants, cocktail parties, and club lounges. Teenagers muttered it under their breath when they passed Jake in the street. Everyone knew Jake was Todd's best friend. There were rumors that Jake was a gigolo too.

John Stirling tried to keep a lid on the case, but the stories leaked out anyway. At bridge clubs and luncheons, people whispered the names of the men and women who'd given Todd money and gifts. The accused fired back, declaring they'd only been friendly with the young man, that he'd lied to them, showed up at their front door asking to use the phone or get a drink of water as a pretext to robbing their house. They were shocked to discover that Todd, the All-American boy, had taken advantage of their hospitality. They accused the police department in general, and John Stirling specifically, of besmirching their reputations. After Todd was released, some went as far as hiring lawyers and bringing litigation against the department. Jake's father was named in all the lawsuits.

Other bombshells were dropped. Todd had been born out of wedlock. He wasn't his father's biological son. Unfounded rumors about the DuBarry's marriage began to circulate— that Miss DuBarry had been ostracized by her own family, a black sheep banished to California for her libertine ways, that her husband was a practicing homosexual, that they'd adopted Todd in his early teens as a sex slave to fulfill both their physical needs. There was no evidence for any of these wilder speculations, but the DuBarry's known interest in modern art, avant-garde theater and the New Left was proof enough for many, clear symptoms of a sickness that might lead to such depravity. There was even some sympathy for Todd, given the godless and immoral homelife he'd been forced to endure. He was a sweet young man, taken advantage of by his parents and others.

Despite the distractions, Detective John Stirling stuck to his findings. He convinced the district attorney to drop the case against Todd DuBarry. Todd's parents sued the police department and the city, lost their case, and were divorced soon afterward.

Jake stared at the notebook, reviewing a chart his father had drawn across two of the pages. It was a list of stolen items and victims, dated in chronological order with a set of initials at the end of each line, either TD or OWL. Jake assumed the TD stood for Todd DuBarry. Touchdown Todd. TD. He didn't know who or what OWL represented. Was it the initials of another suspect or shorthand his father had invented to note some other aspect of the case?

The last time Jake had spoken to Todd was at the beach when Lucy became fascinated with the octopus, when Danny went crazy and called Todd a pervert. Jake pulled Danny away and made him apologize, then sent Danny and Lucy back to the car while he made his own apology, hoping to lessen the distance that had come between himself and his best friend. Todd's only crime had been being too obliging and good-looking. That's what Jake's mother used to say, back when the rumors first broke. Something had changed in Todd since his high school days. A dim confusion had replaced the playful sparkle in his eyes.

Before that day at the beach, Jake had only seen Todd from

a distance, out in a boat or down by the beach, looking weathered and rough, but still as strong and handsome as he'd been in high school when Todd and Jake played on the football team, Todd at quarterback and linebacker, Jake as his back-up and tight end. Jake was too slow to qualify for an athletic scholarship, but Todd had been recruited by both Oregon State and UCLA. Todd hadn't gone to college, though. Soon after the *Creeper* case ended, his parents cut off his trust fund. Todd drifted, doing odd jobs, sleeping on the beach, sponging off rich girlfriends and sympathetic old ladies. Everyone knew what Todd had done or thought they did. Those that required his services knew where to find him. Everyone else could pretend he'd gone away. It didn't seem fair.

Jake closed the notebook and placed it on the nightstand, then walked to the sink and brushed his teeth. He stared at his face in the mirror. It was complicated being a cop in the town where you grew up, a small town where rumors spread like wild mustard on the side of the road. Jake had answered domestic disturbance calls from civic luminaries, confiscated liquor from younger siblings of former classmates, and broken up backseat trysts of married couples—married to other people he knew.

Transgressors who recognized Jake often leaned on their shared familiarity to plead for leniency, but others became hostile. They brought up Jake's involvement in the *Creeper* case, his association with Todd DuBarry, and the shadow of John Stirling's lingering shame. Jake treated the offenders equally, keeping his professional cool. He didn't tell tales. Discretion was part of his job.

John Stirling would be officially dead soon. Jake's mother had submitted her petition. She'd begun to move on with her life. Danny would graduate high school in a couple of years, if he didn't kill himself on his roller board first. Lucy would be a teenager. The town was growing up too. There was talk of a state university that would be built on the mesa above the ocean institute. The professors and graduate students who moved to town would be well-educated and worldly.

Jake planned to leave the past behind too. The police department would transfer him to another district eventually, somewhere in the real world, and he needed to make the best of the time he had left. His feelings toward Millie felt more substantial than he'd felt before. She was different than the girls he'd dated in high school, confounding him with her self-deprecating humor and steely commitment to speaking her mind. Millie wasn't coy or kittenish. She didn't hide her opinions and said no when she meant no. Her divorce would be final by the end of the summer. They could move on.

He turned out the lights, crossed to the window and looked down on the street. It was still dark outside. He checked his watch. The Waffle Shop wouldn't open until six-thirty. He'd go in around eight, eat breakfast for dinner and talk with Millie as much as she'd let him. Then he'd come home and sleep, rise before the light faded and prepare for the night shift. The summer season was getting into high gear. Day trippers and tourists had started filling up the beaches and restaurants, the shops, and the streets. Politicians, movie stars and other various eminences would pass through town like a traveling circus, exotic creatures from another world. It was the busiest time of the year. For waitresses as well as policemen.

5

A crowd of teenage boys and one girl stood on the northwest corner of Nautilus Street and La Jolla Scenic Drive overlooking the Muirlands, or Manure-lands as they liked to call it, an unimproved subdivision near the crest of Mount Soledad, which wasn't really a mountain, just a tall hill. Tomorrow was the first day of summer vacation. They'd trekked up the street together after the final school bell. Each of them had put in a quarter for the privilege of watching Danny Stirling kill himself. The feeling was mutual. Danny hated them too.

Danny sat on the sidewalk, inspecting the wheels he'd attached to a thick plank of wood. He'd stolen the wood from a construction site during spring break, then taken the wheels off his sister Lucy's roller skates and attached them to one side of the plank, building his own version of a contraption he'd seen in Life Magazine. Since then, he'd traveled around town on his homemade roller board, pushing it along with one foot until it picked up enough speed that he could stand on top and coast for a while. It was faster than walking, but not by much. Going down hills was where you got some real speed.

This wasn't the first time Danny had tried to go down Nautilus Street on his roller board, but no one had been there to witness his previous efforts. He'd never started this far up the hill, which meant he'd hit the first curve at a much faster speed. The second curve worried him more than the first. He'd crashed there before, pushed by centrifugal force into the curb.

"This is stupid," said a voice in the crowd. "You'll never make it."

Danny looked over at the crowd. Rachel Shapiro, with her arms crossed, glared at him. She was a big girl, taller than all the boys and thicker than most of them, except maybe Earl Johnson, who was built like a truck and had started on the varsity football team his first year in high school.

"You want your money back?" Danny said, glaring back at Rachel. She'd put up a quarter, just like the boys. It was Rachel who'd dared him to do it in the first place, calling him on his boast. She seemed to be having second thoughts.

"No," she replied. "I'm just saying it's stupid."

"It'll be worth it, Stirling," said Earl Johnson, "just to see your smart ass get smashed."

The rest of the boys laughed. Rachel frowned. Danny stood up and inspected the wheels again.

"Stop stalling," said Earl. Other boys joined in, goading him on. Danny smiled. He had three and a half dollars in his pocket, which was three more than he'd started with that morning. Three dollars he'd taken from kids who would pay to watch a classmate get mangled or killed. They were rich boys, most of them, spoiled jerks whose parents passed out ten dollar bills for a weekly allowance. As far as Danny was concerned, he'd already won by taking their money. Now it was just a matter of surviving his trip down the hill, not breaking any bones. His mother would kill him if he ended up in the hospital. She could barely afford food for the family, let alone a hospital bill.

He walked to the other side of the street and stared down the hill, lining up the first curve. The angle would be better from this side of the street, allowing him to shoot through the first curve without turning. Turning was dangerous. That's when you crashed. The boys hoped he'd crack up. They hadn't yet realized he'd be out of sight after the first curve. None of these dopes had thought of that. Danny sat down on the roller board, bracing it in place with his feet. He adjusted his position then lifted one foot and placed it on the board.

"Hey," Earl Johnson said. "You're supposed to stand on the thing."

"I said I'd go down the hill on it," Danny replied, giving Earl the stink-eye. "That was the bet."

"I think you're yellow. Just like your dad."

The crowd gasped, but no one challenged Earl's assertion. Danny felt the heat rising inside him, the shame. He wanted to bash Earl Johnson's face in, maybe crack him across the side of the head with his roller board.

"Car!" someone shouted. Danny put his foot back down on the street. He couldn't see any cars below, so it must be on the street above, La Jolla Scenic, driving down from the big white cross on top of the hill.

"Cheese it!" another voice said. "It's the cops!"

The crowd chattered and stirred. Danny turned his head and saw the front half of a patrol car pull up to the corner. The rest of the car was blocked by the crowd. He heard a car door open and close.

"Afternoon boys," said a familiar voice. "What's all the excitement?"

No one said anything. Two boys at the edge of the crowd started creeping back down the hill. Rachel turned to look at Danny with an alarmed look on her face. She said the words without making a sound, exaggerating the shape of her mouth to warn Danny, but he already knew.

"C'mon boys," Jake Stirling said. Danny's brother, the cop. His head and shoulders came into view as he stepped onto the sidewalk above. "I know trouble when I see it. What're you up to?"

The crowd turned to look at Danny. Jake followed their gaze. His eyes settled on Danny.

"What the hell are you doing?" he said. Danny stared back at his brother, returning Jake's approbation with a surly defiance.

"Don't even think about it," Jake said. He moved toward Danny, the other boys parting in front of him like a biblical sea. Even Earl Johnson seemed cowed by the young cop. Danny lifted his left foot and placed it onto the roller board as Jake stepped into the street.

"Danny Stirling, I'm warning you," Jake said, pointing his finger at Danny. "You stop there. Right now!"

Danny stared at his big brother, contemplating his options. He had an excuse now, a direct order from a policeman not to go down the hill. On the other hand, the cop was his older brother. Jake had been telling Danny what to do ever since their father had died, when Jake decided he was the man of the house. Danny was sick of Jake's moralizing bullshit and stupid rules. He was sick and tired of everyone—the teachers who penalized him for being disruptive, the spoiled rich kids and their exclusive cliques. He wouldn't let Earl Johnson, or any of them, call him chicken. Something had happened to Danny's father. Something had gone wrong inside his head, a sickness that infected his brain. But he wasn't a coward. Danny didn't want to give the boys their money back either. He turned his head and looked down the hill.

"Danny!" Jake cried, charging at him, but it was too late. Danny pulled his right foot onto the sled and rolled down the hill, eluding Jake's grasp. Someone screamed, probably Rachel. Girls always screamed like that, even smart ones like Rachel.

Danny felt the wind in his face as it blew through his hair. His eyes watered as he picked up speed. He grabbed both sides of the board and hung on, focusing on the midpoint of the first curve below. The only thing on his mind now was survival. If he hit it just right, he could shoot straight through the first curve, if there were no cars headed the other way up the street. The roller board's wheels rattled and screeched as it accelerated. He leaned to the left as he entered the curve, straining to maintain his line, fighting centrifugal force. The sled shot through the inside of the turn, missed the ridge of the sidewalk by less than an inch then careened out of the curve and over the median line into the opposite lane. The kids on the hill would lose sight of him soon. He could put his feet down, brake to a stop and run the rest of the way to the high school. He'd get there before any of the other kids even saw him. He'd win.

He couldn't beat Jake, though. He couldn't outrun Jake's police car. His only chance of escape was to continue down the street at top speed, all the way to the bottom. He shifted his weight to the other side of the board, crossed back over the median line and prepared to enter the big, sweeping curve near the bottom of the hill. The road wasn't as steep there, but the sled had built up a lot of speed. He couldn't shoot through the second turn like he had the first. It was longer, with a tighter angle.

He drifted to the far side of the road, setting up his entry into the turn, then glanced further down the hill. A car appeared below, headed up the other side of the street.

"Shit," Danny yelled. The car wouldn't hit him, but he'd have to delay his drop into the curve, hanging onto the outer part of the turn until the car passed. He hunkered down and gripped the sled tighter, making himself smaller as he entered the curve. The forces of centrifuge pressed against him, pushing out toward the edge of the street.

The car honked and swooshed past. The sled skidded across the asphalt and slammed into the curb, flipping Danny over the sidewalk and into the air. He floated there for a moment, hanging in the sky like Wile E. Coyote in those cartoons at the movie show. Then, just like the coyote, he plunged into the canyon below.

WILLIE DENTON HAD JUST EXITED the concrete bunker embedded in the earth below Nautilus Street when a body hurtled into the sky above him and landed face first in the ice plant. A plank of wood tumbled down the slope and came to rest by his feet.

"Holy cow!" Willie said. "Is that you Danny?"

Danny groaned but didn't move. He kept his face planted in the ice plant.

"Is anyone up there?" he asked.

"I don't see no one," Willie said, checking the street above. Danny pushed himself up to his knees. There was a long streak of blood on his right cheek.

"Jake's going to arrest me," said Danny.

"Shoot," Willie said. Everyone knew Danny Stirling's big brother was a policeman. Willie's parents had warned him not to mess with the police, that cops would arrest colored boys just for breathing. But Danny Stirling was okay. He liked Willie's drawings. Danny said Willie's drawings were a kick in the teeth, *supermurgitroid*. Danny Stirling looked scared now, like a mouse in a cage.

"I know a place you can hide," Willie said. "Follow me."

6

It was just before noon when Caleb Shapiro and his boss, Roger Revelle, walked onto the grounds of the Del Charro Hotel and headed toward the pool. The Del Charro was located at the intersection of Torrey Pines Road and La Jolla Shores Drive, two miles from the village, but only a twenty-minute walk from the oceanographic institute where they both worked. The walk had given Revelle time to fill Caleb in on the men they were about to meet—Texas oil barons Clint Murchison and Sid Richardson, who owned the hotel. Revelle thought Caleb's engineering acumen would be useful to the discussion but claimed ignorance as to the reason for their summoning. Revelle was the institute's captain. He steered it with a strong hand, straight and true, and would probe for an angle that benefitted the bottom line.

According to Caleb's boss, each weekday morning at four o'clock two tables were set up under the umbrellas by the hotel's pool, one table for Murchison and one for Richardson. Two phones were placed on each of the tables. At the other end of the phone lines were secretaries in Dallas, who kept the lines open all day, transcribing letters and transferring calls. The two men had made their fortunes in Texas oil, but they did business all over the country, and had expanded their empire to include racetracks and uranium mines. Dallas was their home, but from opening day at the Del Mar racetrack until Labor Day they resided at the Del Charro. They'd built the hotel for that purpose. Murchison's wife and family sometimes stayed at the hotel with him. Richardson was a confirmed bachelor.

Both men were on the phone when Caleb and Revelle entered the patio. One of the men finished his call, then stood up and walked over to them.

"You Revelle?" he said, extending a hand.

"Call me Roger," said Revelle. "This is our chief engineer, Caleb Shapiro."

"Clint Murchison," said the man, shaking hands with them. "You can call me Clint. Have a seat. Sid will be over just as soon as he gets off the phone."

The three men seated themselves at the table. A waiter in a white coat appeared.

"Good morning, Silvio," said Murchison. "I'll have my usual. Would either of you fellas like something to eat or maybe a drink?"

"Nothing for me," said Revelle.

Caleb shook his head, declining the offer. Men like Murchison made him nervous. Their capitalist arrogance seemed amoral to him, an echo of the German industrial barons who'd turned their factories into war machines for the Nazis, men who lived only for profits and claimed only ignorance when the true nature of their operations became known. Still, this was America, where men were free to make fortunes without interference from government trespass. Those fortunes leaked money and Revelle had a gift for catching the drips. Caleb felt like he had the greatest job in the world—for an engineer, anyway. Every day provided new stimulation—planning and building equipment that would measure the oceans, adding to the store of human knowledge.

He could make room for capitalism and the U.S. military if he needed to. It didn't mean he'd have to vote for Eisenhower.

The other man, Sid Richardson, joined them at the table. As the men introduced themselves, the waiter returned with a glass of brown liquid for Murchison, with plenty of ice.

"Jim Beam," Murchison said, eyeing Caleb after he took a sip. "It's cocktail hour for me. I've been up since three-thirty this morning."

Caleb nodded, hoping he hadn't looked disapproving. People often said he looked disapproving or judgmental when he only meant to be attentive.

"Well, gentlemen," Revelle said, taking that lets-get-down-to-business tone Caleb recognized from institute meetings. "What can we do for you?"

"Undersea oil," said Murchison.

"What about it?" said Revelle.

"They're drilling for it in the Gulf of Mexico, off the Texas and Louisiana coasts."

"Yes," said Revelle. "I'm aware of that."

"You think there's any out here?" said Murchison, waving his hand in the general direction of the Pacific Ocean.

"Possibly," Revelle said. "Probably."

"I've heard there's some fields off the coast of Santa Barbara."

Revelle nodded.

"That's true. But if you want to drill here, you're going to have to go down a lot deeper than they will in Santa Barbara. We've got a deep trench here, just off the coast. The engineering costs alone would be prohibitive."

"But you think there might be oil out there?" Murchison asked.

"No idea," Revelle said.

Sid Richardson leaned forward.

"We understand that you and your scientists have done

some research with atomics, that you exploded an a-bomb in the ocean."

Caleb glanced over at Revelle, wondering how he would respond. Operation Wigwam was still an official secret, but everyone seemed to know about it. There'd been an article in the local newspaper. Revelle tossed the question back to Richardson.

"Where did you hear that?" he said.

Richardson grinned.

"Clint and I have friends in Washington. Hell, I could call Ike up right now and get the information from him, but that seems like a waste of the president's time when we've got someone like you here, someone directly involved with the tests."

"Information about atomic testing is classified," Revelle said. "Top secret. I can't reveal any specifics about the tests I was involved in. If you gentlemen can explain where your interests lie, perhaps I could assist you better."

Richardson leaned back in his chair and looked over at his partner.

"You want to explain our idea to them, Clint?"

Murchison finished his drink, rattled the ice cubes, and set the glass back on the table.

"Sid and I are in the energy business," he said, nodding at his partner. "Our company owns half the producing oil wells in Texas, but it's getting more and more expensive to buy land there and test for new fields. Too many wildcatters and corporations getting into the game. Then Mr. Charlie came along. You heard of him?"

Revelle nodded. Caleb had no idea who they were talking about.

"Who's Mr. Charlie?" he said.

"Charlie's a new kind of drill platform," said Murchison. "They call it a MODU, for mobile offshore drilling unit. You can sail it out to sea, drop anchor and drill. Down to about forty feet, twice as deep as any previous offshore well."

"You'll need to go down more than forty feet around here," said Revelle. Murchison nodded, then continued his explanation.

"We missed out bidding on those gulf leases Louisiana put up for auction back in '45," he said. "California was selling some offshore leases last year, but Sid and I didn't like the way they were priced. Then we heard about this operation you were involved in, this Wigawam thing. You see Sid and I own uranium interests too. We've got access to all the ingredients. We were thinking that you and your scientist friends at the institute might be able to do something for us."

Revelle furrowed his brow and pursed his lips.

"I'm not sure where you're going with this, Mr. Murchison."

Sid Richardson jumped into the conversation again, like an enthusiastic puppy.

"Out there, on the ocean, it's free. Open range, just like the old days in Texas. No leases. No government rules."

Caleb still didn't get it or didn't want to. He didn't like the two men. A light went on in his boss's eyes. Revelle had figured it out.

"You're proposing to drill for oil outside of territorial waters, is that it?" said Revelle. "On the high seas?"

"That's right," said Murchison. "What do you think?"

"I think it'd be a hell of a challenge," said Revelle. "You're the engineer, Caleb. What do you think?"

"Well," said Caleb, stalling for time. It was the most ridiculous thing he'd ever heard, but he needed to be diplomatic. His boss had a way of noodling around on a topic until he figured out some way to get money for the institute, sometimes for research already underway.

"It would certainly be difficult," he continued. "I'd have to study this Charlie rig and see how it works. You'd have to go down hundreds, if not thousands, of feet in the open ocean. I doubt the current technology can scale to that depth."

"Your other problem," said Revelle. "Is prospecting. There's a lot of wild ocean out there. You can't just walk along the shore looking for seeps."

"That's where the a-bomb comes in," said Richardson.

Caleb frowned. He didn't like where this seemed to be leading. Revelle cleared his throat. They both waited. Richardson looked at them both for a moment, then continued.

"We heard some things about these underwater bomb tests," he said. "That they're stirring things up down there. And we got to thinking that maybe one of the things they would stir up would be evidence of where oil fields might be. Under the mantle, where it's weak. We wondered if all of them fancy instruments your scientists use could test for oil coming out of the deep."

Revelle chuckled.

"Well, gentlemen, that is either the most hare-brained idea I've ever heard or it's genius. What do you think, Caleb?"

"I think it's crazy," said Caleb.

"Have we built any tools that could measure for evidence of oil?"

"No, but, well ..."

"Yes?"

"It's probably doable. Some sort of underwater spectrometer might work."

"Excellent," said Richardson. "How much money would you need for something like that?"

Caleb glanced over at Revelle, hoping he wasn't taking this seriously. The institute had far more important things to do than help two cowboys poke around the ocean for oil. Revelle stared at his hands a moment, then spoke.

"Caleb and I can discuss this," he said. "And get back to you. There's some other challenges you'd have to consider."

"Such as?" said Murchison.

"Radiation," said Revelle. "If you blow up a bomb, any oil you release is likely to be radioactive."

"Can't you get rid of that radiation stuff somehow, in the processing?" said Richardson.

Revelle shook his head. "There's no way that I know of," he said. "And all products processed from radioactive oil would be radioactive too. All up the line. It wouldn't be safe for oil workers or consumers."

Clint glanced over at Sid. "I told you it wouldn't work," he said.

Sid shrugged. "Anything can work if you give it enough time and money," he said.

"True," said Revelle. "But I doubt it would be worth your investment. By the time those technical problems were solved, oil may be done for."

"What do you mean, done for?"

"Carbon release," said Revelle. He leaned forward and tapped his hand twice on the table, as if calling a classroom of students to order. "That's the problem with oil."

The two men from Texas stared at Revelle. They looked dumbfounded. Revelle continued his lesson.

"Some of our scientists are working on a new theory," he said. "You see, when we burn coal or gasoline, the carbon that's stored in them gets released into the air. That carbon's now in the atmosphere, not in the earth."

"What about wood?" said Clint Murchison. "People burn wood."

"It's the same," said Revelle. "When you burn wood in your fireplace, the carbon stored in that tree gets released into the air."

"I don't get it," said Sid. "People have always burned stuff, ever since that first caveman invented fire."

"But not at our current rate," said Revelle. "With our automobiles and factories. As the industrial world grows, it's putting more carbon into the air every day. Every year. We may reach a point where there's more carbon being put into the air than is getting stored back into the earth. The molecular composition of the atmosphere will change which means our weather will change. Quite dramatically."

A woman's laugh rang out across the concrete patio. The men turned their heads to look for its source as a lively and glamorous trio—a redhead and a blonde with a dark-haired man between them—exited the lobby and made their way to a waiting limousine. The driver opened the door for them. They climbed in.

"That fellow looks familiar," Revelle said, as the driver closed the door and walked around to the other side of the limousine.

"That was Mr. Arnaz," said Sid Richardson. "From TV. And his wife, Lucille. And their friend, Miss Gabor."

"I meant the driver," said Revelle.

"Todd DuBarry," Caleb said. "He worked for us at the institute. Cleaning the aquariums and checking the diving equipment."

"Good-looking kid, isn't he?" Richardson said. "I let the guests use my limo sometimes. He comes with it."

Clint Murchison cleared his throat. He rattled his ice and glanced up at the sky. "This change in the weather you were talking about, professor. Is it going to get hotter or colder?"

Revelle shrugged his shoulders. "We don't know enough yet to predict that," he said. "Probably both. The first thing we're going to test is the ocean. If this theory about carbon release proves true, the temperature of the ocean will rise over time. That's one of the things we're studying right now."

"Well, that's real interesting, professor," Richardson said, rising from his chair. "We'll take that under advisement. Thank you for coming by."

"Yes, thank you," Murchison said, staring at the ice melting in his whisky glass.

Caleb glanced at Revelle. They'd been dismissed.

7

————

D anny Stirling sat inside the concrete bunker at the bottom of the ravine below Nautilus Street, where Willie Denton had hidden him after his roller board accident. It had been a good place to lie low. Jake and the schoolboys never caught up with him. He and Willie had become friends that day, sitting in the cool darkness of the bunker, comparing rumors about their least favorite teachers, and trying to guess which of the varsity cheerleaders had gone all the way. They'd worked together since then to fix up the place, installing cinder-block bookshelves, empty milk crates for chairs and a cable spool they found in a back alley turned on its side for a table. All in preparation for this day—the first meeting of The Perverted Savants Club. Danny had come up with the name.

Someone tapped 'shave and a haircut' on the metal hatch. Danny slid open the spy window to see who it was.

"Have you brought an oblation?" he asked.

"A what?" Willie said, staring back at him.

"Evidence of perversions," Danny said.

"Oh, yeah," Willie said, holding up a thin, pocket-sized booklet. "I got one of those."

Danny opened the hatch and let Willie in.

"Wait!" a voice called. Danny shut the hatch. There were the rules. Club members had to follow protocol. Something went 'thunk' in the bushes outside.

"Shit," a voice said. Willie giggled. Danny slid open the spy window, saw Rachel Shapiro lifting herself off the ground. She wore a white blouse, a green-checked dress and saddle shoes. A drop of blood dribbled down her left knee.

"What happened?" Danny asked.

"What do you think?" Rachel said. "I tripped and fell. Now let me in."

"You have to do the secret knock."

"Just open the door, you jerk. I hurt my knee."

"No knock. No entry."

"Forget it," Rachel said, turning away. "I'm leaving."

Danny opened the hatch.

"Have you brought an oblation?" he asked. Rachel reversed direction and stalked back toward him.

"Here," she said, thrusting a small paper bag into his hands. "Let me in."

The boys drew back as Rachel stomped into the room. She was bigger than either Willie or Danny. Neither of them wanted to get in her way.

"What's this?" Danny said, inspecting the bottle nestled inside the bag.

"Manischewitz," Rachel said, surveying the room. She hadn't been inside the bunker since the day Danny had crashed his roller board. Jake and the other boys might have raced past that day, but Rachel had lingered on her way down the hill. She'd spotted Danny exiting the bunker to check if the coast was clear, accosted him and demanded her winnings. He'd extracted her promise not to tell anyone where he'd been hiding. She'd insisted on looking the place over. Willie spilled the beans on their plan for a clubhouse.

"What's Manischewitz?" Willie asked.

"Kosher wine," Rachel said. "It's Jewish. My parents drink it at Passover."

"Oh," Willie said. He scratched his nose. "Is it pervy?"

"What?"

"Your offering is supposed to be pervy."

"It's horrible stuff."

"We can use it for the initiation oath," Danny said.

"I can't stay long," Rachel said, taking the bottle back from Danny. "I got a summer job, working for my dad at the institute, cleaning the aquariums."

"I'm cleaning windows with my dad," Willie said. "What about you, Danny? Did your mom get you that job at the Cave Store?"

"Yeah." Danny nodded. "I have to start tomorrow."

They arranged themselves around the cable spool table, sitting on the overturned milk crates.

"Okay," Danny said. "The first meeting of the Perverted Savants Club is called to order. As president, I will make the first offering."

"Who made you president?" Rachel said.

"I did," Danny said. "I thought up the club. I get to be president."

"Seems like we should vote for the president," Willie said. "If we don't vote, you're like a dictator."

Danny sighed. "Ok, then, let's vote," he said. "Raise your hand to vote for me as president."

"To make it official, you have to be nominated," Rachel said.

"Okay, somebody nominate me," Danny said.

"I nominate you," Willie said.

"You have to say his name," Rachel said.

"I nominate Danny for president of the Perverts Club."

"The Perverted Savants Club."

"Yeah. That."

"I second the nomination," Rachel said. "Now we can vote."

"Okay," Danny said. "If you want me for president—"

"Say all in favor and your name."

Danny took a deep breath. He wondered if he'd made a mistake letting Rachel into the club. Girls made things so complicated.

"All in favor ..." he said, checking with Rachel for approval, "of electing Danny Stirling president of the Perverted Savants Club raise their hands."

He raised his hand. Rachel and Willie raised theirs.

"It's unanimous then," Danny said. "I'm president. Now, for the first oblation—"

"Are there going to be other officers?" Rachel said. "If it's a real club, it should have officers. You can appoint them."

"Jeez, Louise," Willie said. "Are all the meetings going be like this?"

"No," Danny said. "Willie you're vice-president."

"Cool, daddy-o."

"Rachel, you're the secretary."

"Why am I the secretary?"

"Because secretaries are girls," Willie said. "Everybody knows that."

Rachel set her mouth and crossed her arms.

"Dag Hammarskjöld is Secretary-General of the United Nations," she said. "He's not a girl."

"That's different," Danny said. "Listen, you can be secretary-treasurer. That's two jobs. More than either of us. How's that?"

"Fine," Rachel said. "But I'm not taking notes."

"Yeah, yeah, okay," Danny said. "You don't have to take notes. Can we start the meeting now?"

Rachel nodded.

"Okay," Danny said. "The first offering." He pulled a paperback book from his back pocket and presented the front cover.

"This is a book called The Killer Inside Me. It's a really sick book. I'm going to read a page from it."

He opened the book to a dog-eared page, squinted his eyes and started reading the section where Sheriff Ford beats his prostitute girlfriend to death. He finished the section and looked up at his friends. They looked suitably traumatized.

"That's horrible," Rachel said. "How can you read that stuff?"

"Yeah," Willie said. "That guy's really messed up."

"He's a psychopath," Rachel said.

"Yeah," Danny said. "That's what's so interesting. The story's told from his point of view. He was sexually molested when he was a kid. That's what makes him a pervert. He kills his regular girlfriend too."

"Yuck." Rachel shivered.

Danny turned to look at Willie.

"It's your turn," he said. "What'd you bring?"

"This," Willie said, placing a little booklet on the table. "It's this comic book. They call 'em Tijuana Bibles. It's just like other comics with the same characters except these are dirty. They're drawings of naked cartoon people. Like Blondie and Dagwood, or Mickey and Minnie. They're doing it."

"They have Mickey Mouse doing it?" Rachel said.

"Yeah. Here, I'll show you."

Willie flipped through the magazine, found the page he wanted and held it out in front of them. Danny laughed. Rachel covered her mouth.

"Oh my God!" she said. "Mickey's got a big penis."

Danny laughed again. "That is so great," he said. "Let me see it."

Willie passed the Tijuana Bible over to him. Danny leafed through it, giggling with a kind of maniacal glee.

"Where do you find things like that?" Rachel said, still in shock.

"Downtown," Willie said. "They got a lot of them at the sailor arcades by the plaza."

"My parents would never let me go there."

"You got to know how to ask for the right thing," Willie continued. "They keep these behind the counter where you buy cigarettes and gum. They got all different types of them bibles down there. Some of them have movie stars."

"Real movie stars?" Rachel said.

"Yeah, but, you know, drawings of movie stars. Not photos or nothing."

"But they ... you know, do they show ... I mean, like Mickey?"

"Oh yeah. The movie stars are all having sex and stuff."

"That's pornography," Rachel said, shaking her head in disbelief.

"I think it's great," Danny said. "Okay Rachel. It's your turn."

Rachel looked at the brown bag in her lap.

"I don't think I want to be part of this club anymore," she said. "My parents would kill me if they found out about this."

"I know my mom would kill me," Willie said.

"That's the whole point of the club," Danny said. "My mom tried to get rid of that book I read to you. Our parents, our teachers, the ministers, and politicians. All the adults. They don't want us to see this kind of stuff. They think they're protecting us."

"Protecting us from what?" Willie said.

"Real life. What really goes on in the world," Danny said. "It's a big front, a fake. Why do you think they put us all in the same class?"

"Cause we're perverts?" Willie said.

"I'm not a pervert," Rachel said.

"It's because we don't follow the rules," Danny said. "We don't act like they want us to."

"I follow the rules," Rachel said.

"No, you don't," Danny said. "You argue with teachers all the time."

"I do not."

"Yes, you do," Willie said. "You're always asking questions the teachers don't want to answer and telling them they're wrong about stuff. And you don't say God when we do the pledge of allegiance."

"Face it," Danny said. "We're all troublemakers. One way or the other. Too weird to fit into the system. They put us in that class together so they could keep an eye on us."

"They told my parents I was special," Willie said. "That's why I'm in the class. I like it. I get to work on my drawings."

"Yeah," Rachel said. "Who wants to be in the normal class? Those kids are all dopes."

"That's what they told us, wasn't it?" Danny said. "That we were special. That it was all for our own good. It's a lie. They're afraid of us."

"Who is?" Willie said.

"The system. The establishment. The people in charge."

"Oh."

"Think about it," Danny said. "Willie draws weird stuff all the time. Rachel asks a lot of questions and I'm trying to crack everyone up. The system can't handle kids like us, kids who don't act like sheep. We're in that class together because none of us fit in. We're a threat to their provincial way of life."

"What's that mean?" Willie said. "Provincial?"

"It means small town," Rachel said. "Narrow minded."

"It's worse than that," Danny said, bringing his voice down as if he were just now getting to the important part.

"What?"

"Well ..." Danny paused.

"What?"

"It's just that ... Rachel, you're Jewish. And Willie's colored."

"I'm not colored," Willie said. "I'm half-colored, half-Mexican."

"You really think that's why they put us in the same class?" Rachel said.

They were silent a moment.

"What about Bobby Bell?" Willie said. "He's colored. He's not in our class."

"Bobby Bell plays football," Danny said.

"So?"

"That's like a magic ticket," Danny said. "If you're good at sports, they let you in."

"Yeah. I guess. I'm terrible at sports."

"But what about you, Danny?" Rachel said. "You're white. Your brother's a policeman, for Pete's sake. Why did they put you in the class?"

Danny shrugged.

"Maybe it's because of your dad," Willie said.

"What about my dad?" Danny snarled, feeling the hot gorge rise in his chest, an anger he couldn't restrain.

"I don't mean nothing," Willie said, flinching at Danny's sudden ferocity. "It's just, you know, something my parents said."

"What did they say?"

"Calm down, Danny." Rachel tried to intercede, but Danny was still hot.

"What did your parents say about my dad, Willie?"

Willie cleared his throat and stared at the floor, looking penitent.

"Tell me." Danny persisted. Willie looked up at him.

"They said your dad might as well been a Negro, the way this town treated him."

Danny surveyed the room. The first meeting of the Perverted Savants Club hadn't gone as he'd hoped. It was supposed to be fun, but he'd run off at the mouth again and screwed things up. He and Willie had put a lot of work into the clubhouse, making it nicer inside. Cool and dark and secret. A place you could escape to and think about important things.

"Forget it," he said. "I'm sorry. You guys still want to be in the club?"

"Yeah," Willie said, brightening. "I like this place."

They both looked at Rachel. She glanced around the room, assessing Danny and Willie's decorative efforts as well as her own secret thoughts.

"Okay. For now," Rachel said. "I'll still be in the club."

Danny felt relieved. He hadn't totally messed up. With great ceremony, he placed the Killer book and the Tijuana Bible on the bookshelves he and Willie had assembled from scrap and painted with a coat of marine varnish.

"This is going to be our personal library," he said. "Our private collection of perversity. Stuff you can't find in the regular library. The truth they won't tell us. You can add more stuff to the shelf anytime. Anyone in the club is allowed to come in and read it."

Rachel opened the bottle of Manischewitz. She poured the wine into three little Dixie cups she'd brought with her and passed them out. Danny raised his cup.

"A toast," he said. "To the Perverted Savants."

"To the Perverted Savants," the others said, then bolted back their drinks. Willie coughed. Danny soured his face.

"I told you it was horrible," Rachel said.

8

Jake Stirling pulled his patrol car into the parking lot of the Del Charro Hotel in The Shores neighborhood. Three years ago, it had been nothing but horses and a barn, but two oilmen from Texas had purchased the property from Mrs. Marechal and turned it into a luxury resort, with a crescent-shaped swimming pool and a fancy restaurant called The Jacaranda Room, named for the magnificent, purple-flowering tree that served as its centerpiece. The main attraction for the hotel's more famous guests were the individual bungalows scattered about the property, private and discreet. Guests rarely interacted with the locals, but tonight one of the guests had been robbed and the manager had called the police.

Jake opened the door, climbed out of his patrol car, and headed for the registration office, located in a two-story building that overlooked the pool and its patio full of brightly colored umbrellas. The door to the registration office opened as Jake approached. The hotel's manager stepped out to meet him.

"Good evening, Mr. Witwer," Jake said. "Did you call the police?"

The manager placed his index finger against his lips. "Please keep your voice down," he said, "I don't want to disturb the guests."

Jake nodded.

"Come with me," Witwer whispered. Jake followed the manager past the lighted swimming pool, then down a winding concrete path that wound through a half-dozen darkened bungalows. They turned in at a bungalow with a light on over the front door. The manager paused on the stoop.

"You understand, officer," he said. "Our guests expect a certain amount of discretion when they stay here. The hotel prides itself on the privacy we are able to provide."

"Yes, of course," Jake said. He adjusted his hat, trying to look serious and professional.

"It's just that ... well, nothing like this has ever happened before," Witwer said. "We've never had a robbery or any sort of criminal activity. It's a sensitive matter for the owners."

"We'll do our best," Jake said. All he'd really do was take a statement and write a report. It was up to his boss, Captain Lennox, to keep the report under wraps once detectives were assigned to the case.

Witwer tapped on the door.

"Miss Gabor," he said. "It's the manager. Mr. Witwer. I've got a policeman with me."

The front door opened. A short woman in a powder-blue satin gown and a wreath-like coif of platinum blond hair examined the two men on her doorstep. She lifted her chin with an aristocratic tilt as she spoke.

"Thank goodness you're here," she said, drawing out syllables with a husky, European tonality.

"Can we come in?" said Mr. Witwer. The woman hesitated. Witwer continued. "I think it would be better if we discussed this inside. Privately."

The woman nodded. "Yes, dahling. Of course."

She opened the door wide and closed it behind them as Jake followed Mr. Witwer into the room.

"Please have a seat," she said, indicating an easy chair and a sofa near the door.

"Thank you," Jake said. "I'll stand for now, in case there's something I need to look at." He pulled his notebook from the breast pocket of his uniform.

"I'm Patrolman Jake Stirling," he said, his pencil hovering above the paper. "It's Miss Gabor, right?"

"That's correct."

"And your first name?"

The woman gave Jake a strange look, like he was stupid.

"Zsa Zsa, of course," she said. Jake wrote the name in his notebook. He wasn't sure he'd spelled it right, but he didn't want to ask. He felt like he'd done something stupid already.

"I understand something's been stolen from the premises," he said.

"It was a diamond necklace from my first marriage."

"And you're sure it was stolen?"

Miss Gabor raised her eyebrows. She seemed to raise the rest of her body up too. "What do mean by that?" she said.

"I mean ..." Jake paused. "Are you sure you didn't misplace it?"

"Certainly not," said Gabor.

"Was anything else taken?"

"My train case. The necklace was in the train case, along with my make-up and some earrings."

"I see," Jake said, jotting notes with his pencil. "A train case. That's one of those little round cases, like a large purse?"

"Yes, a powder-blue train case. The same shade as my gown."

"When did you last see the case?"

"This morning. After breakfast. I left around noon. With Mr. and Mrs. Arnaz. It was a splendid day to be by the ocean and watch the horses run."

"When did you get back?"

"It was after ten. I went to dinner after the races."

"Where did you eat?"

Miss Gabor sighed. She seemed annoyed. "At the Jacaranda Room, of course. Here at the hotel. Would you like to know what I ate?"

Mr. Witwer chuckled.

"No ma'am," Jake said, feeling chagrined. He wasn't a detective. He was just a beat cop. He shouldn't be asking so many questions. He just needed to file a report. "That won't be necessary. Why don't you just walk me through what happened after you got home."

"Very well," said Miss Gabor. "I came back to my room after dinner. It must have been ten-thirty or so. I went into the bedroom to change out of my clothes, then to the bathroom to do my toilette and prepare for bed. That's when I noticed the train case was missing. I'd placed it on the bathroom counter, you see, where I put on my makeup this morning. I returned to the bedroom to look for it, checked in the closet and under the bed. The train case was gone, with my necklace inside it."

Jake scribbled in his notebook.

"Was anything else missing?" he asked.

"No. Nothing else was disturbed in the least."

Jake finished scribbling. He surveyed the room. There was an open doorway leading to a small kitchen. Another interior doorway was shut.

"Is that the bedroom?" he said. "Do you mind if I take a look?"

"I would prefer that you didn't."

Jake raised his eyebrows a notch. Miss Gabor noticed.

"A lady's boudoir is her private place," she said. "I don't want strange men in my bedroom, running their hands through my delicates. Even an attractive young man like you."

"Yes, well," Jake said, feeling his face flush. "I mean ... is there ... a suspect? Can you think of anyone who might have stolen the necklace?"

"Oh yes," said Gabor. "It was Nicky. I saw him yesterday out by the pool."

The manager cleared his throat.

"He's not checked in as a guest," said Witwer.

"Who's Nicky?" Jake said.

Miss Gabor took a deep breath. Jake couldn't help noticing her curvy figure as it shifted under the silk nightgown. She was strange and exotic, unlike any woman he'd ever met. Miss Gabor brushed a wisp of hair from her face.

"His full name is Conrad Hilton Jr.," she said. "Everyone calls him Nicky. He's the son of my first husband, Conrad Hilton Sr. Nicky had quite a crush on me, which he confessed to me just before I married his father. He's always been angry with me for going through with the marriage. I had to fend him off several times when Conrad Sr. was out of town. Nicky's a gambler and a drunk. He's abusive. Just ask poor Elizabeth. He was astonishingly cruel to her."

"Who's Elizabeth?"

"Elizabeth Taylor, the actress. You do know who she is, don't you?"

"Yes. Is she staying here too?"

"No," said Mr. Witwer. "Miss Taylor is not one of our guests. Not at this time."

"Yes, well," said Gabor, distracted for a moment. "Elizabeth was married to Nicky, poor girl. She was a replacement for me, I suppose, in Nicky's heart and his bedroom. That's neither here nor there, I suppose. Cat in a sack, as my mother would say."

"Ma'am?"

Miss Gabor stared at Jake a moment, as if she'd forgotten he was there. "Yes?"

"Why do you think Mr. Hilton stole your necklace?"

"Nicky gave it to me when he was pursuing me. He asked

me to give it back about a year ago. He said I owed him that much, that it would be the honorable thing for me to return it. As if Nicky had any honor. He needs money, I expect. His father cuts him off from the family funds every so often when Nicky runs up his gambling debts."

"How much is the necklace worth?"

"Something in the range of ten thousand dollars."

Jake wrote in his notebook as Miss Gabor described her necklace—graduated round diamonds set in white gold with a three-carat stone in the center. The necklace was worth twice as much as Jake made in a year.

"Aside from yourself and Mr. Hilton, who else knows about the necklace? Who else might have known it was here?"

"Mr. Corcoran, of course," said Gabor.

"Who's Mr. Corcoran?"

"My dinner companion. He seemed very angry when I told him the train case was missing. He went looking for Nicky."

Jake read back through his notes. Something was wrong with the timeline Miss Gabor had given him.

"You're saying Mr. Corcoran was here when you found the necklace was missing?"

"Yes."

"I'm a little confused then," Jake said. "You said earlier that you were getting ready for bed when you found the necklace missing."

Miss Gabor smiled. "Yes. I was changing into my nightgown when I discovered the missing necklace. Mr. Corcoran was waiting for me."

"Oh," Jake said. "I see. So, he hadn't left yet?"

Mr. Witwer cleared his throat. Miss Gabor chuckled.

"Such a dahling young man," she said. "Are all the policeman here as delightfully innocent as you?"

Jake flushed again, feeling embarrassed. He'd only dealt with a couple of women like Miss Gabor before, spoiled wives and daughters who tried to use their sex to distract him from doing his job, women who thought they could get out of a speeding ticket by flirting with him. He'd heard some cops fell for that kind of thing, but a bribe was a bribe, no matter the wrapping it came in. He scribbled in his notebook for a moment, reasserting his authority. Miss Gabor didn't wait for him to finish.

"Artie, Mr. Corcoran that is, ran off when he found out the train case was missing," she said. "I didn't realize he would be so upset. He gave it to me. The case, I mean."

"Do you know where he went?"

"Well, I told him I suspected Nicky. Artie can be quite territorial."

"So you think Mr. Corcoran went looking for Nicky?"

"Yes, I believe so."

"Do you have any idea where Nicky might be?"

"Me? No. Artie has some connections here. No doubt he's making some inquiries about the local gambling operations."

"Gambling is illegal in San Diego."

"Yes, of course dear. But if there's a card game going on somewhere, Nicky will find it. Artie also knows people who know where to find such things."

Jake looked at his notes again. He couldn't think of anything else to ask.

"I think that's all I need for now," he said, closing his notebook. "I'll file the report tonight and detectives will take it from there. They'll want to talk to Mr. Corcoran as well, I expect."

Miss Gabor nodded.

"My apologies again, Miss Gabor," said Mr. Witwer. "We've never had something like this happen before."

"I should hope not," she said. "It's most upsetting, knowing someone was able to get in and root around in my boudoir."

"Yes, yes," said Witwer. "Most unsettling. I would appreciate it if you didn't say anything to the other guests. And please lock up after we leave."

"I intend to," said Gabor. She shivered, rubbing her exposed arms.

Witwer opened the front door and ushered Jake out. They walked back along the lighted path, past the pool and out to the parking lot.

"How soon do you think we'll hear something?" said Witwer.

"Hard to say," Jake said. "A detective will come by tomorrow morning, unless they're too busy."

"I'd like to be able to tell Mr. Murchison something in the morning."

"Who's that?"

"One of the owners. I decided not to wake him. He gets up at 4 a.m. to do business back east."

"Well, I doubt we'll have much by then. Unless this Corcoran fellow finds Mr. Hilton and takes care of things for us."

"You might try the La Valencia. I expect that's where Mr. Hilton is staying, since he's not staying here. It's the only other place in town a man of his means would find acceptable."

Jake nodded. "I'll stop in and check. What can you tell me about Miss Gabor's friend, Mr. Corcoran?"

"What do you mean?"

"What kind of man is he? Is he likely to go after Mr. Hilton in some violent way?"

"Oh no. I don't think so, anyway. Although ..."

"What?"

"As Miss Gabor mentioned, Mr. Corcoran is quite well-connected. He's a lobbyist in Sacramento, helps arrange deals for his clients. I've heard—only heard, mind you—that some of those clients aren't so nice."

"What do you mean?"

"Mr. Corcoran works for racetrack owners and liquor concerns, that kind of thing. That's what I've been told, anyway.

He knows people who know people who might be ... a bit rough."

"I understand," Jake said. "Thanks."

He opened the door to his car and climbed in. Mr. Witwer looked like he still had something to say. Jake rolled down the window.

"What is it?" he said. Witwer rubbed his temple.

"About Mr. Corcoran," he said. "I saw him tonight, speaking to one of the other guests. It was shortly after Miss Gabor reported the robbery. The Director. Bungalow A."

"Perhaps I should talk to him."

Witwer rubbed his stomach as if some bit of food wasn't sitting right.

"I hate to disturb Director Hoover and Mr. Tolson. I know they retire early. It's just that Mr. Corcoran seemed very angry with him."

"Wait," Jake said, "Are you talking about J. Edgar Hoover? The FBI Hoover?"

"Yes," said Witwer, nodding his head. "Mr. Corcoran was shaking his fist at the director. If I didn't know better, I'd say he was threatening him."

9

FBI Director J. Edgar Hoover looked different in person. He was shorter than Jake expected him to be. Older too. Then again, no one looked like their official photograph when they were preparing to tuck in for the night. Hoover had answered the door in his pajamas, slippers, and a yellow silk robe. His smashed bulldog face had the same imposing visage Jake had seen in newspapers and books, but the man himself seemed softer and weaker than his public persona. The snarl in Hoover's voice sounded more petulant than tough.

"What is it?"

"Please excuse me, Mr. Hoover," said the hotel manager, Mr. Witwer, practically curtsying on the doorstep. "It's just that ... I'm afraid to report there's been a burglary."

"What do you expect me to do about it?" sneered Hoover. "Call the FBI?"

Witwer gave the director a thin smile, unsure if it was a serious question or a joke.

"No sir," said Witwer. He glanced toward Jake. "This officer is filing a report. He asked if he could speak with you."

"Officer Jake Stirling," Jake said. "Of the San Diego Police Department. It's an honor to meet you, Mr. Hoover."

Jake saluted. Hoover stared at him a moment, sizing him up.

"You're a good-looking young fellow," said Hoover. "Do all San Diego cops look like you?"

Jake wasn't sure how to respond.

"I don't know sir," he said. "I've only been on the job for a year."

"How tall are you, son? I'd guess at least six-two."

"Six-three and a half, sir."

"You like being a cop?"

"Yes, sir. I find it very rewarding."

"Good for you. The law needs more young men like you. Big. Handsome. Virile. Serving and protecting."

"Yes, sir," Jake said, feeling both flattered and somewhat uncomfortable. Meeting the head of the FBI was a bigger deal than meeting a movie star as far as he was concerned, but the moment didn't feel like he'd imagined it might be. The FBI director's appearance and demeanor had thrown him for a loop. He opened his notebook to where he'd left off with Miss Gabor, trying to concentrate on the subject at hand.

"Do you know a Mr. Corcoran, sir? Artie Corcoran?"

Hoover's left eyebrow wrinkled. The corner of his mouth twitched.

"Corcoran," he said, drawing out the syllables of the name. "There's an oily bastard."

"You know him then?" Jake said.

"Sure, I know him. I fired that piece of dog shit from the bureau three years ago."

"He was an FBI agent?" Jake said.

"Started out as an agent. Became an associate director. I appointed him congressional liaison for the bureau. Fired him after I discovered he was feathering his own nest and selling us out."

Jake nodded. The conversation was getting away from him

again. He looked over at Witwer, who remained attentive but silent.

"Mr. Witwer says he saw you and Mr. Corcoran having a conversation tonight."

"More like an argument," said Hoover. "A one-sided argument. I opened the door and Corcoran started screaming his head off at me. I couldn't make heads or tails of what he was saying. He was hopping mad about something."

"What did he say?"

"He called me a lot of names first, then babbled on about some case. I know for a fact that Corcoran's a drug addict. It's in his file. Cocaine and marijuana."

Jake noted the director's assertion, writing "confrontational" and "uses illegal drugs" next to Corcoran's name.

"This case Mr. Corcoran talked about, what did he say about it?"

A man entered the living room behind Hoover, shuffling in from another part of the bungalow. The man was both taller and younger than Hoover. He wore a silk robe and pajamas that matched the director's outfit.

"What's going on?" the man said.

"Nothing," said Hoover without turning to address the other man. "Go back to bed, Clyde."

"I want a glass of milk."

"Go back to bed," Hoover said, his jaw setting like a block of concrete.

The other man squinted at them for a moment, scratched his head, and strolled back to his room.

"Anything else?" said Hoover.

Jake stared at his notes.

"This case you mentioned," he said.

"What case?"

"The one Mr. Corcoran talked about. What did he say about it?"

"Hell if I know. Something about a deal for the case. I

figured he was talking about some old FBI case, something he'd worked on, maybe something we worked on together when he was back at the bureau. He said it was his ticket."

"Was it a train case he was talking about?"

"You mean like a piece of luggage?"

"Yes."

"How the hell would I know? The man was incoherent, a hopped-up rodent. Why are you so interested in Corcoran anyway?"

Witwer, the manager, cleared his throat.

"What is it, man?" said Hoover, glaring at him. "Speak up!"

"Pardon me, sir. Please don't share this with our other guests. A woman's train case has gone missing. A friend of Mr. Corcoran's."

"You mean that Gabor woman? The one Artie's screwing?"

Witwer gave Hoover a tight smile and cleared his throat, maintaining his dignity. "Upon learning of the robbery," he continued. "Mr. Corcoran took it upon himself to go looking for the culprit. Miss Gabor kept a rather expensive necklace in her train case."

"We thought Mr. Corcoran might have said something to you," Jake said, hoping to take control of the conversation again. He glanced at his notes. "Maybe something about a man called Nicky Hilton?"

"Nicky Hilton?" said Hoover. "That fool kid? He's part of this too?"

"Possibly," Jake said. "Mr. Hilton gave the necklace to Miss Gabor as a gift, then demanded she return it."

Hoover flared his nostrils and curled his lip, as if a putrid smell had floated off the pages of Jake's notebook and infiltrated his brain.

"Trash with money," he said. "That's what you're dealing with here, son. A drug addict, a spoiled brat, and a Hungarian whore. They're weak people. They erode our moral system and give the communists something to gloat about. Rich degenerates. If I were you, I'd leave the whole thing alone. Don't waste your time on these perverts. Help out the honest, law-abiding citizens who deserve your protection."

"Yes, sir," Jake said. "I'm just here to file a report. That's all. Is there anything else you can think of that might be of use to us regarding the robbery?"

"No," said Hoover. He looked past Jake's shoulder at something outside. "You have any corroborating evidence that it was Hilton who stole the necklace?"

"No," Jake said. "Only Miss Gabor's statement."

"No other suspects?"

"Not at this time," Jake said. "Detectives will be assigned to the case after I file my report. They'll do more digging into the details. It's out of my hands after that."

Hoover nodded. "Well, son, you might want to write this down. I saw some black Sambo hanging around Miss Gabor's place this afternoon, before we went to the races. He looked kind of suspicious to me."

"You saw a Negro man loitering near Miss Gabor's bungalow? Is that what you mean?"

"More like a boy. Fourteen or fifteen. Spindly little black kid."

"What was he doing that made you suspicious?" Jake said.

"Looking in the windows, over there," said Hoover, pointing at the back wall of Miss Gabor's bungalow. "I watched him nose around for a bit, then chased him away. Figured he was trying to get a peek at the hoochie-coochie."

Jake penciled in the note, then glanced over at the manager, Witwer, who looked contemplative, stroking his chin.

"Was this boy cleaning the windows?" Witwer asked. "We had the windows washers in this afternoon. Mr. Denton's company. Most of his staff are Negroes. There are a couple of Mexicans too."

"He did have a bucket or something," said Hoover. "But this kid wasn't doing much cleaning, not while I was watching him.

He had his hand on the window, like you do when you're trying to look inside."

Hoover cupped his hand to his forehead to demonstrate. Jake added another note to his book, then paused. Danny's friend. Mabel Denton's kid. Willie. Jake wrote the name down in his notebook, added a question mark.

"Anything else?" he asked.

"That's all," said Hoover. "You find that little pickaninny and make him explain himself."

"I will," Jake said. "Thank you for your time."

"Yes, thank you, director," said Witwer. "I'm sorry we had to bother you."

"Always happy to help out my fellow lawmen," said Hoover, though he didn't look particularly cheerful as he shut the door in their face. He just looked tired. So much, Jake thought, for meeting one's heroes. He and Mr. Witwer returned to the path and made their way back toward the parking lot.

"I hope none of Mr. Denton's people are involved in this," said Witwer. "They do excellent work, but the owners might cancel the contract if they hear about this. I don't know where I'd find someone else."

"We'll call Mr. Denton," Jake said. "If he's got a peeping Tom working for him, I'm sure he'd want to know."

"Yes," said Witwer. "I'm sure you're right."

Willie Denton's mother and father were model citizens, leading lights of La Jolla's colored community. Their oldest daughter had won a scholarship to UCLA. But Jake knew that some apples fell farther from the tree. His brother Danny was one of those outlying fruits. Danny had been put in a special class for kids with anti-social tendencies. Willie was in the class, too.

Jake doubted that Willie was bold enough or resourceful enough to break in and rob one of the bungalows, but teenagers were easily led astray. Willie might have been casing the place for someone more corrupt, a professional thief or one of those slick manipulators who took young people under their wing and step-by-fateful-step entrapped them into a life of crime and moral decay. Jake had learned in cadet training that juvenile delinquents were well on their way to becoming hardened criminals. You saw it all the time in the movies and on police shows like Dragnet. Jake wanted to help kids like that, to save them from themselves. It was an important part of his job. No one had stepped in to help Todd DuBarry.

10

J ake pulled his patrol car into a valet parking space
outside the La Valencia Hotel on Prospect Street,
opened the door and climbed out. La Valencia was the
center of the social scene in La Jolla, a six-story edifice
that breathed old money and generational entitlement, the
grand matron of La Jolla hospitality, situated on a rise above
Cove Park and the rocky beaches below. Movie stars looking for
peace and privacy didn't book rooms at the La Valencia, especially during the summer. There were too many tourists in
town during the day and too many parties at night.

La Jolla residents used the amenities for weddings, tea
socials, after-theater celebrations, and debutante balls. The
hotel's restaurants featured al fresco dining, where clientele
consumed lobster and asparagus salads surrounded by terra-
cotta gardens of dark green succulents beneath swaying palm
trees. Tendrils of purple bougainvillea scaled the arched
columns on the terrace and spread across the Spanish-style
tiled roof. The exterior of the building had recently been
painted Pepto-Bismol pink, which local wits joked was to
settle the stomachs of lushes leaving the bar. The police

substation was only a block away, on the other side of the street.

"I'll just be a couple of minutes," Jake said to the valet who stepped out to greet him. The valet nodded and returned to his station. Jake walked up the sidewalk, turned in at the Saltillo-tiled patio, and entered the lobby. The night clerk stood at the reception desk, sorting through papers.

"Good evening, officer," said the clerk. "Can I help you?"

"I'm looking for someone named Nicky Hilton," Jake said. "I've been told he's a guest here."

"Let me check," said the clerk. He opened a drawer and flipped through a stack of registration receipts, found the one he wanted. "Yes. Mr. Hilton is still registered with us. I can have the operator put you through to his room, if you'd like. Just use the phone over there."

The night clerk indicated a curved vestibule where a black phone sat on a circular side table. Jake crossed the lobby, picked up the receiver, heard the desk clerk speak to the operator.

"Guest lobby to Suite 501 please, Agnes," said the clerk. Jake waited as the operator connected. A phone rang at the other end of the line. It continued to ring—four, five, six times. After the seventh ring, the operator disconnected the line.

"Your party doesn't appear to be in," she said. "Would you like to leave a message?"

"Yes," Jake said. "Tell him that officer ... never mind. I'll try later."

Jake hung up the phone. If Hilton had stolen the necklace, a message from a police officer would only tip him off. He returned to the reception desk.

"Did you reach Mr. Hilton?" said the night clerk.

"No," Jake said. "He's not in."

"I'm not surprised," said the clerk. "Mr. Hilton is quite the night owl. He often doesn't come back until four or five in the morning."

"Where does he go?"

The desk clerk gave Jake a tight smile.

"I couldn't say, sir. We don't keep tabs on our guests."

"No, of course not," Jake said. "Have you seen Mr. Hilton tonight? Did you see him go out?"

The clerk looked thoughtful, as if trying to remember if he'd seen Hilton, or perhaps deciding what to say if he had.

"I haven't seen him tonight, but you might enquire at the valet station. That's where taxis pick up our guests. The valet may have seen him."

"Thank you," Jake said, scribbling notes. "Anything else you can tell me about Mr. Hilton? How long is he planning to stay?"

The night clerk checked the registration card.

"It's listed as an open-ended stay on the card, sir. There's no checkout date."

"Is that unusual?"

"Not really," said the clerk. "Many of our summer guests do the same. The regulars, anyway. You might check next door in the lounge."

Jake pointed his pencil toward the front door.

"The Whaling Bar?" he said.

"Yes, sir," said the clerk. "Mr. Hilton is a regular there."

"Thank you," Jake said. He closed his notebook, put it back in his pocket and headed toward the street. The Whaling Bar was the liveliest and most public wing of the hotel, a dark, leathery den of alcoholic fraternization patronized by La Jolla residents as well as hotel guests. A large painting hung on the back wall, a room-length rendering of whales, ships, and harpooners that wouldn't have been out of place in a drab New England pub but seemed at odds with the hotel's sunny frippery.

Jake turned in at the side entrance. The room was noisy and crowded. He heard someone call his name, turned to look for the voice. A man waved at him from a back corner table. Max

Miller, the writer from the diner. Jake made his way over. There were three other men at the table.

"Good evening, Jake," bellowed Miller. His ever-present ruddiness seemed even more flush than usual. Jake gave a tiny nod and touched the brim of his hat.

"Good evening, Mr. Miller. How can I help you?"

"I want you to arrest the men at this table."

"What for, sir?"

"They have committed outrageous literary crimes."

There was an outburst of laughter from the men at the table. Jake twitched his jaw. He didn't understand the joke. He didn't want to be the butt of it, either.

"I don't have the authority to arrest someone for that," he said.

The men laughed again. Jake didn't have time to play games with drunkards, even ones as well-heeled as this group appeared to be.

"Let me introduce you to my friends," said Mr. Miller. "If you arrested us all, you would singlehandedly reduce the published output of our little village about ninety percent. I'll start over here, with the youngest, an ink-stained wretch still working under the oppressive thumb of his city editor. Jake, this is Neil. Last name Morgan. Young Morgan hopes to someday throw off the yoke of his task masters and write a real book. Something about the new California and its bright-eyed achievers. Neil, this is Jake Stirling. I have now provided you with an honest contact in the San Diego Police Department. You're welcome."

The man with reddish-blonde hair nodded at Jake.

"Pleased to meet you, officer," he said. Jake nodded back.

"And across from me is Ted Geisel," Miller continued. "Who writes a few small words, mostly for children, and gets paid extravagantly for them. That's the only reason we let him in the group. He also draws very strange pictures."

Geisel nodded at Jake. He was older than Morgan, with flat graying hair and a sharp hooked nose.

"And I believe you've met our most senior member before," said Miller, indicating the man who sat at the corner of the table closest to Jake. The man tilted his gaze up from the table, turning his face toward the light.

"Mr. Chandler," Jake said. "I thought you'd moved to England."

He started to offer a handshake, but Chandler waved it away.

"It was too damn cold there," the old man grumbled. "Nothing but faded gentry who paw at me during parties and refer to me as that American genius."

"Yes," said Miller. "Apparently Ray's books have convinced the literary cognoscenti of England that Americans all speak like gangsters and use overwrought similes."

"Better overwrought similes than overblown travel brochures," said Chandler, glaring back at Miller.

"Touché, Ray," said Miller. "You haven't lost your ability to shoot a dead scribbler straight in his pocketbook."

"Perhaps it's time for us to go home," said Morgan.

"Yes," said Geisel. "I'm afraid our grinches are showing."

"There you go again, Ted," said Miller. "Making up words. None of my editors would let me get away with a word like that."

"Nor mine," said Morgan.

"They might soon," said Geisel. He winked at Morgan, who nodded back, as if the two men shared a secret.

"What brings you in here, anyway, Jake?" said Miller.

"I'm looking for a man named Nicky Hilton," Jake said. "Do any of you know him?"

"You mean that spoiled brat who married Elizabeth Taylor?" said Morgan.

"Yes, sir." Jake nodded. "I believe that's correct."

Max Miller leaned forward, addressing Morgan.

"Was he the one who got in that kerfuffle after the Playhouse soirée?" he asked. Mr. Morgan nodded in agreement.

"When was this?" Jake said.

"Two nights ago," said Miller. "He was screaming at somebody out by the valet station."

"Any idea who he was screaming at?" Jake said.

Max Miller looked over at Neil Morgan. They both shook their heads.

"Check with the valets," said Mr. Morgan. "They might remember."

"Thank you," Jake said. "Goodnight, gentleman."

He turned on his heel, left the bar and headed back to his car. Writers were a strange breed of men. Back at the valet station, the kid in charge sat on a stool next to the key cabinet, biting his fingernails. He glanced up as Jake approached. The boy looked familiar, perhaps someone Jake had encountered on patrol, but Jake couldn't remember the name or situation. He saw a lot of familiar faces while on patrol. Some made a stronger impression than others. He pulled out his notebook. The valet looked nervous.

"I'm looking for a hotel guest who might have ordered a cab," Jake said. "His name's Nicky Hilton."

"Yeah." The valet nodded. "I know that guy. He gets a cab every night. About the same time."

"Did he go out tonight?"

"Yeah." The valet nodded. "I heard him say something about Van Nuys."

"Van Nuys," Jake said, scowling as he jotted the name in his book. "Isn't that in Los Angeles?"

The valet shrugged. "I dunno. That's what I thought he said. Check with the cab company."

"I will. Were you here two nights ago?"

"Yeah. So?"

"I heard there was some sort of incident. Mr. Hilton yelled at someone?"

"Oh yeah," said the valet. He chuckled. "He got really nasty with that lady, calling her all sorts of names—slut, whore, that kind of stuff."

"Do you know who this woman was?"

"Sure. She was in that Martin and Lewis circus flick. Real glamour-puss. Zaa Zaa something?"

"Zsa Zsa Gabor?"

"Yeah, that's her. He, Mr. Hilton I mean, he went kind of crazy. He called her a ... he called her a cunt. Can you believe that, right out here in public? I don't know what she would've done if TD hadn't stepped in."

"TD? Todd DuBarry?"

"Yeah. Big Todd. You know him, right? Todd grabbed that Hilton guy and gave him the bum rush halfway up the street."

Jake scribbled in the notebook, then reread his notes to make sure he'd captured the important details. Nicky Hilton sounded like a real piece of work. A car pulled into the spot next to his squad car. The valet climbed down from his stool, preparing to greet the driver. Jake wondered how Todd had managed to get involved in all this. It seemed important, but he didn't know why.

"Does Todd work here?" Jake said. "At the hotel?"

"Oh no," said the valet, stepping off the curb. "Todd was driving that lady's big Cadillac. He was her chauffeur."

11

A sound outside awakened Mabel Denton. She sat up, then glanced over at her husband in bed. He continued to saw logs, fast asleep. If the gates of hell opened up in the backyard one night and flying devils poured out of it, Willie Sr. would sleep through the whole thing and ask where the hole in the ground came from the next morning. Her husband worked hard, six days a week, running his window-cleaning service. Mabel worked hard too, cleaning and cooking for wealthy families. The money she and her husband had saved would soon be enough to make a down payment on a new house, a real home in some other part of town, not the broken-down three-room shack they lived in now, with gaps in the walls that let in the noise and cold air.

She heard voices outside—rough men's voices, garbled and mean. She glanced at the alarm clock on the nightstand. A little past midnight. One man passing through the neighborhood at this hour could be Mr. Bell or Mr. Davis, returning home from restaurant jobs. Two men or more could mean trouble.

Life in this California village was a paradise compared to the dusty town in Texas where Mabel had grown up.

No one had been lynched or attacked by a mob. No one had been dragged out of their homes. The racism wasn't as visible or as vicious. But it was still present, floating under the surface of polite society like a deep ocean current. Two white boys in a Chrysler Imperial had torn through the neighborhood a month ago, knocking down mailboxes and tearing up Mr. Bell's nice new picket fence. The month before, someone had spray-painted "nigger" on the sidewalk, with a message telling them to go back to Africa.

Fear crept into Mabel's heart like the foggy mist that surrounded her house most every morning. She climbed out of bed, put on her robe and slippers, and walked into the front room. Willie Jr. stood by the window, looking outside.

"Who's out there?" Mabel whispered.

"There's some men out behind the Pig," said Willie. The Little Pig BBQ sold ribs, pork sandwiches and fried pickles from a pick-up window on Draper Avenue. The smell from the smokers in back permeated the neighborhood at night, tomorrow's meals cooking low and slow on grills the proprietor, Mr. Parker, had built out of discarded Army oil drums.

"What're they up to?" asked Mabel, joining her son at the window.

"They're carrying something," said Willie. Mabel watched the shadows of two large men struggle with something near the Little Pig's trash cans. One of the trash cans tipped over, bouncing off another with a metallic clang and spilling its contents onto the ground. The light over the back porch of the restaurant blinked on.

"Who's out there?" shouted Mr. Parker, who slept in a back room. The light from his porch threw the men into vivid relief, providing a clearer view of what they were doing.

"Gee whiz!" exclaimed Willie.

"Oh dear," said Mabel.

Two large men, dressed in fedoras and trench coats, had

stuffed a third man into one of the trash cans. Mabel and Willie could see the victim's feet sticking out of the top.

"You get away from my meats," shouted Mr. Parker. "I got a shotgun."

The two men stepped back from the trash and looked at each other. The one on the left pointed his thumb toward the street. They hurried away, around the side of the Little Pig, then climbed into a car parked on Draper. The tires squealed as they pulled out and sped off. The back door of the Pig opened. Mabel saw Mr. Parker step out into the light. She moved to the front door, put her hand on the doorknob.

"Willie Senior?" she called to the back room. There was no response.

"Go wake your father," she said to Willie Jr.

Willie scampered off to his parents' bedroom. Mabel opened the front door.

"Are you okay, Mr. Parker?" she asked.

"I'm fine, Mabel. Do you see what I see?"

"It looks like they dumped some man in your trash," she replied.

"That's what it looks like to me too," said Mr. Parker. "I'm gonna call the police 'fore I do anything."

Parker stepped back into his building. Mabel pulled her robe tighter and stepped down from the porch.

"I'll be over at the Little Pig," she called back to the house, then set out for the trash cans. "That man needs our help."

Two more porch lights went on as her neighbors awoke. Doors opened.

"What's going on, Mabel?" Mr. Buchanon called from his front stoop.

"They dumped some man in the Pig's trash cans."

"Who did?"

"I don't know. Two big fellas. They're gone now. Mr. Parker's calling the police."

Mabel continued toward the trash cans. The man's feet

wiggled in the air as he struggled to climb out, his black patent shoes circling above the rim like two giant horse flies. The trash can swayed in widening circles, then tilted toward Mabel and crashed to the ground. She stopped, leaned forward, and stared into the opening.

"Are you okay, mister?"

The man groaned. Mabel heard footsteps behind her, then turned and saw Mr. Buchanon approaching. Willie Sr. exited the front door of their house.

"I brought a flashlight," said Mr. Buchanon. He flicked on the light, walked up beside her, and pointed it at the man in the trash can. Blood drained from the man's nose and down his chin. His left eye looked puffy.

"He don't look too good," said Mr. Buchanon.

"Fuckers," the man whimpered. He twisted his hips and reached for the edge of the trash can. Mabel took a step toward him.

"Don't touch him," said her husband, Willie Sr., striding in from behind.

"The man needs our help," said Mabel.

"Charlie and I can take care of him," said Willie Sr. "You hold the light."

Mabel took the flashlight from Mr. Buchanon and aimed it toward the man in the trash can as her husband and Mr. Buchanon leaned down to look at him. Another person walked up beside Mabel.

"What happened to him?" said Willie Jr.

"You don't need to be out here, Willie Jr.," said Mabel. "You just get back in the house."

"Who is he?"

"None of your business," said Mabel. "Now get back to the house and close the door."

Mr. Parker exited the back door of the Pig.

"The police are coming," he said. "Let's get this fellow offa' my property. I don't need this kind of trouble."

"Hold the can steady," said Willie Sr. "While Charlie and I pull him out."

Mr. Parker stabilized the trash can while Willie Sr. and Mr. Buchanon grabbed the man inside and dragged him out onto the ground. The man rolled over on one side as if to rise, then gave up and rolled onto his back. The lapels of his dark tuxedo jacket looked slick and wet. A loosened bow tie hung from his neck. His white shirt was covered in blood.

"Fuckers," the man groaned, closing his eyes. Mabel shooed Willie Jr. away with a wave of her hand. That kind of language wasn't allowed in her house. She didn't want Willie Jr. hearing it anywhere else, either. He turned back toward the house then stopped and picked something up off the ground.

"Get this fool out to the street," said Mr. Parker, collecting the spillage and replacing the trash can in its original spot.

"He's hurt," said Mabel.

"I don't care," said Parker. "I don't want policemens all 'round my back yard, getting up in my smokers just because some white man got himself mugged. There's very strict procedures I got to keep."

"Mister?" said Willie Sr., leaning in close to the man on the ground. "You think you can get up and walk?"

The man opened his eyes and stared at Willie Sr.'s face for a moment.

"Just bring the car 'round for me, Rochester," he said and gave a weak giggle.

Willie Sr. glanced back at his wife. She'd seen that look before. Her husband had worked as a chauffeur for three years before starting his window cleaning business. He'd hated driving rich people around, hated waiting for them while they went to their doctor's appointments and luncheons. He hated the way they talked to him—most of them, anyway. Mabel leaned over the man on the ground.

"Are you hurt, sir?" she said. "Is anything broken?"

The man turned his head toward her and squinted at the light.

"I'm fine," he said, rolling over onto his side again, then pushing himself up to his knees. "Good as new."

Willie Sr. and Mr. Buchanon helped the man up. Once on his feet, he shook off his helpers, adjusted his jacket and took a step toward the street. His next step sent him sideways. Willie Sr. and Mr. Buchanon stepped in to support him, escorted the man out to the street. Mabel followed them.

"Fool's drunk," grunted Mr. Parker, as she passed. "White man getting himself beat half to death on my property. Bad for business, if this gets around. It'll be bad for all of us, Mabel."

Mr. Parker was right, but Mabel didn't want to think about how this would affect the neighborhood. The police would arrive soon. They'd interrogate everyone, if not tonight, then tomorrow. They'd start patrolling this part of town more often, keeping an eye on the colored folks, looking for signs of trouble and hassling anyone who seemed the least bit suspicious. The police here gave Black people room to breathe, but an incident like this could change their minds. She worried about Willie Jr. He had a knack for getting in trouble and doing dumb things.

"Let's sit him down here," said Willie Sr., indicating a picnic table located in front of the restaurant, below the pink painted pig sign. Mabel's husband and Mr. Buchanon helped the man turn around, then lowered him down on the bench. The man groaned, spread his knees, and lowered his head.

"Mr. Parker will have a fit if you get sick on his property, mister," warned Willie Sr.

The man lifted his head. He looked back and forth between the two men, as if seeing them for the first time.

"I told those boys," he said. "And I'm telling you. I don't have the damn thing."

Willie Sr. and Mr. Buchanon exchanged glances.

"Have what thing?" said Willie Sr.

The man wagged his finger at them.

"Oh no," he said. "You can't fool me with that innocent act. I know how the man works. You can't fool me."

"What's he talking about?" asked Mr. Buchanon.

"Don't hurt me," the man said. He touched his nose, testing it. "Just don't hurt me anymore, okay?"

"No one's going to hurt you, mister," said Mabel. A siren wailed in the distance. "The police are on their way. You're safe now."

The man looked up at Mabel. He looked surprised to see her. Then he started to cry.

"Mammy," he said. "Don't let them hurt me anymore."

12

The fog had lifted by the time Caleb Shapiro walked out of the engineering building at the Institute of Oceanography and gazed at the dazzling blue expanse of Pacific Ocean that lay less than a hundred feet from his door. His wife would arrive later with their daughter, Rachel, bearing a picnic basket for the whole family. They planned to eat lunch together on the bluffs overlooking the beach. Caleb needed to take the ocean's temperature before they arrived. He walked across the lawn and headed out toward the end of the pier.

As he strode across the pier's wood planks, he peered down through the cracks at the waves crashing below. A brightness welled up in him that he wouldn't have thought possible ten years ago after the war, when he'd learned that his parents and sister, his aunts and uncles, had all died in the Nazi camps. He was the only member of his family who'd escaped the Shoah, obtaining a visa to study electrical engineering at MIT just before the pogroms began.

As he continued along the pier, he looked across the water to the point of land where the village of La Jolla extended out into the sea. Even in this sunny paradise there were traces of the ancient affliction, genteel reminders that he and his people were never fully welcomed. The country club with a golf course on the hill and the beach club just down the coast from the institute had signs at their entrances: Gentiles only. There was an understanding among local real estate agents that any house for sale with the porch light on during the day was not to be shown to the children of Israel. Or the children of Africa. Or anyone not of white European ancestry. Local residents employed Negroes and Mexicans as cooks, cleaners, and gardeners. A less-desirable part of the village had been designated as the neighborhood where those workers and their families could live. But the Jews who came to town arrived with more money in their bank accounts, with ACLU cards in their pockets, and college degrees on their resumes. They were a different kind of threat to the blue-blooded order of things.

The Institute was a safe haven for Caleb, a pocket realm of science and intellectualism, separate from the town in both politics and geography. A new neighborhood of graduate students, scientists and their families had sprung up around the Institute, with houses constructed on the flat spread of land next to Shores Beach and on the slope of the hill that rose above it. His boss, Revelle, had begun lobbying for a public university to be built on top of that hill, where the U.S. Army still maintained a shooting range at Camp Matthews. Some townspeople expressed concerns about having a university so close to their little kingdom by the sea, warning of paradise lost and liberals at the gates. All agreed a university would change the town's character, for better or worse.

Caleb reached the end of the pier and stood staring out at the far edge of the Pacific Ocean. Just over a year ago, he'd sailed across that horizon with Revelle and other scientists from the institute on a Navy ship five hundred miles from where he stood now, to watch a nuclear bomb explode underwater. Operation Wigwam. Caleb had designed and built some of the instruments that measured the physical effects of the blast. But there were no instruments that could measure the anxiety and foreboding it had released in his thoughts.

The Institute's scientists had selected the site, but the U.S. Navy had been in charge of the test. A Mark 90 nuclear bomb nicknamed Betty had been suspended from a Navy barge, two-thousand feet below the surface of the ocean. Dummy submarines, equipped with cameras and measuring devices floated beneath the surface of the ocean at varying depths and distances from the bomb. Everyone had theories on how the submarines and sea life would be affected by the blast.

Caleb pictured the explosion now, saw it in his mind, a huge cone of water erupting from the ocean's placid surface and shooting two thousand feet into the air, a fleeting white mountain born from the sea. Concentric waves rolled out from the bomb's ignition point, lifting and dropping the ship on which he stood more than five miles away, forcing him to brace himself on the deck. It had been the most exhilarating and terrifying thing Caleb had ever experienced, intoxicating and sobering at the same time, witness to the power that created the universe. God's all-consuming power, now in men's hands.

"Good morning, Caleb," said a booming voice from behind him. A hand clapped his shoulder. His boss had caught him daydreaming again.

"Good morning, Roger," said Caleb, glancing over at Dr. Revelle, then turning back to the ocean. "I was just getting ready to take the ocean's temperature."

"Ah yes," said Revelle. "Plotting the data points. You looked like you had something on your mind."

"I was thinking about Wigwam. Last year, when we met."

"It's a terrifying thing, Caleb," said Revelle. "The power of the atom. Mankind has opened the box. We need to make the best of it and learn as much as we can. Mark my words, the atomic bomb is going to be a wonderful oceanographic tool."

"If it doesn't kill us all first."

"Well, that's one of the things Professor Goldberg is investigating with his mackerel studies. You see, bacteria in the water will absorb radioactive isotopes that were released from that bomb. Those isotopes will get passed on to the creatures that eat the bacteria and continue to get passed up through the food chain."

"I might need to check my lobster dinner with a Geiger counter?"

"It's not just the radiation effects we're studying. Hans thinks we may be able to assess changes in CO_2 levels, as well. Have faith in the science, Caleb."

"It's not the science I'm worried about. It's the U.S. Navy."

Revelle chuckled. He was a big man, at least six-four, an undeniable force of personality who could talk anybody into anything. He'd persuaded brilliant scientists to leave the hallowed halls of Stanford and Princeton for a motley set of run-down buildings at the edge of western civilization, with only an isolated outpost of blue-blood conservatism nearby for cultural refreshment. He'd talked Caleb into taking this job. Revelle had sold them all a vision of scientific freedom and sunshine that few could resist.

"At any rate," said Revelle. "I wanted to get your take on our meeting yesterday. With the Texas oilmen."

"It's a ridiculous idea," said Caleb. "Using nuclear bombs to activate oil deposits."

"Absolutely," said Revelle. "I was thinking more along the lines of searching for oil underwater. It sounded like you had an idea. For one of your gadgets."

"Well," said Caleb. His engineering mind was engaged now. He let it run. "Some sort of underwater spectrometer might do the trick. I'd have to work with one of the scientists to research the molecular structure of oil, pinpoint its chemical signature, then build and tune the spectrometer for outputting that signal. You could attach the spectrometer to a cable running from a ship, lower it to specific depths and navigate the ship along a geographic grid. Then analyze the data and search for spikes at specific points in the grid."

"Excellent," said Revelle. "Write that up for me. Not a full proposal, just plain language, a page or two, something I could present to those fellows."

"You're still going to pursue this?"

"There's no stopping the oil business, Caleb. Not now. There's no reason to. Not until we find something to replace it. Those cowboys are two of the richest men in the country. A week of their income would keep this place running for years."

Caleb nodded. Fundraising was always on Revelle's mind. Preeminence in the new field of oceanography wouldn't happen without lots of money.

"I'll have something for you next week," he said, acceding to the Institute's financial realities. Scientific inquiry was never as pure as he wished.

"Great," said Revelle, clapping him on the shoulder. "I knew I could count on you."

Revelle headed back down the pier, while Caleb made his way over to a wood hut at the edge of the pier. He opened the door, grabbed a nylon rope that dropped down through a hole in the floor. He hauled up the float at the end of the rope and checked the thermometer attached to it. The temperature of the water beneath the pier had been measured three times a day, every day of the year, since 1916. It was the institution's oldest experiment.

Today the reading was 65.4 degrees Fahrenheit. Caleb dropped the float back into the water and marked the temperature on a clipboard that hung on the wall. He stepped outside and closed the door. It would take years of data to corroborate the scientists' theory, that carbon gas was changing the atmosphere, that if an atomic fire didn't wipe out humanity first, the atmosphere itself would someday shrivel and die, and turn the planet to dust.

That was the future, though. Today Caleb would work on

the plans for a new research aquarium, trying to figure out the best way to filter the water it needed, piped in from the pier. He'd eat lunch with his family on a grassy bluff above a sunny beach. Tonight, at home, he'd sketch out ideas for an underwater oil spectrometer. Life wasn't perfect, but it felt like the greater darkness was behind him. Today was brighter than so many that had come before.

He checked his watch, then set off down the pier at a faster clip than he'd taken on the way out. His wife and daughter would arrive soon with the picnic basket. He passed a large wooden locker, about halfway down the pier, then stopped and stared at it. Something was wrong. The locker's padlock was missing. He lifted the lid, checked the contents inside.

The Institute stored diving gear in the locker—masks, flippers, wetsuits, and snorkels. Six Aqua-Lung tanks were also stored in the locker, along with their hoses and air regulators. He counted the oxygen tanks, then counted again. There were only five.

Scientists at the Institute were some of the smartest people he'd ever met, but they could also be absent-minded, their brains so energized with new ideas and research that they neglected their more mundane responsibilities. Like using the proper procedures to check out diving equipment. And check it back in. Theft had never been a problem at the Institute, but Caleb's mind wouldn't rest until he found the missing equipment. He'd review the check-out sheet back at the office, then search the building and question the staff. If nothing turned up, he might have to call the police. Those Aqua-Lung contraptions weren't cheap.

13

Willie Denton Jr. was in trouble. Big trouble. His mother had always said he would get himself in a real pickle someday, that she wouldn't be able to rescue him. Today was that day, the pickle of all pickles. He'd been arrested, hauled away in the back of a policeman's squad car. Now he sat in the holding cell of the La Jolla police substation, sweaty and thirsty, afraid to even ask for a drink of water.

His father and other men in the neighborhood often talked about how colored men were treated by the police, how the cops liked to give black boys the third degree. Willie had no idea what the third degree was, but he imagined some sort of medieval torture device like he'd read about in his history books. The police had let him call home, but no one had answered the phone. His parents were both working today. He didn't know where. And his sister had gone off to college last week. He was alone. He was scared.

He'd been delighted at first when his father gave him the day off, reveling in his unexpected freedom. Now he regretted that liberty. If he'd been out with his father's window-washing crew he wouldn't have started snooping around town, sneaking down alleys and picking through people's garbage. The policeman had spotted him in an alley behind the flower shop, pulling things out of the trash can. Willie didn't think he'd done anything wrong. People only threw away things they didn't want. It shouldn't count as stealing if you took something from a trash can. They were sending that stuff to the dump anyway.

Soon after they'd brought him to the station, the police captain came to Willie's cell and started asking about a diamond necklace that had been stolen. Willie told the captain he didn't know about any necklace. The captain asked about the item they'd found in Willie's pocket, a photograph like the kind fathers kept in their wallets, pictures of wives and children. The photo in Willie's pocket wasn't a family portrait, though. It was a picture of a naked lady, a white lady from the movies who had blond hair and big boobies. The police captain called Willie a pervert and wanted to know who gave him the picture. Willie told the truth, that he'd found the photograph last night, on the ground next to the Little Pig's overturned trash cans after that white man had been mugged.

The captain had asked Willie if he'd ever seen that white man before last night. Willie said no. It wasn't a lie, but it wasn't the truth either. Willie had seen the man earlier in the evening when he was out with Danny Stirling. He hadn't told the captain about Danny. Or the Perverted Savants Club. He'd hoped to show that photo to Rachel and Danny at their next meeting.

"Willie?" said a man's voice. Willie looked up from his cot. The man pulled a chair up to the cell door. "Do you know who I am?"

"Yeah, I know you," said Willie, wiping his eyes with his shirt sleeve. "You're Danny's brother."

"That's right. I'm Jake. I'm a policeman."

"Where's your uniform?" said Willie.

"I'm not on duty right now."

"What're you doing here?"

Jake smiled and nodded in that way adults did when they were going to explain something to you. Danny Stirling had a word for when teachers did that in class. He said they were patronizing.

"Your mom called my mom," Jake said. "She was worried about you. My mom called me. I called the station. They said you were here and that I could talk to you."

"Does my mom know I'm in jail?"

"Someone saw you get into the squad car, I guess, and told your mom."

"I didn't do nothing to no one," said Willie. "I didn't hurt no one."

"I know," Jake said. "Do you understand why the police brought you in? Why you're here?"

"They said I was indecent or something."

"The charge is possession of indecent materials," Jake said. "You shouldn't be looking at pictures like that. You shouldn't be carrying them around. They're obscene."

"I didn't mean nothing by it."

"I'm going to help you out get out of here, Willie," Jake said. "I know your parents. They're good people. I think you want to be a good person too. But I need you to tell me the truth. Okay?"

Willie nodded. He stared at the floor. Jake lowered his voice.

"Did Danny have something to do with this?" he said. "Are you protecting him?"

Willie continued to stare at the floor. Jake continued, speaking with a soft voice through the bars.

"My mother told me you went out with Danny last night. She said Danny acted strangely when he came home. My mom notices things like that, you see. She's pretty smart. She caught me with some pictures like yours once. I had a magazine under my bed, back when I was in high school."

"What'd your mom do when she found out?" said Willie.

"She talked to me. She said it was normal for a boy my age to want to look at things like that. She said that the women in those magazines are exploited, that they're mistreated by the men who publish those things. She said anyone who bought one of those magazines was supporting prostitution and white slavery."

Willie had never heard of white slavery before. He thought it was only people who looked like him who'd been slaves in the South before the War Between the States, and Abraham Lincoln.

"Did your mom punish you?" he said.

"No," Jake said. "She didn't. She said she'd let me decide for myself if I wanted to keep the magazine. I threw it away."

"Your mom's a nice lady," said Willie. "She's nice to us at the grocery store."

"Where'd you go with Danny?" Jake said.

"We was just driving around," he said. "Just goofing off."

"Okay," Jake said. "Why was Danny acting so strangely when he got home?"

"I dunno."

"C'mon Willie. You want to get out of here, don't you? Tell me what happened."

Willie continued to stare at the floor.

"Can I get a drink of water?" he said.

"You bet," Jake said. He stood up, walked out to the front of the station, and returned with a paper cup and passed it to Willie between the bars. Willie drank all the water in the cup and passed it back to him.

"Thank you," he said. Jake stared at him for a moment, then nodded.

"Okay," he said. "Now are you going to tell me what happened with Danny?"

Willie shrugged. "We was just messing around. That's all."

Jake frowned. He put the cup on the ground and leaned forward but didn't say anything. Willie felt like he'd done something bad, but he hadn't lied. He and Danny were just messing around, Willie on his bicycle pulling Danny on his roller board. They went all the way down to Pacific Beach. They stopped and looked at a house that was down there.

"I seen that lady before," said Willie. "In a movie with Jerry Lewis, the funny one where he goes to the circus. She got a funny name too."

"Zsa Zsa?" Jake said.

"Yeah, that's it," said Willie. He smiled.

Jake leaned back in his chair. "You work with your dad, don't you Willie? You clean windows for him?"

"Yes, sir," said Willie. "In the summers, and sometimes on Saturdays, when I'm not in school."

"Not today, though?"

"No. He didn't need me today."

"Were you cleaning windows at the Del Charro Hotel a couple of days ago, you know that fancy place near the Shores?"

Willie nodded.

"Did you see that lady there? The one in the photo? Zsa Zsa?"

"Huh?" said Willie, jerking back like a baseball player dodging a high heater. "You mean the naked lady?"

"Yes," Jake said. "I thought maybe you saw her at the hotel. Maybe she was in her bedroom, didn't have any clothes on there either? I'm sure it's hard not to peek sometimes when you're doing the kind of work you do."

"No, no," said Willie, shaking his head. "I didn't see no naked lady, I swear."

"I know you looked in her window," Jake said. "A man told me he chased you away."

"I remember that man," said Willie, feeling deflated. The white man with the bulldog face had shouted at him. "He called me a pickaninny."

"What were you looking at?" Jake said. "Were you spying on Miss Gabor?"

Jake pitched that one too close. Willie felt something break in his chest, move up his shoulders and into his neck. He started to cry.

"My pop's going to kill me," he said, snuffling. "He always tells me you just do your job and don't look in the windows. And don't look at no white woman."

"Take it easy now," Jake said. "It must be hard not to look sometimes, especially when there's someone in there who looks like she does. Just tell me what you saw through the window."

"It wasn't no lady," said Willie, recovering his composure. "It was a man."

"Was it someone you recognized?"

Willie nodded. He wiped his nose with his sleeve.

"It was TD."

"Todd DuBarry?"

"Yeah. That All American guy. He's got all kinds of money. His family I mean. His mom lives in that house with all those big windows."

"You saw Todd DuBarry in Zsa Zsa Gabor's room at the Del Charro?"

"Yeah. It was him. I didn't know it was that Frenchie lady's room though. I swear it."

"Okay, okay," Jake said. "Was anyone else in the room besides Todd?"

"No, it was just him."

"What was he doing?"

"He was carrying this little suitcase. That's why I was watching him. It made me laugh. Seeing Big Todd with that little blue case."

14

Jake opened the front door of Scripps Hospital. Willie Denton Jr. was with him. They'd walked the half-mile from the substation together. Captain Lennox had called in to the station, discovered Jake was there and asked him to bring Willie over to the hospital. Nicky Hilton, the man who'd been assaulted the previous night outside the Little Pig Barbecue, was well enough to talk to the police.

"You ever been inside a hospital before?" Jake said to Willie as he reached for the front door.

"Nah," said Willie. "Is it icky? Is there blood and guts everywhere?"

"Not really," Jake said. "It's kind of dark and smells funny."

They walked inside and over to the reception desk. Jake showed his badge and asked for Mr. Hilton. The nurse directed them up the stairs to a room on the second floor. Captain Lennox stood waiting for them outside the door.

"Jesus, Stirling, what are you doing?" he said.

"Sir?"

"No restraints on the suspect?"

"We walked over. He promised he wouldn't cause any trouble. Right, Willie?"

"No sir," said Willie. "I told you I wouldn't run. I don't have nowhere to go anyway."

Lennox looked Jake and Willie over for a moment, as if trying to decide which of them was the biggest idiot. Jake hadn't even considered putting cuffs on the prisoner. Willie was Danny's best friend, just a scrawny, scared kid. He wasn't dangerous. The walk had given Jake time to think about what Willie had told him, to ask some more questions and try to figure out why Todd DuBarry might have taken Miss Gabor's train case.

"Let's get to it then," said Lennox, taking a look inside the manila envelope he held in his hands. "This shouldn't take long, either way."

Lennox peeked through the door window, knocked once on the door, and then opened it. Jake guided Willie into the room, following the captain. Nicky Hilton sat propped up in the bed. His black hair looked matted and sweaty. His left eye socket was purple and swollen. There was a long bandage across his nose. A glass of water with a green straw sat on the table next to the bed.

"Whoo boy," Hilton grumbled. "Here comes the cavalry." He sounded groggy. There was a drip bag attached to his arm.

"Mr. Hilton," said Lennox, "I'm Captain Lennox of the La Jolla division of the San Diego Police. You remember me?"

"How could I forget?" said Hilton, bringing his hand up to his forehead as if attempting a salute, but not getting it far enough to really qualify. Lennox waved a hand at Jake.

"This is Patrolman Jake Stirling," he said. "He was on the scene last night and called in the ambulance that brought you here."

"Fuck you very much," said Hilton.

"Excuse me?" Jake said. He didn't know what he'd expected from Hilton, but it wasn't rude hostility.

"I said fuck you," said Hilton. "I can take care of myself."

Captain Lennox pulled a single sheet of paper from the manila folder.

"I'd appreciate more respect for my officers, Mr. Hilton. It says here you've got a broken nose and two cracked ribs, along with other deep contusions and cuts. I'd say you owe Officer Stirling a word of thanks."

"Fuck it," said Hilton.

"You got a potty mouth, mister," said Willie.

"Who's this little lawn jockey?" said Hilton, turning his attention to Willie.

"Have you seen this boy before, Mr. Hilton?" said Lennox. "Do you recognize him?"

"Maybe," said Hilton. "Maybe you shined my shoes, was that it, boy?"

"No sir," said Willie. "I don't shine nobody's shoes except mine."

Lennox reached in the folder again, pulled out a wallet-sized photograph, and handed it to Nicky Hilton.

"Is this your photograph, sir? Have you seen it before?"

Hilton gave a little smirk as he looked at the photo. He seemed almost pleased. "Yeah, I've seen it before," he said. "I took this photograph. Where'd you find it?"

Lennox pointed at Willie. "This young fellow had it on him when we arrested him."

Hilton locked his eyes on Willie.

"Where'd you find this?" he said.

"In the trash," said Willie.

Hilton sneered. "You like those big titties, little man? You wanta jerk your little pud on 'em?"

"Mr. Hilton," said Lennox, trying to intercede, but Hilton kept going.

"That is a top-shelf piece of ass there, little man. You got to have a lot of money to get a taste of that pussy. I took this picture. I got me a piece. I fucked that bitch six ways to Sunday."

Jake stepped across the floor, grabbed Hilton's hand, and ripped the picture away.

"Shut up!" he hissed, squeezing Hilton's wrist.

"Jake!" yelled Captain Lennox. "Take it easy."

Jake released Hilton's wrist. He stepped back from the bed, feeling foolish. He'd lost his head. It wasn't like him to do something like that. It wasn't right for an officer of the law to lose control. Never. He turned, handed the photograph to Captain Lennox.

"I'm sorry, sir."

Lennox nodded, took the photograph, and put it back in the manila folder.

"That's my photograph," said Nicky Hilton. "You give that back to me."

"Yes. Thank you for clearing that up, Mr. Hilton," said Lennox. "It's also pornography."

"It's my private property."

"It's still pornography, which you may have distributed to minors."

"What are you talking about? You heard the kid. He found the photo in the trash. Those guys took my wallet. The ones who attacked me. They tossed my stuff everywhere."

Lennox nodded. "You still don't know who attacked you?" he said. "You don't remember what they looked like?"

"I told you. It was two guys. I didn't really see them."

"You told Officer Stirling last night they were colored men. Negroes."

Nicky Hilton looked from Captain Lennox to Willie. Jake followed his gaze, saw Willie tremble. Hilton finally understood what Lennox wanted. He laughed.

"You think this little dipshit mugged me?" he said, pointing at Willie, his voice dripping with disdain. "Christ, you cops are dumber than dirt."

"Just for the record, Mr. Hilton," said Lennox. "You're saying this fellow here was not one of the men that attacked you?"

Hilton stared at Willie for a moment, looking aggrieved.

"That's what I'm saying," he said. "I've never seen this kid before. And, for the record, I didn't say they were Negroes. I said their faces were dark."

Hilton looked up from Willie and settled his eyes on the door. The look on his face changed. Jake swiveled to follow his gaze. A man's face loomed in the door window outside, then disappeared. Jake looked back at Hilton.

"Who was that?" Jake said.

"Who was who?" said Hilton. There was a scream from outside in the hall.

Jake ran to the door. He opened it and stepped into the hallway. No one there, except for two nurses. One of them reached down to help the other climb up from the floor.

"What happened?" Jake said.

"That man ran into us," said the upright nurse. "He didn't even stop to apologize, just kept right on running. Down the hall, that way."

Jake started down the hall.

"Stirling! What the hell are you doing?"

Jake stopped and looked back to see Captain Lennox standing in the doorway of Hilton's room.

"There was someone looking in the window," he said. "He ran away when I saw him."

Lennox glanced over at the nurses. "Are you ladies okay?" he said.

"We're fine," said the nurse who'd just climbed up off the floor. "What's going on?"

"Nothing to worry about, ladies," said Lennox. "Police business."

"Captain?" Jake said, tilting his head in the direction the runner had gone.

"He's long gone now, Stirling. Get back in here."

Jake returned to the room, feeling chastised. Captain Lennox handed the case envelope to Jake, then moved to the foot of the bed. He crossed his arms and glared down at Hilton.

"You want to tell us what that was all about?" he said.

"I've got a headache," said Hilton.

"We'll have a nurse get you some aspirin," said Lennox. "But first you tell me who was out there."

"I don't know what you're talking about," said Hilton.

"Stirling, reach in that envelope and pull out your incident report from the Del Charro Hotel."

Jake flipped through the papers inside the envelope, found the incident report.

"Got it," he said.

"What was the name of the guy who's staying at the hotel with Miss Gabor?"

Jake glanced over the document. "Corcoran, sir. Artie Corcoran."

"Miss Gabor told you Corcoran was looking for Mr. Hilton, right?"

"Yes, sir. That's right."

"Was that him, Mr. Hilton? Outside the door. Was that Artie Corcoran? Did you know he was looking for you?"

"I don't know what you're talking about," said Hilton.

"Was it Corcoran's boys who attacked you last night? We can file charges against him."

"Fuck off," said Hilton.

"Captain?" Jake said, glancing over at Willie, who still looked in shock.

"What is it?" said Lennox. He didn't move an inch, his back to Jake as he stared down at Hilton with the black look that Mac the desk sergeant referred to as "getting the Wade eye."

"Maybe I should take the prisoner back to the station, process him out," Jake said. "We're letting him go, right?"

Lennox turned back to Jake, looked over at Willie.

"Yeah, get him out of here. Have Mac sign him out. Take the

case file with you too. I'm going to talk with our friend here a little longer."

Jake turned to Willie, gave him a wink. They started to leave. Lennox barked at them. They stopped and turned back.

"Willie," said Lennox. "I hope this'll teach you not to go nosing around in the trash anymore."

"Yes, sir," said Willie. "I won't do it again."

"And you won't be telling anyone about that picture you found, will you?" Lennox waved his finger. "You just forget about that."

"Yes, sir."

Lennox waved them away. Jake and Willie left the room, walked down the stairs, and exited the hospital into the sunlight. They walked a few blocks in silence, both of them processing what had just happened. As they passed the Balmer schoolhouse, Jake looked over at Willie, who didn't look particularly happy for someone who'd just been set free.

"It's okay, Willie," Jake said. "We're letting you go."

"Yeah, I know," said Willie. He still looked worried.

"Is something bothering you?" Jake said.

"That man," Willie said. "The one at the hospital. I seen him before."

"That's right. At the Pig last night. I saw you there."

"I mean before that," said Willie.

Jake stopped on the sidewalk. Willie stopped too.

"When was this?" Jake said. "Where else did you see him?"

Willie stared at the ground.

"C'mon, Willie," Jake said. "You need to tell me."

"I can't," Willie said. "Danny made me promise. He said we'd get in trouble if anyone knew."

Jake leaned down and put his hand on Willie's shoulder. Willie shook it off.

"Where did you go with Danny last night, Willie?" Jake said. "I won't tell Danny it was you that told me."

Willie wriggled a moment, wrestling with his conscience. It

was hard to decide what to do when all his choices seemed equally bad.

"There was this house in Pacific Beach. Danny said they had girls there—you know, girls you can pay to do stuff."

Jake resisted the impulse to grab Willie. It wasn't Willie he really wanted to shake. It was Danny. He knew Danny had instigated the trip.

"Did you go into the house, Willie? Did Danny?"

Willie guffawed. "Nah. We was too scared to go in. Even Danny. We just sat and watched from across the street. We saw some people go in. We didn't see any girls."

Jake narrowed his eyes. "Was that where you saw Mr. Hilton? You saw him go into the house?"

"We didn't see him go in. But we saw those two guys dragging him out of there."

15

FBI Director J. Edgar Hoover and his Associate Director Clyde Tolson, sat by the pool at the Del Charro Hotel sporting cream-colored business suits and brown satin ties. Sid Richardson, Texas oilman and fifty-percent owner of the hotel, sat with them. He'd put on his best summer suit as well, with a silver bulls-head bolo tie around his neck and a cowboy hat on his head. The men sat like statues, bunched together under the shade of the umbrella and staring in silence as Jake and Captain Lennox approached from the parking lot. Sid Richardson was the first to acknowledge the policemen, tipping his Stetson brim like a bird dipping its beak in a puddle of rainwater.

"Good afternoon, officers," he said. "How can I help you?"

Captain Lennox pulled up six feet from the table and nodded back.

"Good afternoon, Mr. Richardson," he said. "Director Hoover. Director Tolson. I believe you've met Officer Stirling."

"We have indeed," said Hoover. "You have a good eye for men, captain."

"I'll say," said Richardson, lifting his eyebrows and staring at Jake in a way that felt slightly carnivorous.

"I'm here to follow up on the incident a couple of nights ago," said Lennox.

"Ah yes," said Richardson. "Our movie star robbery. Did you find Miss Gabor's necklace?"

"Not yet, sir. I hoped we could talk to her. And her companion. Mr. Corcoran?"

"I'm afraid you just missed them," said Richardson. "They're off to the races, as we soon shall be."

"Gone with the spick and his redheaded bitch," said Hoover. Sid Richardson grimaced.

"I've asked you before, Edgar," he said. "Please refrain from referring to our guests with these crass nicknames. At least not in public."

"We're among friends here, Sid," said Hoover, looking to Lennox for confirmation. Captain Lennox didn't confirm the affinity. He didn't deny it either. Wade Lennox gave nothing away.

"Miss Gabor and Mr. Corcoran have gone to the races as guests of Mr. and Mrs. Arnaz," said Richardson.

"That Cuban bastard keeps asking me to back his TV show about the bureau," said Hoover. "He wants to make a hero out of that drunk, Purvis."

"I still think it's a good idea, Eddie," said Mr. Tolson. "Especially if you introduced each episode. It'd be great public relations for the bureau."

"I'm not working with Hollywood deviants," said Hoover. "They're all communists."

Clyde Tolson rolled his eyes and stared off toward the lobby. Captain Lennox took the lead again, turning his attention to Director Hoover.

"I understand that Mr. Corcoran worked for the FBI at one time."

"That's correct," said Hoover. "Until he got too big for his britches."

"Would you say he's a violent man? Is he capable of violence?"

"Yes and no. Artie's the kind of man gets others to do his dirty work."

"You're saying he might hire thugs?" asked Lennox. He glanced at Jake as if to confirm the relevance of the question.

"It's more like Artie has friends who employ thugs," said Hoover. "They might do him a favor."

"What's this all about?" said Tolson, interested in the conversation again. Lennox turned his attention to Tolson.

"A man named Nicky Hilton was attacked last night. He's in the hospital. We're looking for the assailants. Miss Gabor and Mr. Corcoran suspect Mr. Hilton of stealing her necklace."

Hoover started to laugh. "I'd like to see that fight," he said between chuckles. "A couple of sissies like Hilton and Corcoran scratching each other's eyes out over some slut."

"Have you found the necklace yet?" said Richardson.

"No sir," said Lennox.

"What about that colored boy I saw?" said Hoover, looking at Jake. "What'd you find out about him?"

"We've interviewed the young man," Jake said. "He's been cleared."

"Cleared of the assault on Mr. Hilton," said Captain Lennox, frowning at Jake. "He hasn't been cleared in the robbery case yet."

"Yes, that's what I meant," Jake said. He hadn't yet told Lennox about Willie seeing Todd DuBarry in Miss Gabor's room the day her necklace was stolen. The captain would have the whole department out looking for Todd if he found out about that. The repercussions from the *Creeper* case had left a bad taste in the mouth of San Diego's Finest, and Todd's blithe freedom was its bitterest note. Anyone on the force would jump at a chance to arrest him, to prove once and for all that Todd DuBarry was a degenerate and a thief. Jake wanted to find Todd before that happened, to give Todd a chance to explain himself before some cop with a grudge got a hold of him. Jake owed that much to his old teammate. Todd had been nice to Lucy, letting her look at the octopus. He hadn't punched Danny's lights out when Danny called him a pervert.

Sid Richardson checked his watch, then rose from his chair.

"Excuse me, gentlemen," he said. "I'm going to check on our limousine. It should've been here by now."

Richardson walked to the lobby and went inside. Director Hoover watched the door close behind Richardson, then turned to Captain Lennox. He had something on his mind.

"Captain," he began. "My friend Sid there is a true Texas patriot, but he's a civilian and he's got a big mouth. What I'm going to tell you next is a matter of national security. I'm counting on you and your young officer to be close-lipped about this."

"Absolutely," said Lennox. "What is it?"

"The FBI has been watching Miss Gabor for some time. We have information suggesting she may be working with a foreign intelligence agency."

"I see?" said Lennox. "Who is she working for?"

"That information is classified," said Mr. Hoover. "But I think this robbery may be a ruse, a diversion. Corcoran's behind it, I'm sure, but that Hungarian cunt is the key."

"Key to what?" said Lennox.

"The two of them are in possession of classified documents which would be of great interest to our nation's enemies. To communists."

"Geez," Jake said, not sure if he were more shocked by the director's assertion of spies in their midst or the vulgar language he used to describe them. Captain Lennox gave Jake a peevish glare, making Jake feel even more like a rube, an unsophisticated country cousin to these mature, professional men, the top lawmen in the nation. Hoover and Tolson had brought down John Dillinger and Pretty Boy Floyd. Jake was stupid and soft in comparison. Millie would chide him for using that kind of language. His mother would kill him.

"What would you like us to do?" said Captain Lennox, returning his attention to Hoover and Tolson.

"We're interested in the train case," said Hoover. "Clyde and me. I'd like you to keep us both in the loop with your investigation."

"Certainly."

"Is anyone else working the case, other than you and Officer Stirling?"

"None so far. No detectives have been assigned yet."

"Good. Let's keep it that way." Hoover turned to his partner. "Clyde, give the captain our number."

Tolson reached in his jacket pocket, removed a pen and a business card, wrote a number on the back of the card, and passed it across the table.

"That's our private line," he said. "Bungalow A. Call that number directly. Don't go through the hotel switchboard. We don't want hotel staff hearing any of this."

"I understand," said Lennox.

"Any information related to that necklace or the train case, you bring it directly to us," said Hoover. "No one else. Anything about Artie or the Hungarian bitch, you tell it to us, especially if you find any papers in the train case. Those documents are property of the United States government, for FBI and selected officials' eyes only. You don't even look at them. Is that clear?"

"Yes, sir," said Lennox, retrieving their business card from the table. Jake could almost hear the gears turning in the captain's mind.

"I assume you also have FBI agents working on this," Lennox said, turning the card in his hand.

"Of course," said Hoover.

"Can we meet them? To coordinate? I wouldn't want to get in their way."

Hoover looked over at Tolson. The assistant director shook his head.

"I'm afraid that's not possible," he said. "Our agents are working this case from another direction. They can't be too visible."

"We're counting on your discretion, captain," said Hoover. "You and your boy here. To do what's best for the country."

Lennox nodded. The door to the hotel lobby opened. Sid Richardson walked out just as a Cadillac limousine pulled into the parking lot.

"Looks like our ride's here," said Tolson. He and Hoover rose from their chairs.

"Thank you, captain," said Hoover. He glanced over at Jake.

"Both of you are welcome to join us at the track sometime, if you're free. Just call that number Clyde gave you. We've got our own private box there. We go most days the horses are running."

"Thank you, sir," Jake said, feeling an odd thrill. The director of the FBI, J. Edgar Hoover, had invited him to the horse races. He doubted he'd get a chance to take the director up on his offer, but it would be a good story to tell Millie. He and the FBI were working the same case. The fate of the nation could be in Jake's hands. One tiny sliver of it anyway.

"Gentlemen," said Richardson. "It's time. Our chariot awaits."

Richardson herded the other two men to the parking lot. The chauffeur climbed out of the limousine and opened the passenger door for them. Voices spilled out from inside the car as the three men climbed in, a party already underway. The chauffeur closed the door and walked back around to the driver's side of the car. He glanced back at Jake from across the shiny black roof of the Cadillac, pausing to give a small wave before disappearing behind the tinted windows like a squirrel darting into its burrow.

"It's Todd," Jake said.

"Hmm?" said Captain Lennox.

"Nothing," Jake said. The limousine backed out of the driveway. "Just someone I used to know."

16

"What'd you think of him, Jake?" said Captain Lennox. They still stood by the pool at the Del Charro Hotel. J. Edgar Hoover and his retinue had just driven away in their black limousine, headed for the racetrack in Del Mar.

"You mean Mr. Hoover?" Jake said.

"Tough son-of-a-bitch, isn't he?"

"Yes, sir."

"He seems to have taken a shine to you."

"If you say so, sir," Jake said. Lennox was testing him, to see if Jake had any fancy ideas about joining the bureau. Jake wasn't FBI material. Not yet anyway. And Lennox would be there to take him down a notch if he forgot. The captain moved in closer and lowered his voice.

"You understand, Officer Stirling," he said. "Not a word of this to anyone. Not your family, not your friends, not your waitress girlfriend. If I find out you've told anyone about what the director just told us, you'll be on graveyard shift the rest of your career. You understand?"

"Yes, sir," Jake said, wondering how Lennox knew about

Millie. La Jolla was a small town, he supposed. Everyone knew everything about everyone. The captain knew what everyone else knew and a few things they didn't.

"You interviewed this Gabor woman," said Lennox. "What do you think?"

"About what, sir?"

"You think she's a spy?"

Jake shrugged.

"She's got a funny accent, I guess."

"Did she attempt to seduce you?"

Jake felt his face flush. "No, sir. I don't think so."

Lennox chuckled. "You wouldn't even know where to start with a piece of ass like that, would you, Stirling?"

"Sir?"

"Never mind," said Lennox. "Let's talk to the manager. Unless he's gone to the races like everyone else."

They turned and walked across the concrete patio toward the office. A pale-skinned young man in a crisp short-sleeved shirt approached them.

"Excuse me," he said. "Is one of you Officer Stirling?"

"He is," said Lennox, giving a quick tilt of his head in Jake's direction.

"Yes. Thank you. Officer Stirling, my name is Don Santry. I came over from London with Mr. Chandler. He'd like to speak with you. Over there."

Santry pointed toward the other end of the pool, where the famous writer sat at a table under the shade of an umbrella. Jake glanced over at his boss. Lennox nodded.

"Go ahead," he said. "I'll talk to the manager."

Lennox walked to the registration office. Jake followed Santry.

"Do you work for Mr. Chandler?" Jake asked.

"Yes," said Santry. "I'm his nurse. I should warn you, he's in one of his moods. I shouldn't have let him go out last night."

"I saw him with some friends at the Whaling Bar," Jake said, recalling the foursome of writers he'd encountered last night.

"He shouldn't be drinking at all," said Santry. "But it's good for him to get out once in a while and socialize. He gets so gloomy when he sits in the house all day. I thought getting him out here by the pool for a while might brighten his mood. We'll see."

Jake and Santry arrived at the table. Chandler lifted his head and stared up at Jake through thick glass lenses set in heavy black frames. He looked a lot older than the man Jake had saved from shooting himself a year ago. He looked even older than he had last night, when the touch of alcohol had brightened his dismal countenance. Chandler slumped in his deck chair like a supercilious lizard, impeccably dressed in a dark suit, white shirt, and tie. His black shoes were spit shined and bright, but his face gave off the dull grayness of lead.

"So you're Stirling," he said.

"Yes, sir," Jake said. "Officer Jake Stirling. We met last night at the Whaling Bar. You were at the table with Mr. Miller."

"You and I met once before, didn't we?"

"Yes," Jake nodded. "At your home, last year." It wasn't Jake's place to say anything else about that night. Not unless Chandler wanted to talk about it.

"Have a seat," said Chandler, waving his arm at the other chairs like a penguin with an errant flipper. Jake sat down across from Chandler. The nurse, Santry, lowered himself toward the chair in between them.

"Get lost, Santry," said Chandler. The nurse froze, halfway seated. "This is a private matter, between the cop and me. It's not for your damn memoirs."

"Yes, Mr. Chandler," said Santry, returning to standing. "Is there anything I can get for you?"

"A couple of gimlets," said Chandler. "And one for my cop friend too."

"No alcohol today, Mr. Chandler. Doctor's orders."

"Go away then."

Santry hesitated. "I'll bring some ice water," he said. "It's hot out."

"Yes, yes, go away," said Chandler, flapping his arm. Santry retreated and headed back toward the bungalows.

"Son of a bitch," said Chandler. "I brought that fellow back with me from England and now he thinks he's in charge of my life."

"He's just trying to do his job," Jake said. "How can I help you, Mr. Chandler?"

Chandler leaned forward. "What'd you do with my gun?"

"Excuse me?"

"It was you that was there, wasn't it? When I shot up the bathroom."

Jake nodded. "Yes, sir. I took the gun away from you and removed it from the scene. Standard procedure in a situation like that."

"When a gin-soaked hack tries to eat a bullet, you mean?"

"Yes, sir."

"So where is it?"

"The gun?"

"Yes. My service revolver. The gun. What'd you do with it?"

"I put it in an evidence bag and turned it in at the station."

"What happened to it after that?"

"Well, it might've stayed at the station a couple of days and then gotten transferred to our central evidence facility. It would stay there until the case is closed or there's a trial."

"How do I get my gun back?"

"Just go to the station. Fill out a request form. There should be a record on file. It might take a few days."

"That's what I thought. What did you really do with it?"

"Sir?"

"I filled out those forms already. They can't find the damn gun."

Jake turned his head and looked down the path toward the

bungalows, hoping that Santry would reappear soon with the ice water. He wondered if the nurse knew about Chandler's attempt to reclaim his old revolver. Perhaps that was why Chandler had sent the nurse away. It was Santry's job to keep Chandler healthy. Alive. The pistol was a danger to him, especially when combined with alcohol.

"They must've misfiled it or something," Jake said.

"Yeah," said Chandler. "Or some cop needed a plant."

"Excuse me, sir?"

Chandler coughed. He pulled a handkerchief from his breast pocket and covered his mouth, then coughed some more, a dry hack that sounded like a rusty gearbox slipping a shift. Jake glanced toward the bungalows. Santry hadn't appeared yet. He looked over at the lobby entrance. Captain Lennox was still inside. Chandler coughed again.

"Are you all right, sir?" Jake said, leaning forward.

Chandler nodded his head and held up his hand, indicating he would recover. He coughed again, folded up the handkerchief and slipped it back into his pocket. He slumped even lower into his chair.

"That was my service revolver you took from me, Stirling," he said, rubbing his temples with the thumb and fourth finger of his right hand. "I carried it with me in the Great War. The first world war, I mean, not the mechanized slaughter of civilians that was the last one. It was soldier against soldier back in my day. Still a bit of the old chivalry. Soldier against mud. Soldier against hunger and disease. I shot my first German with that gun. I shot him from as close as you are to me now, changed a man from a light to a lump with a squeeze of the trigger. This was before the Nazis arrived, before Truman dropped the bomb, before murder became just another form of industrial waste. Killing was a personal thing back then. They've taken all the fun out of it now."

Jake didn't know what to say. He wondered if writers were always like this, spewing big words and dramatic pronouncements. Mr. Miller liked to talk too, but at least Jake could understand what Miller said most of the time. Miller seemed a lot happier than Mr. Chandler. He was certainly more agreeable, anyway. Mr. Miller was everyone's friend. Chandler acted like he wanted to drive people away.

"What did you mean," Jake said. "About a cop needing a plant?"

"Christ, Stirling, you really lay it on thick, don't you?" said Chandler.

"I don't know what you mean."

"This honest, upstanding cop act. It's hokum."

"It's not hokum, sir. It's just the way I try to do my job."

Chandler stared across the table at Jake, as if sizing him up, then surveyed the pool and the bright-colored umbrellas dotting the patio. A cool breeze blew through the palm trees. The fronds fluttered and clicked like needles at a tropical knitting party. Chandler grunted.

"Hell, maybe I'm dead already and this place is heaven," he said. "What a bore. The weather's the same every goddamn day. People sit around the pool, making piles of money by waving their fingers and talking on the phone. The cops are all six-foot-two and models of virtue. Okay, Stirling. I believe you. You're a straight arrow. Born of immaculate conception. And your mother's a virgin."

Jake stood up. He didn't care how rich or famous the man was, Chandler was just another foul-mouthed drunk.

"Excuse me, sir," he said, sliding his chair back under the table. "I need to get back to work."

"A word of warning, son," said Chandler, flapping his twisted flipper again. "You're in over your head."

"What do you mean?"

"Hoover's the greatest faker since Moronica Lake."

"You mean Veronica Lake."

"No. Believe me. It's Moronica. I worked with her on a movie."

Jake stared at the faded gray man in the expensive black suit.

"You don't like people much, do you, Mr. Chandler?" he said.

"I saw you talking to the director. To Hoover. What'd he want with you?"

"It's police business. That's all. I can't really talk about it."

"No, of course not. The director took you into his confidence, didn't he?"

"Yes."

"He asked you and the captain to keep things on the hush-hush. Report only to him."

"Yes."

"About that stolen necklace."

"How'd you know that?" Jake said, then regretted it.

"I wasn't sure," said Chandler, giving Jake a thin smile. "Until now."

Jake felt something twist inside him, a knotted panic. Chandler had caught him off guard, had manipulated their conversation the same way Captain Lennox did, pointing out holes in the path ahead, then knocking Jake off-balance with a blow from the rear. It made Jake angry.

"That wasn't fair," he said. "You tricked me."

"Duplicity and deceit," said Chandler, holding one hand up like a gun, thumb up and index finger extended. "An old man uses the weapons he has left to him."

"Please don't tell the captain I told you that," Jake said, fearing he'd said too much.

"Wouldn't dream of it, Officer Stirling. I wouldn't give Lennox the time of day. Besides I like you."

"You do?"

"Sure, I do. Not many like you out there. And because I like you, I'm going to give you one last piece of advice. Some information about the director. For your personal protection."

"What's that?"

"Hoover's a cocksucker, Jake. He's queer as a three dollar bill."

Jake saw the nurse, Santry, walking down the path toward them with a pitcher of water and two small glasses. He shook his head in disgust at Chandler's grotesque and ludicrous accusation.

"I have to leave now, Mr. Chandler. You're a sick man."

He turned on his heels and headed toward the lobby entrance. Chandler tossed out one last volley before Jake walked out of hearing range.

"You're right, Stirling," crowed Chandler. "I'm sick. I'm a sick, drunk, crazy old bastard. But it's the truth."

17

J ake turned his patrol car off Torrey Pines Road onto Princess Street, drove down to the end of the block and parked in front of the house at the end of the cul-de-sac. The DuBarry mansion. He'd officially been on duty for less than an hour, but he'd been working all day—interviewing Willie Denton at the substation, confronting Nicky Hilton at the hospital, and accompanying Captain Lennox to the Del Charro Hotel. None of that work had been part of his assigned shift. He wouldn't get paid for it. That was the life of a cop, as his father had often complained. Too many hours for too little pay.

Despite the long hours he'd already put in, Jake felt enlivened and excited. The outside world, the real world, had reached its hand into his little town, shaken it like a bottle of warm root beer and popped the cap. Working the La Jolla beat had never felt so urgent and fizzy.

He sighed. There was nothing urgent about answering a call from Miss DuBarry. It was a regular chore. He climbed out of the car, walked to the front door, and rang the doorbell. He heard the pad of bare feet across the foyer. The door opened and Miss DuBarry appeared, dressed in a tiki-print muumuu.

"Oh, Jake, I'm glad it's you," she said. "I'm so frightened. Come in."

Jake nodded but didn't move. Crossing the threshold into the DuBarry house was an invitation to unhappy memories or, at the very least, an unsettling journey into an alternate world. People in town said Miss DuBarry was colorful, flamboyant, free-spirited. Some called her one sandwich short of a picnic. Jake's mother said that Miss DuBarry lived her life without a filter, which was as good a description as any.

"What happened, ma'am?" he said.

Miss DuBarry squeezed her lips together, a tiny pout. She preferred to be addressed by her first name, Candace. She didn't correct him though. Her lips settled into a serious line.

"Someone's been in the house," she said. "I'm sure of it."

"What makes you say that?"

"I can't put my finger on it. Everything just seems out of place. It's almost like … God, I don't even want to say it."

"What?"

"It's like the *Creeper*."

Jake wrinkled his nose and hoped Miss DuBarry didn't notice. There'd been no report of the *Creeper* in the three years since Todd's arrest, a correlation that many said pointed to Todd's culpability. But Jake's father had insisted on Todd's innocence. No other suspect had ever been identified and it seemed odd that Miss DuBarry, Todd's mother, would bring it up now.

"Is anything missing?" Jake asked.

"No. Everything just feels … disturbed. The sliding door to the front patio was open when I came home. I'm sure I closed it before I went out."

Miss DuBarry's house sat on top of the cliffs halfway between the main village and Shores Beach. There were no other houses nearby. If someone had come in through the patio door it meant they'd taken the old Indian trail that snaked along the edge of the cliffs. Daytime visitors hiked the trail for its magnificent views of the coast, but there wasn't much to see late at night. It was dangerous, too. High school boys might still make the trip on a dare, like they did in Jake's day, hoping to catch a glimpse of the orgies Miss DuBarry was rumored to host in her living room. None of these bacchanalias had ever been witnessed, but boys who took the challenge had on occasion been rewarded with a glimpse of Miss DuBarry lying naked on her patio, soaking up moonlight and smoking a cigarette clamped in a long tortoise shell holder.

"You're sure you didn't leave the sliding door open?" Jake said.

"Yes, I'm sure," said Miss DuBarry. "I left at five-thirty for the final dress rehearsal at The Playhouse. I got back half an hour ago. I knew something was wrong as soon as I opened the door. Two men came by this morning."

"What's that?" Jake said, confused by Miss DuBarry's non sequitur.

"Big men in dark suits," she said. "They came to the front door this morning. They said they were FBI agents. They were asking about Todd."

Jake's heart skipped a beat. Hoover and Tolson had agents out searching for the necklace and train case. Did they know Todd had been in Miss Gabor's room? Did Todd know they were looking for him? If Todd had stolen the necklace, he'd need to hide it somewhere. Perhaps here, in his mother's house.

"Has Todd been here recently?" he asked.

"I haven't seen him for months," said Miss DuBarry. "He doesn't speak to me anymore."

"Does he have a key to the house?"

"I suppose he might. I never changed the locks. Is he in trouble again?"

"I don't know," Jake said, shaking his head. "What did the FBI men say?"

"Very little. I found them quite vulgar."

"How so?"

"They were coarse, dirty, and rude. They wouldn't respond to my inquiries."

Jake scratched the back of his neck. Something wasn't right. Director Hoover's foul mouth aside, his agents were said to be scrupulous squares—often arrogant, but well dressed and businesslike.

"You're sure these men were with the FBI?" he said.

"That's what they claimed." said Miss DuBarry. "They flashed some sort of badges at me. Rather furtively, I might add. I didn't let them into the house. There was something about them that gave me the creeps."

"I understand," Jake said. There was more to this than Miss DuBarry's usual need for attention. "I can take a look around, if you'd like me to."

Miss DuBarry stepped back from the doorway. Jake entered the foyer. It had been at least three years since he'd been in the house, back in high school when he and Todd were still friends. The DuBarrys had built the house shortly after they'd arrived in town, giving license to a local architect to indulge his wildest modernist schemes. The mansion's austere style had caused some consternation amongst the town's traditionalists. They said it was too severe, that it lacked decorative flair, all right angles and windows. Few of those know-it-alls got invited to Miss DuBarry's parties, which may have contributed to their disdain. Sour grapes, as Jake's mother would say.

Miss DuBarry flipped on the lights and led Jake across the living room to the patio door.

"You see there?" she said. "How it's open?"

Jake inspected the gap in the sliding glass door. It was as wide as it needed to be, just enough for a man to slip through.

"You're sure you didn't leave it this way?" he said.

"Absolutely," said Miss DuBarry.

"And no one else has been in the house today? A maid or a cleaning person?"

Miss DuBarry shook her head.

"What about Mr. DuBarry?" Jake said.

"You mean Harry?"

"Yes, sorry," Jake said. "I mean Mr. Smith." Candace DuBarry had reverted to her maiden name after the divorce, dropping the hyphenated DuBarry-Smith. The money came from the DuBarry side of the family, after all. She paid the bills. She kept the name.

"Harry is far too polite to break in," said Miss DuBarry. "He always calls first if he wants to visit one of his paintings."

Jake turned from the door and surveyed the living room. The interior furnishings were as modern as the rest of the house. Large abstract paintings hung on the walls—gobbed-on paint and mashes of color. Pieces of sculpture were displayed on free-standing bases, twisted pieces of metal and stone that hinted of strange appetites, but not so much they could get you arrested. He remembered how uncomfortable he'd felt when Todd had first brought him over to the house, how Miss DuBarry had explained all the art to him, telling him what each artist was trying to say. He felt like he understood the art after that, but he didn't like it any better. He didn't like art much in general. He turned back to Miss DuBarry.

"You're sure nothing's been taken?" he said.

"Not that I've been able to find. I checked the valuables in my bedroom closet and bureaus. Do you want to take a look?"

Poking around Miss DuBarry's bedroom was the last thing Jake wanted to do. He pulled out his pencil and his notebook, creating some professional distance.

"I suppose I should," he said, not wanting to give away his suspicions. "For my report."

Miss DuBarry led him down the hallway to the master bedroom where a king-sized bed sat with its headboard against the back wall facing out toward the ocean. A second hallway led past the walk-in closet to the master bath. Nothing looked out of place.

"Where do you keep your jewelry?" Jake said.

"In the closet here," said Miss DuBarry. She opened a slatted accordion door in the hallway, waved her hand at the contents inside. The abundance and extravagance of Miss DuBarry's clothing contradicted the spareness of her house. The selection of dresses, skirts, blouses, and scarves hanging in the closet outdid the inventory of the I. Magnin store. Jake wasn't an expert on women's fashion, but he expected it was more valuable, too.

"You see," said Miss DuBarry. "Everything's normal. Just like it was."

She crossed the floor and opened the top drawer of a waist-high bureau, polished wood burl and ebony.

"This is my jewelry drawer," she said. "I can't find anything missing. If they were thieves, you'd think they'd just grab it all, wouldn't you?"

Jake nodded, jotting in his notebook.

"Maybe you surprised them before they got this far," he said. "Did you hear anything when you first arrived?"

"No," said Miss DuBarry. "Mr. Marvin dropped me off in his car. I asked him in for a drink, but he declined. Bus Stop opens tomorrow."

"Who's Mr. Marvin?"

"He's an actor. He's in the show at the Playhouse. He was in that Spencer Tracy movie. Bad Day at Black Rock. The rehearsal ended at eleven."

"Uh huh," Jake said. He checked his watch. 11:45. "So it would have been just after eleven when you came in?"

"Yes."

Jake wrote down the time. He tapped the eraser end of the pencil against his cheek a couple of times. He didn't want to ask but he had to.

"What about Todd's room?" he said. "Have you looked in his closet?"

A shadow passed across Miss DuBarry's eyes, like a seagull

crossing the late afternoon sun. She touched an orange scarf that hung from a nearby hook and tilted her head as she rubbed the fabric between her fingers.

"Do you mind if I take a look?" Jake said.

"What's that?"

"In Todd's room. Is it okay if I look around in there?"

"Todd hasn't stayed there in years."

"Yes. I know. I just want to check something."

"Yes, of course, dear." Miss DuBarry seemed far away now.

He left her with her clothes and jewelry, walked back down the hall, across the living room, down another hall and opened the door to Todd's old bedroom. The faded smell of absence drifted up to his nose, the sterile scent of a room left untouched by human activity. He flipped on the light switch. The room looked like he remembered it—a twin bed, nightstand, floor lamp and closet.

Inside the closet was a built-in bureau of drawers. The first time Jake had visited, his first year in high school, Todd had opened the closet door, pulled out the bottom drawer, reached back into the opening and retrieved a Cohiba cigar box wrapped in green rubber bands he kept hidden there. He showed Jake all the stuff he kept in the box—cigarettes, amphetamine diet pills Todd had stolen from his mother, a small flask of whisky, numbers tickets, and a folded-up girlie magazine—the magazine Jake's mother had later found under Jake's bed. Jake had fudged the story a bit when he shared that youthful indiscretion with Willie. He hadn't thrown the magazine in the trash after his mother had found it. He'd returned it to Todd.

Two years later, when cops arrived with a warrant to search the DuBarry house, they found something more valuable than dirty magazines behind the bureau drawers. They found jewelry—gold rings, pearl earrings, and diamond bracelets. They felt sure they'd captured the *Creeper*. Until Jake told his father what Todd had told him, that certain members of the town's moneyed class—older men and older women—had given these trinkets to Todd out of gratitude, a kind of payment for services rendered. Detective John Stirling made some discreet inquiries, checking Todd's story. Those who were willing to talk confirmed what Todd had said. Which meant Todd wasn't the *Creeper*. He'd been other places when the *Creeper* struck.

Jake knew Todd had chauffeured Miss Gabor around town, had physically defended her from Nicky Hilton. Willie Denton had seen Todd in Miss Gabor's bedroom with the train case. And Director Hoover had suggested, in rather colorful terms, that Gabor and her friends followed a loose moral compass. It all sounded familiar to Jake, like the gossip that rolled through town three years ago. But Todd was in even bigger trouble than he'd been back then. Spies and G-men were looking for him now.

Jake opened the closet. He knelt down in front of the bureau and pulled out the bottom drawer, put it to one side. He pulled out his flashlight, flipped it on, then leaned down to a point where his face almost touched the floor. He pointed the light into the opening. The cigar box was gone. In its place was a bright sparkle of diamonds. It looked like the necklace Miss Gabor had described to him.

18

The low-slung building at the end of Van Nuys Street looked like any other California ranch-style house. It sat near the mouth of a canyon on the backside of Mount Soledad at the southernmost edge of Jake's patrol area, just as Willie had described it. The house didn't look like a den of iniquity, but there were no other houses on the street, just empty lots and acres of scrubby vegetation. No streetlights. No nosy neighbors. Jake counted a dozen automobiles, curved metal shadows, parked in the cul-de-sac. Someone was throwing a party.

The diamond necklace he'd found in Todd's closet was now locked in a safe at the La Jolla substation, placed there by Mac, the night sergeant. Jake had suggested they call Captain Lennox, but Mac had demurred, saying it could wait until morning. Jake had six hours left on patrol duty before he needed to check in again. He hoped he could find Todd before then, ask him about the necklace, give Todd a chance to explain himself. It would be better for them both if he brought Todd in. Jake still hoped there was an explanation that didn't call for an arrest.

He climbed out of the car, adjusted his gun belt, and took a deep breath. The La Jolla Cab company had confirmed a fare last night from the La Valencia Hotel to this address. This was where Nicky Hilton had been abducted the previous night. Hilton had given the necklace to Miss Gabor, then tried to take it back. Perhaps he'd asked Todd to steal it for him.

He started across the street, preparing to knock on the door. Two loud pops broke the silence, muffled explosions from behind the house. There was a third pop, then a scream. The front door burst open. A jumble of human silhouettes scurried out from the house like ants disturbed from their nest. One of them spotted Jake.

"It's the cops!" the man shouted, riling the crowd even more. People darted in all directions, knocking others down, yelling and slamming car doors. The mob parted around Jake as he advanced. He passed through the doorway and spotted a young woman in a short red dress quivering in the foyer. She looked over at Jake.

"They shot him!" she screamed, holding her hands out in bloody supplication. "They shot him!"

Adrenaline rushed through Jake's body like gas igniting on a stove. He dodged another wild-eyed escapee, then unsnapped his holster and pulled his gun. He grabbed the woman's arm.

"Who did they shoot?" he shouted, pulling her into a hollow vestibule on one side of the foyer. "Where is he?"

The woman pointed to the back of the house.

"The boss," she said as others continued to escape. "They shot the boss."

"Who did it?" Jake said. "Did you see who it was?"

The woman shook her head. The house had gone quiet. Jake raised his gun again and peeked down the hallway. No one was there. He pulled the woman with him as he advanced farther into the living room. Shattered glass and playing cards covered the floor. Tires screeched outside as the last of the crowd made their escape.

"Let me go," said the woman in the red dress, pulling against his grip on her arm.

"Is he dead?" Jake said.

"Let me go." The woman tore at Jake's grip with her bright red fingernails, scraping the back of his hand. He let go.

"Ma'am, I need you to ..." he said, but the woman was out the front door before he could finish whatever he'd been planning to say. He glanced at the back of his hand, the red scratches she'd left there. He raised his gun again and took cover behind a wall.

"This is Officer Jake Stirling," he called down the hallway. "San Diego Police. Is anyone back there? Is anyone in the house?"

No one answered. Jake waited, called again.

He peeked down the hall. There were four doorways, two on either side, and a fifth one at the end of the hall. He thought about calling for backup, but the wounded man might still be alive, the only man who could identify those who had shot him.

He advanced down the hall, pausing beside each doorway, then peeking inside. The rooms were small and austere, with just a bed, a lamp, and a chair. The beds were unmade but there were no bodies in them. The room at the end of the hall was larger, like an office, with a sturdy desk in the middle and shelves of liquor against the back wall. An open safe sat in one corner of the room. A man leaned back in a chair next to the safe, a look of surprise on his face and three ragged holes in his chest.

Blackout curtains covered the near side of the room, the one closest to Jake. He elbowed the curtains aside and found a sliding glass door behind them. The door was open and the concrete patio outside was empty. There was no one in the house, no one except the dead man and Jake. It was time to call in.

A siren keened down the block as Jake headed toward the front door. By the time he reached the front stoop, there were patrol lights flashing outside. He holstered his gun and walked out to meet them.

Three patrol cars had pulled up to the curb, aiming their headlights at the front stoop. Three patrolmen crouched down defensively behind their driver side doors, pointing pistols at the house. Jake raised his hands as he stepped outside.

"I'm a police officer," he shouted. "Officer Jake Stirling."

The officers kept their guns trained on him. A voice floated out from behind them.

"He's one of mine, boys," said Captain Lennox. "Put down your weapons."

The policemen lowered their guns. Lennox emerged from the darkness behind them. He walked up to Jake, stopped, and placed his hands on his hips, asserting command.

"What the hell are you doing here, Stirling?" he asked as the patrolmen holstered their weapons and moved in behind him. "How'd you get here so fast?"

"I was patrolling the area, sir. I heard shots fired from the house."

"Go on."

"People started running out of the house. I pulled my weapon and went in, found a woman with blood on her hands. She said a man had been shot. I searched the house and found the victim in the back room. He was dead by the time I arrived. Three shots to the chest."

"Have you identified the victim?"

"No, sir. The woman referred to him as the boss."

"Where is this woman?"

"She escaped, sir. Got away from me while I was searching the house."

"Anyone else inside?" said Stirling.

"No, sir. It appears to be empty, except for the victim."

Lennox nodded, then turned and barked instructions to his men.

"One of you call for an ambulance. And tell dispatch we

have a shooting death so they can notify detectives. The other two go check inside the house. Be careful. Don't touch anything. Just confirm the victim and that there's no one else inside."

The policemen scrambled to their duties. Lennox put a hand on Jake's shoulder, looked him in the eye.

"You okay, patrolman?"

"Yes, sir," Jake said, "I'm fine."

"Good work, young man," said Lennox. He slipped his arm around Jake's shoulders and led him toward a darker patch of sidewalk, away from the house.

"Now tell me what really happened," he said, his voice low in Jake's ear, conspiratorial. "What the hell were you doing down here?"

"It's just like I told you sir," Jake said. "I was on patrol in my car, when I heard the shots fired."

"A coincidence then? You just happened to be in this area at that exact moment?"

"Yes, sir."

Lennox turned his head and looked at the house, then turned back to Jake.

"All right, officer," said Lennox. "You stick to your story. But if I find out it's any different, I'm going to have you kicked off the force."

Jake nodded.

"I know what goes on in that house," Lennox asserted, woodpeckering Jake's sternum with a long, bony finger. "If this is some kind of protection racket you're running, you're done. If you were gambling or drinking or taking a kickback, you're dead to me. Hell, even if you were just sitting out here having one of those gals polish your gearshift, you're done. I won't abide dirty cops. Do I make myself clear, patrolman?"

"Yes, sir," Jake said. "I didn't know about this place. Not until tonight."

Lennox paused his jackhammer finger. His eyes glinted

with tiny needles of light, reflecting the headlights of the patrol cars.

"Christ, Stirling," he said, shaking his head in disbelief. "Every cop in town knows about this place. Would it hurt you to have a beer with the other boys sometimes?"

"I'm sorry, sir. I don't drink."

The captain sighed. Jake felt stupid, thinking he'd been the first cop to discover the house of sin. Everyone in town seemed to know what went on there. Everyone except him. None of the transgressions the captain had accused him of had even crossed Jake's mind. He needed to explain his actions more thoroughly.

"Nicky Hilton was here last night," he said. "Two men dragged him out of the house and took him away in their car."

"Yeah. I know," said Lennox. "I got Hilton to crack. How'd you find out?"

Jake stared at the ground for a moment. Willie had told him about Hilton. If he told the captain what Willie had said, the poor kid would get dragged in for another interrogation, maybe a rougher one. Willie would tell the cops about Danny. There was no way around it. Danny had to learn there were consequences for his actions.

"I was trying to protect my brother," Jake said.

Captain Lennox tilted his head like a hawk, listening. His eyes seemed to sharpen and glisten. Jake sighed.

"Danny was out here last night. He saw what happened to Mr. Hilton. Danny's not a bad kid. He's just ... I don't know, he's drawn to bad things. My mother can't keep him in line. She can't control him. And with my dad gone, you know, I'm trying to do what I can. I thought, well I don't know what I thought. I was looking for the men who attacked Mr. Hilton."

"You were going to knock on the door and politely inquire if they were in?"

"I'm not sure what I planned to do. I was walking towards

the door when I heard the shots and people screaming. I just reacted."

Lennox nodded. "Did your brother go into the house last night?" he asked.

"No, sir. He saw the two men dragging Mr. Hilton out of there though. I think it scared him."

"Yeah, I'll bet." Captain Lennox chuckled.

"I was going to tell you," Jake said. "I wanted to take a look at the place first."

"Did you get an official statement from your brother?"

"Not yet, sir. But I will."

"All right, Jake. Good work. But you can't go around acting like the lone ranger. You're a patrolman, not a detective. I understand your frustration, but a situation like this can take time to get figured out. There's a lot of ... politics involved. You need to work with the rest of the force. Get your statements. Identify witnesses. Let the detectives take it from there. You don't get to wear the white hat. Is that understood?"

Jake nodded and looked back at the house. "I found Miss Gabor's necklace," he said, hoping for redemption. "I think it's hers anyway. Mac put it in the safe at the station. I was going to call you, but Mac said it could wait until morning."

The captain stared at Jake for a moment. Jake couldn't tell if he was angry or impressed.

"Does anyone else know about this?" the captain asked.

Jake shook his head. "No, sir. It was earlier this evening. Miss DuBarry called in, said someone had been in her house while she was out. I looked around. I found the necklace behind a bureau. In Todd's room."

"Todd DuBarry? *Creeper* Todd?"

Jake nodded. "Miss DuBarry saw the necklace, but she doesn't know where it came from."

"Any sign of that train case?"

"No, sir."

Another set of flashing lights appeared down the street, the ambulance. Captain Lennox glanced at his watch with the radium dial.

"It sounds like TD's our man," he said.

"He works at the Del Charro," Jake said. "He was driving that limousine."

"Yeah, I know," said the captain. "I checked with management while you were talking to Mr. Chandler out by the pool. Todd DuBarry is Mr. Richardson's chauffeur. He got in some kind of scrape with Nicky Hilton outside the La Valencia a couple nights ago. Miss Gabor was there."

"I'd like to bring in Todd on my own, captain," Jake said. Lennox seemed to know everything he did. "If you can give me a day or two to find him, maybe I can convince him to turn himself in."

"Yeah," said Lennox, stroking his chin. "That might be best. Director Hoover wants us to keep this thing under wraps anyway. Remember, it's just you and me on this, Jake. Now get back to your beat. I'll take care of things here. I'll talk to Mac too, tell him to keep his mouth shut."

"Yes, sir," Jake said. The ambulance arrived. He watched Lennox walk over to greet the medics, then returned to his car.

He started the engine, then circled the cul-de-sac and headed back down the street, glancing in the rear-view mirror, and watching the flashing lights recede from view. Something bothered him, something at the back of his mind that he couldn't quite figure. He checked the clock in the dashboard. A half hour had passed since he'd first parked across from the house. It felt like two hours. He couldn't have spent more than five minutes inside the house, but Lennox and the other cops had arrived by the time he walked out. How had they all managed to get there so soon? And why was the captain there with them?

19

"What do you think?" asked Millie.

"About what?" Jake said.

"The play, silly. Do you like it?"

Jake surveyed the crowd milling about the entrance to the high school auditorium. It was a different crowd from the last time he'd been here, attending his own graduation. The theater audience dressed up like the folks you'd find at the La Valencia Hotel on Friday and Saturday evenings, high society in tuxes and evening gowns. He felt awkward, but Millie seemed pleased to be there, which made him happy. She didn't need an evening gown to look beautiful.

"It's pretty good, I guess," he said, turning back to Millie. "That guy who plays the cowboy, he's the one who gave you the tickets?"

"Yes. That's Mr. Marvin. Lee. He eats at the diner every day. He says it's the best place in town."

Jake felt a twinge of jealousy, fearing that Mr. Marvin, the Hollywood actor who'd rebuffed Miss DuBarry's advances, was making a play for his girl.

"What movie did you say he was in?" Jake asked.

"The Wild One. That motorcycle movie with Marlon Brando. Lee played the bad guy."

"Oh yeah." Jake wrinkled his nose. He'd seen the movie, but he hadn't liked it much. He thought it glorified criminals. Marlon Brando wasn't exactly a good guy in the movie. He was just better than the other guy, Mr. Marvin. The gang members were all punks, one rung above juvenile delinquents on the criminal career ladder. Danny had seen the movie too and seemed to admire the characters' renegade lives. Jake glanced at his watch. It was 8:05. Millie said the play ended at nine, which would give him an hour to walk her home, go back to his apartment, change clothes and report for duty at 10:00. He was cutting it close, but he wanted to please her. And he wanted to make sure this Lee Marvin character knew she was spoken for, that he could look elsewhere if he wanted a summer fling. Miss DuBarry was probably still available.

"Oh, gosh," Millie said. She leaned in close to him and whispered. "Isn't that Lucy from TV? And Desi?"

Jake glanced in the direction Millie had indicated. A glamorous redhead stood by the trashcan, smoking a cigarette, giving the side eye to a dark-haired man who stood next to her. The man waved his hands in front of his face, expressing his enthusiasm to a petite blonde who stood with her back to the crowd.

"Yes," Jake said, remembering the group from the Del Charro. "I think that's them. They're in town for the races."

"She looks so beautiful in person," said Millie.

"I guess," Jake said. It was all too much for him, the buzzy glamour and high society chatter. He felt out of place. The blond woman talking to Desi and Lucy looked over her shoulder and smiled at him. Jake dropped his head and stared down into his Dixie Cup of Hawaiian Punch.

"Who's that?" said Millie.

"Who?"

"The blond woman with them. She's waving at us."

Jake looked up at Millie, then over at the group.

"Her name's Zsa Zsa Gabor," he said. "She's an actress. I met her on duty."

"She's coming over here," said Millie. She sounded excited, but Jake only felt doom approaching. He lifted his shoulders and set them in place, prepared to meet the situation head on. Miss Gabor floated across the concrete floor toward them, an ethereal, bosomy sprite. Jake recognized the diamond necklace that encircled her throat. She must have retrieved it from the police station earlier in the day. Or the captain had returned it to her in person.

"I thought that was you," Gabor cooed, dangling one hand in the air as she approached. "I thought that was my young policeman. Hello, dahling."

"Good evening, Miss Gabor," Jake said. "How are you?"

"I'm well. Enjoying the play. Fred and Benay are wonderful, of course. I've known them for years. Lovely people. Are you going to introduce me to your lady friend?"

"Oh, yeah ... um ..."

"I'm Millie," said Millie. "Millie Nelson. Lopez, I mean. Millie Lopez. Nelson was my husband's last name."

Miss Gabor swatted away Millie's verbal stumble.

"Oh, dahling. I understand. I've been through two husbands already. It gets confusing for everyone. I just say Zsa Zsa and let them work out the rest for themselves."

Millie laughed. Miss Gabor laughed. Jake tried to smile. He felt like an awkward schoolboy between the two women, a goody two shoes, out of his depth.

"That's a remarkable necklace you're wearing," said Millie.

"Oh this?" said Gabor, patting the jewels on her skin. "Thank you. Your young man found it for me."

"He did?"

Miss Gabor leaned in toward Millie with a conspiring whisper.

"He hasn't told you about us, has he, Millie?"

"Not exactly," Millie whispered back. She arched an eyebrow and looked over at Jake. "He said he met you on duty."

"Jake is my knight in shining armor," said Miss Gabor. "You see, this necklace was stolen from my boudoir two days ago. I never thought I'd see it again. Then a handsome young police officer came to interview me. He made little notes in his book and less than forty-eight hours later ... Voilà! Like a magic trick."

"I got lucky," Jake said. "Just doing my job."

"Such a modest young man too," said Miss Gabor. "Your captain tells me you're quite enthusiastic about your work. He said he's keeping an eye on you."

Jake didn't doubt what the captain had told Miss Gabor. To his ears it meant something different than how she might have heard it, the difference between a promotion and just keeping his job. Millie smiled at him with something that looked like pride, as if she thought the captain's remarks were a compliment too. Jake wasn't sure.

"When did you see Captain Lennox?" he asked.

"This afternoon. He brought me the necklace. Now, I hate to bother you, with everything you've done for me ..."

"What is it?" Jake said.

"Do you think you might still be able to find the train case? Your captain seemed rather noncommittal when I asked. A bit churlish. He said the department had other priorities. I don't mean to seem ungrateful, but the case was a gift from Artie. Mr. Corcoran. He's still angry with me."

"It's not your fault the train case was stolen," Jake said. He knew the captain had lied to Miss Gabor, playing down their involvement. Captain Lennox wanted to find the train case as much as Jake did, to recover its secrets and return them to Director Hoover. It was their patriotic duty to assist the FBI in its investigation. He wondered how Millie would react if he told her about Mr. Hoover's accusations—that Miss Gabor was a communist, perhaps even a spy.

"Do you know Todd DuBarry?" he asked, then wished he hadn't. He wasn't on duty and the captain had asked him to keep Todd's name under wraps. Now both Millie and Miss Gabor had heard it.

"I don't think I know anyone by that name," said Gabor. "What does he look like?"

"He's the same age as me, a little bigger, blond hair," Jake said. It was too late for misgivings. "Someone told me he drove you to the La Valencia a couple of nights ago, that he intervened on your behalf with Mr. Hilton."

"You mean the chauffeur? That Todd?"

"Yes. Todd DuBarry."

"Ah yes. Like Madame DuBarry, the French courtesan. Such a gallant young man. And handsome too. What is it they put in the water here? Such valorous and attractive young men all about."

Millie glared at Gabor for a split second then gave a curt laugh.

"There's plenty of attractive ones around," she said, with an edge in her voice Jake had never heard before. "Valorous, not so many."

"Just like in the movie business," Miss Gabor replied. "The good-looking young actors are scoundrels."

Jake felt unsettled by the tone the conversation had taken.

"What can you tell me about the incident with Mr. Hilton?" he asked, turning the discussion back to something more decipherable, his police work.

"Well, I have to say, Nicky was being quite awful. He called me the most horrid names. The chauffeur, this Todd fellow, it was when Nicky grabbed me that he intervened. I was wearing the necklace, you see, and Nicky decided he would take it by force. I rather enjoyed seeing him hauled along the sidewalk by the seat of his pants."

"And Todd drove you back to the Del Charro afterwards?"

"Yes. Of course."

"Did you discuss the incident? Did he say anything?"

"I thanked him, of course, and told him I'd put in a good word with Mr. Richardson. When we got back to the Del Charro, I asked him to walk me to my bungalow, which he did. I felt quite unsettled, after what had happened with Nicky. I wanted to give him a tip, as well, a token of my appreciation. He waited in the living room while I went back to my bedroom and raided Artie's stash of bills. I gave him ten dollars. I really was grateful."

"How long was Todd in the living room?"

"No more than two minutes."

"Was Mr. Corcoran there?"

"Artie had some other business that night. He didn't come home until later."

The lights in the courtyard flickered twice. The crowd stirred and moved toward the entrance. Jake knew he didn't have much time. He had to spill the beans.

"Miss Gabor," he said. "Can you think of any other time Todd might have been in your bungalow? Any reason he might have been in your bedroom?"

"Jake!" Millie gasped. Miss Gabor seemed more nonchalant.

"I can think of all sorts of reasons, dahling," she said. "Some of them rather appealing. Why do you ask?"

"That afternoon when you were at the races, someone claims to have seen Todd in your bedroom."

"Oh dear. No, that couldn't be. Quite impossible. He drove us to the races that day. The four of us—Artie, Lucy, Desi and me in Mr. Richardson's limousine. He was waiting for us when we left the grandstand to go home."

Jake knew the first race started at 2 p.m. The last one finished around five. The driving time from La Jolla to Del Mar would be forty-five minutes at most. An hour and a half to travel both ways. That gave Todd plenty of time to drive back to town, enter the bungalow, grab the train case and stash it some-where before returning to the racetrack. With no one the wiser.

"Are you sure he was at the racetrack the whole time?" Jake said, hoping for something that would let Todd off the hook. "Did you see him anytime between when he let you off and when he picked you up?"

Miss Gabor turned her head and waved at Desi and Lucy, who were walking toward them. Jake remembered Hoover's warnings and wondered if he'd divulged information he shouldn't have. To a communist spy. A Mata Hari. But Todd was in trouble and Jake had to find him.

"I saw him speaking with Mr. Hoover," Gabor said, returning her attention to Jake. "At the races, I mean."

It wasn't an answer Jake expected to hear.

"Director Hoover?" he asked. "Of the FBI?"

"Yes. Mr. Hoover sits in Mr. Richardson's box with his friend Mr. Tolson. There were some gorgeous young fellows sitting there with them."

"You're sure it was Todd you saw speaking to the director?"

"Oh yes, dahling. Rather heatedly it seems to me now. Does that help?"

"I don't know," Jake said. He glanced down at his cup of Hawaiian Punch. A tiny moth had landed in the sugary liquid and struggled to free itself. Todd had chauffeured Richardson, Hoover, and Tolson to the races the day after driving Miss Gabor and her friends there. It didn't mean there was a connection. Mr. Richardson might have loaned his limousine, and its driver, to any number of hotel guests. The lights flickered again.

"We need to go in now," Millie said, an anxious note in her voice.

"I'll be quite disappointed," said Miss Gabor, "if this Todd fellow has been rooting about in my boudoir."

Desi and Lucy arrived and after a brief introduction, disappeared with Miss Gabor into the auditorium. Jake went to dump his Hawaiian Punch in the trash then joined Millie at the back of the herd.

"Zsa Zsa," said Millie. "That's an unusual name. She's

funny. She was in that circus movie with Dean Martin and Jerry Lewis. Do you really think Todd stole her necklace?"

Jake stopped in his tracks. The captain had warned him. He'd shouldn't have asked so many questions, not with so many people around. He might've given Todd up to a communist spy.

"Please don't tell anyone else about this," he said, looking Millie in the eye so she'd know he was serious. "About Todd. About Miss Gabor."

Millie nodded. They continued toward the door. Millie stopped.

"Did you notice her makeup?" she asked.

"What's that?"

"Miss Gabor. Her makeup, around her left eye."

"What about it?"

"She really powdered things up on that side, but you could still tell. I couldn't help noticing."

"Noticing what?"

Millie sighed. The house manager waved for them to come in, anxious to close the door and get the second act started.

"It's probably nothing," Millie said. "Just that you're a policeman and I thought you'd want to know. I've seen it before. It's what we women do. She's covering a bruise. I think someone hit her."

The house manager beckoned. Jake looked at Millie, trying to process what she'd just told him. Millie smiled and headed into the theatre. Jake followed, his mind racing. What had she meant about covering bruises with makeup, what we women do? Was there some dark moment in her past she hadn't told him about? Had her soon-to-be ex-husband beat her?

"I can't believe it," Millie said, her voice brightening as they took their seats. "I got to meet Lucy and Desi. It's like I'm at a Hollywood premiere."

The lights dimmed. The play began. The audience laughed. Jake didn't laugh with them.

20

Jake walked Millie home after the show. She lived in a tiny one-bedroom apartment two blocks from the La Valencia Hotel, in the front unit of a duplex located halfway down a long stairway that dropped down from Prospect Street to Cove Park. It was a great location, in the heart of the village, but still private and out of the way, with easy access to both town and beach.

He'd managed to set aside his internal turmoil long enough to enjoy the second half of the play, especially the ending where the hick cowboy, played by Mr. Marvin, and the showgirl he'd met on the bus set off for his ranch to get married. In some ways it reminded him of his own relationship with Millie. She wasn't a showgirl, of course, but Millie had seen more of the world than Jake had. There was something in her eyes that said life wasn't a game anymore, that she understood loss and felt its pain. Millie laughed easily, but she wasn't like the girls he'd dated in high school, who were nice but frivolous, enraptured by the false assurance of sunshine and privilege that surrounded them. Millie lived in the real world. And someone had hurt her.

They walked down the stairs and stopped outside Millie's front door. She searched in her purse for her key, found it, and unlocked the door.

"Thanks for taking me to the play tonight," she said. "I had a wonderful time."

"Me too," Jake said. "I'm glad I could make it."

"I'm glad too," said Millie. "I got to meet your famous friends."

"They're not really my friends," Jake said, shrugging his shoulders.

"I'm joking," said Millie. "You get to watch me at work all the time. It's nice to be on the other side."

Jake started to say something then stopped. Their conversation felt distant and detached, as if a glass curtain had been lowered between them. He didn't know what Millie expected of him, if she worried that revealing the troubles of her past would make him pull away or cause his affection to diminish and fade. Danny said Jake was judgmental. Did Millie feel that way too?

"What is it?" she asked, like a peek through the curtain. Jake needed to break through the glass and let the pieces fall where they may.

"What you said about Miss Gabor?" he said. "Hiding her bruises. Did that happen to you? Is that how you knew?"

Millie sighed and put her key back in her purse, snapped it shut.

"I'm sorry," said Jake. "I don't mean to be nosy."

"It's okay," Millie said. She looked up at him and started to say something but was interrupted by shouting from the street below. They both turned to check on the noise. A well-dressed crowd had assembled under a streetlight on Coast Boulevard, near the retaining wall that looked down over Cove Beach. A man in a dinner jacket and tie spotted Jake and Millie above.

"Jake, is that you?" the man called, megaphoning his hands.

"What is it, Mr. Miller?" Jake asked.

"Sorry to bother you. It's Candace. Miss DuBarry. She's at it again."

"What's she doing?"

"She's had a few too many. She took my boat. We're trying to get her back in."

Jake looked back at Millie, as if to apologize. She nodded.

"Duty calls, Officer Stirling," she said. "Looks like you'd better get down there."

"I'm not on duty," Jake replied, sounding churlish. Millie smiled.

"We both know you'd feel bad if you didn't help out," she said. "That's who you are."

Millie leaned forward and kissed Jake on the lips, lingered there for a moment, then pulled away. "You're a good man, Jake Stirling," she said. "It's okay to ask me about my marriage or divorce or anything else that's on your mind. I'll tell you anything you want to know. I'm not ashamed of anything in my life."

"Thank you," Jake said, feeling tongue-tied. He wished he could think of something less formal to say, something that expressed how he felt about Millie, how much he needed her. If he could only be half as smart as Danny was with words it would suffice, but "I'll see you soon," was all he could muster.

"Go now," said Millie, almost laughing it seemed. She turned and entered her house, closed the door. Jake hustled down the stairs. Millie's kiss lingered on his lips like an invitation for the next time they were together.

He reached the bottom of the stairway and crossed the street toward Mr. Miller. The crowd at the wall were dressed in formal evening clothes. A few had drinks in their hands.

"What happened?" asked Jake as he approached

"We were all at a party, after the show, up at the Valencia," said Mr. Miller. "Candace announced that she was going for a swim, that if anyone wanted to join her, they could come along. You know how she gets."

"I know," Jake said. Miss DuBarry was often the life of a party, especially after a drink or three. Alcohol gave her magical powers that helped her convince otherwise taciturn people into doing outlandish things. Todd could do that too, even without the alcohol.

The group parted as Miller led Jake to a spot by the retaining wall. In the dim light, Jake could make out the crescent-shaped beach below and the white crests of waves coming in.

"Out there," Miller said, pointing out past the breakers, where the ocean turned to indigo ink. Jake spotted the dark shape of a small power boat bouncing on the water. A forlorn-looking figure sat in the boat, Miss DuBarry. It looked like she was wearing a cowboy hat.

"Candace was halfway out before I realized what she was doing," said Mr. Miller. "I think she killed the outboard engine, can't seem to get it started again. She's drifting."

"How'd she get a hold of your boat in the first place?"

"She found it down here on the beach."

"You put in there?"

"No. That's just it. When we came down from the hotel, I saw a boat, bumping up against the shore like it had drifted in. I realized it was The Grunion, my boat. I loaned it to Todd the other day. I shouldn't have said anything. Now Candace thinks something's happened to him."

"When did you see Todd?" Jake asked, wondering where Todd might have gone if he'd brought the boat in here, if he'd be back for it.

"I didn't see him," said Miller. "He called and asked if he could borrow the boat. I didn't think much about it. He's used it before. He knows where I keep it."

Jake felt his chest tighten. Todd had become a kind of phantom, an apparition who seemed to be everywhere, but still unseen. Had he tried to escape in Mr. Miller's boat? Had he fallen from it and drowned?

A shout went up from the crowd at the wall as Miss DuBarry stood up in the boat. She leaned down in the back of the boat and yanked at the engine pull. Once, twice. The third time she yanked lost her grip and fell back into the boat. The crowd roared, a sound halfway between alarm and laughter.

"I'd better get down there," Jake said.

"I'll join you," said Miller. "This tux is due for a cleaning, anyway."

The two men walked down the steps. Jake felt the sand kick up into his shoes as they crossed the beach. They reached the flat, wet stretch of beach that marked the tideline, then stopped and looked out toward the boat. Miss DuBarry spotted the two men on the beach. She stood up and waved both her arms. Jake took a step forward.

"Be careful," he called, but it was too late. The boat wobbled. Miss DuBarry fell over the side and into the water. A woman in the crowd above screamed. Jake pulled his wallet and keys out of his pocket, tossed them on the sand, ripped his shoes off, and sprinted into the waves. He dove into the water and swam toward the spot where Miss DuBarry had surfaced, a wet mop of blond hair. The current pushed against him, but he kept his head down and stroked hard. He ducked underwater to avoid Miss DuBarry's flailing limbs, came up behind her, reached around her waist and pulled her into him

"I've got you, Miss DuBarry," he said. "I've got you."

"Where's Todd!" she sobbed. "Did you find Todd?"

The rip current tugged against them as Jake tried to pull Miss DuBarry back into the beach, kicking furiously and stroking the water with his free arm. Her body had gone limp, and he wondered if she'd fainted. Close to shore, Mr. Miller stood in the water up to his knees, beckoning them.

"Kick, Miss DuBarry," Jake shouted. "You need to help kick."

Jake felt a surge of water below. Miss DuBarry stirred in his arms, conscious now, kicking, and helping him fight the current. The ocean rose, the rip released, and the force of a new wave carried them in toward Mr. Miller. Jake put his feet down, found sandy bottom and pushed. Mr. Miller grabbed Jake's hand, pulling him into the shallower water and together the two of them hauled Miss DuBarry onto the beach. The tipsy peanut gallery cheered.

Jake knelt on the sand to check on Miss DuBarry. It was only then that he noticed her clothes—a rhinestone-encrusted skirt, vest, and a bolo tie with a large turquoise pin. Her cowgirl hat clung to the side of her head, leather strap pulled up under her chin.

"Are you okay, Miss DuBarry," he asked. "Are you hurt?"

"He's gone, Jake," she said. "I can feel it. He's gone."

"Who's gone?"

Miss DuBarry turned her face to look at him. "My son, Jake. Something's happened to Todd."

Jake looked up toward the street, her premonitions darkening his thoughts. That wasn't a place he wanted to go. Not yet. He turned back to Miss DuBarry.

"You know how Todd is. He'll show up eventually. Are you hurt? Do you need to go to the hospital?"

Miss DuBarry looked as if she might cry, then held back. Her face settled into a pasty stillness. "I want to go home," she said.

"Sure, sure," Jake said. "We'll get you home. Let's get you up on your feet."

Jake and Miller helped Miss DuBarry stand up. She brushed the sand off her fancy cowgirl outfit, adjusted her hat and then glanced at the crowd above.

"I guess I made a fool of myself again," she said.

"No more than usual, C," said Miller. "No one will remember anything, anyway. They're all drunk."

Miss DuBarry adjusted her vest and smoothed the front of her skirt. "I'm all wet," she said, as if she'd just realized her clothes were soggy.

"So am I," Jake said. He leaned over, put his shoes on, and picked up his wallet and keys. "Let's get you home."

"I can take her, Jake," said Miller. "Let me secure the boat first."

Jake looked back toward the ocean, saw Miller's boat drifting in. He nodded. Miller walked into the water to retrieve the boat, pulled it up onto the sand. He reached into the hull, fidgeted with something, then beckoned to Jake.

"Come have a look at this," he said.

Jake walked over and looked in the boat. Miller pointed at something under the seat—a silver tube with rubber hoses extending out of a valve on the top.

"That's not mine," said Miller.

"What is it?" Jake said.

"An Aqua-Lung," said Miller. "For diving underwater. Now where did Todd pick up something like that?"

"From Scripps Pier," Jake said, remembering the report he'd read before starting his shift yesterday. Mr. Shapiro, from the ocean institute, had reported the theft of an Aqua-Lung.

21

J ake entered the police substation, reporting for duty.

"You're late, Stirling," said Mac, the desk sergeant, staring down at the chess board on the reception counter. Mac always had a game going. Most of the time he played against himself or the captain, but locals like Mr. Miller sometimes stopped in for a match.

"Sorry," Jake said. He checked his watch. Five minutes past ten. He'd never been late before but rescuing Candace DuBarry had disrupted his already tight schedule. He'd gone home, taken a shower to rinse off the sand and saltwater then changed into his uniform. That's why he was late.

"How was the party?" Mac asked.

"What party?"

"I heard you went for a swim with the theatre crowd."

"Miss DuBarry got herself in a pickle," Jake said. "I had to help out."

Mac gave Jake a sympathetic grunt. Another escapade in the colorful life of Candace DuBarry. Everyone at the station had stories to tell. Mac looked up from the chess board. "Someone's here to see you," he said.

Jake turned to discover a woman sitting in one of the chairs along the wall. She wore a tight-fitting emerald-green dress under a gray overcoat. Last night the dress had been red. The woman stared at Jake for a moment, then looked at the floor.

"Friend of yours?" Mac inquired, lifting his eyebrows.

"She gave me these," Jake said, displaying the pink tracks across the back of his left hand.

"Meow," said Mac.

"She asked to see me?" Jake said.

"Not by name," said Mac. "Said she wanted to talk to the officer she met last night and apologize. Said the guy was young and good-looking. I told her we didn't have any officers that fit that description, but you were probably the closest."

"How long has she been here?"

Mac glanced at the clock on the wall. "Came in about ten minutes ago."

"Did she say anything else?"

"Nope. Just wanted to talk to you."

Jake walked over to the woman. "Officer Jake Stirling, ma'am," he said, tapping the brim of his hat. "How can I help you?"

The woman leaned back in her chair and drew her overcoat tighter, covering up. "You remember me?" she said.

"Sure," Jake said. He held out the back of his left hand. "You gave me these."

The woman looked at Jake's hand, then nodded.

"I'm sorry," she said. "I had to get out of there. I never seen anyone shot before."

"Do you want to make some kind of statement?"

The woman glanced around the room, as skittish as a feral cat.

"Can we get out of here?" she said. "Jails make me jumpy."

"This isn't a jail," Jake said.

"Yeah, right," she said. "What do you call that cage in the back?"

"That's a holding cell," Jake said. The woman shivered.

"It gives me the willies," she said. "I don't like that guy at the desk either, giving me the eye. Is there some place else we can talk?"

Jake surveyed the room and considered his options. The station house was one big room, quiet at this time of night but far from private.

"I know who did it," the girl whispered, staring down at the floor. "I saw him." She looked up at Jake with pleading eyes. He glanced over at Mac, who moved his white queen across the board and pretended not to listen.

"Hey, Mac," Jake called, crossing over to the sergeant's desk. "Give me the car keys, will you? I'm going to take this young lady home."

Mac reached under the desk and pulled out a set of keys. Jake wrote the time in the register and signed his name, took the keys. He turned back to the woman, who'd already risen from her seat.

"Have fun, kids," said Mac as they exited through the front door.

Jake unlocked the passenger side door of the patrol car and the woman climbed in. He shut the door, got in on the driver's side, started the engine, checked his mirrors, and pulled out on to the street.

"Okay," he said. "First off, what's your name?"

The woman looked out the window. "Lola," she said.

"Okay, Lola," Jake said. "Who shot your boss?"

"I don't know his name," she said. "But I've seen him around."

"Okay then," Jake said. "Just tell me what happened last night. What you saw."

Lola continued to stare out the window, checking the sidewalk as Jake drove along Prospect Street. There were no pedestrians on the sidewalk. The restaurants and shops were all closed. Except for the La Valencia Hotel, the town had rolled up and closed for the night.

"Where are you taking me?" she said.

"Nowhere in particular," Jake said. "The car just seemed like the best place to talk. Just you and me. I'll drop you off wherever you like. After you tell me what you know. I might need an official statement at some point, but we'll talk about that later. Just tell me what you remember from last night."

"I need money," the girl asked. "I lost my job."

Jake wondered if Lola was asking him for money. Detectives might have extra money for paying off informants, but patrolmen like Jake didn't rate that kind of allowance.

"What kind of work did you do?" he asked, avoiding the topic.

Lola turned and stared at Jake for a moment. "I was a hostess," she said. "At the club. I got people drinks. And cigarettes. Other things."

"You've got experience," Jake said. "I'm sure you'll find something soon."

The woman laughed. "Yeah. Sure." She looked out the window again. "I'll find something. There's always work for someone who does what I do."

They drove in silence for a few blocks. Jake thought about the dressing down he'd received from Captain Lennox last night, the accusations of sexual impropriety. He remembered the story Willie had told him, the reason Danny had wanted to check out the house. Girls you can pay to do stuff.

"There's services," he said. "You know, for women in your situation, if you want to, you know, get out."

"What?" Lola looked back at him.

"We could check you in to social services. There's a Catholic shelter on Sixth downtown and a women's home in PB—"

"Don't make me barf," said Lola, practically hissing. "I'll tell you what I saw and then you drop me off. Not at the station. I'm not signing any statement. I can take care of myself."

"Okay, okay," Jake said, flustered. "Just tell me."

They fell silent again. Jake waited. Lola cleared her throat.

"There's this guy, about your age, he comes to the club sometimes. Not a regular customer, but I've seen him more than once. Last night he was in back with the boss. I didn't see him come in."

"There's a sliding glass door in the back room," Jake said. "He might have come in that way."

Lola nodded. "Yeah. People come in that way all the time. Not the regulars. People doing business with the boss."

"What kind of business?"

Lola shrugged. "I dunno. The boss didn't like us going back there. The door was locked most of the time. He bought and sold stuff. Cigarettes. Liquor. Other ... things."

"What kind of things?"

"Whatever people bring in." Lola looked out the window again. "The bar was running low on bourbon, so the bartender asked me to get him some more from in back. I knocked on the boss's door. He went and grabbed a couple of bottles, left the door open. That's when I saw this guy sitting at the desk across from the boss, like they were doing business. I got the bottles and left. It wasn't more than a minute later the shooting started."

Jake turned right off Prospect Street, looping back toward the village.

"You said you've seen this guy before at the club?"

"Yeah. You know, with other people."

"What kind of people?"

"Regular people. Customers."

"You know any of their names?"

Lola shook her head. "No names. That's one of the rules. We don't use their names."

"You must hear some names though. With the regulars?"

Lola sighed. "I'm not giving you any names. I can't afford to. Not in my business. Okay?"

Jake nodded. He pulled over to the side of the road, just past the lot where they were building the new Christian Science Church. It was dark. There weren't any lights on this street. He glanced over at Lola, then down at her legs. None of the girls he knew wore dresses that short. She caught him looking.

"You going to act like a real cop now?" she asked.

"What?"

"Let's make a deal, sweetheart?" Lola snickered. "You're not the first cop I've sat in the dark with, you know. Sometimes they ask me to sit on their lap."

"No, no, that's not it," Jake said, feeling embarrassed again. He hadn't even thought of how the situation would look to her. He only wanted to solve the case, to find out who'd shot her boss.

"Ready Eddie," said Lola. "That's what they call him at the club. This guy I saw with the boss."

"His name is Eddie?"

"No, stupid," said Lola, exasperated. "That was just a nickname we gave him. He's a good-looking young guy who shows up at the club with rich old ladies hanging on his arm. That's how he got the name. He's in the same business as me."

A bandsaw of light cut through the confusion in Jake's brain. "He's a gigolo," he said.

"Jigga what?"

"A man who … escorts women for money," he said, remembering Danny's explanation of the term his mother had used. That wasn't exactly how Danny had explained it, of course. Escort was a euphemism. Danny had taught Jake that word too. Euphemism.

"He escorts them, huh?" said Lola. "I like that. Maybe I can get into that racket. Bet he gets paid better too."

"Yeah, I guess," Jake said. He knew the distinction was slim. "Listen, this guy you saw with the boss, this Eddie? You say he was about my age?"

"Yeah. I guess."

"Big guy, like a football player?" Jake said. "All-American. Blond, looks like that actor, Tab Hunter?"

"That's him. That's the guy."

Jake felt a rumble start up inside him. Thoughts began to circle his brain like race cars running pace laps for the Indianapolis 500, gaining speed with each pass. If Todd was a regular patron, why had he come in through the back door of the house last night? What kind of business was he doing with the boss? Lola had intimated there was some sort of fencing operation run from the house, dealing in contraband and stolen goods.

"When you saw this guy," Jake said. "Back in the room with your boss, did you see anything else, was he carrying anything?"

"You mean a gun?"

"Did you see a gun?"

"Yeah, but he wasn't holding the gun. It was sitting on top of the desk in between them."

"What kind of gun was it?"

"I dunno." Lola shrugged.

"A pistol? A rifle? A shotgun?"

"A pistol. One of those cowboy-type guns."

"A revolver?"

"Yeah. The guy, Ready Eddie, he had a little suitcase in his lap."

"Like a woman's train case?"

Lola looked over at him.

"Yeah," she said. "That's right. A little blue train case. I think he had something in there he wanted to sell to the boss."

22

Danny Stirling turned his key in the lock of the Sunny Jim Cave Store and opened the front door. This was only the second time he'd opened the shop by himself. He didn't like going to work at eight-thirty in the morning. His afternoon shifts, Thursday to Sunday from eleven to four, were painful enough, but the owners had decided to give him more responsibility. More money too. They handed him a key, gave him instructions, and assigned him to opening duties twice a week. His mother seemed pleased when Danny informed her of his new responsibilities, seeing it as a sign of someone else's faith in her son, but Danny just figured the owners wanted to sleep in. The shop kept them busy. It was open seven days a week during the summer. He had to get up by seven-thirty, dress and eat breakfast, then walk forty-five minutes to get to the store and have it open by nine.

The shop's main attraction was the reason for its name. The original owner of the cliffside building had tunneled down to a sea cave below, then built a wooden stairway down to an observation deck at the bottom of the cave where visitors could stand and look out through the craggy opening and watch waves rolling in. Swimmers could enter the cave from the ocean, but crosscurrents and jagged rocks made for a treacherous approach that only the most skillful or foolish were willing to attempt. Taking the stairs down from the shop would cost you a quarter, but it was a safer and wiser choice. The shop also sold various collections of things Lucy liked to collect—cowrie shells, scallop shells, sand dollars, starfish, anemones, and other seaside bric-a-brac displayed in flat bins. Salt-water taffy and local curios filled out the additional shelves.

Danny locked the shop door behind him and turned on the lights. He opened the blinds to let in more light, stepped behind the sales counter, stashed his roller board and bologna sandwich, and retrieved the key to the cave entrance. He undid the padlock on the gate, flipped the switch on the fuse box and headed down the stairs. The cave had to be inspected every morning, checked for rotting wood, extruded nails, fallen rocks and any debris that might have drifted in overnight.

As he made his way down toward the mouth of the cave, the damp smell of the sea-encrusted walls grew more intense. He thought about the movie he'd seen with Willie and Rachel last night. *Creature from the Black Lagoon*. The creature's lair probably smelled like this too. He embraced its stink.

He reached the bottom of the stairs. All the steps seemed solid and safe. He tramped out to the edge of the deck and stood watching the ocean come in. The high tide had crested. Waves roared as they crashed into the rocks, bursting into sheets of white spray. Drops of salt water spattered his face. He liked standing here, before the shop opened, before the screaming kids and fat tourists invaded the place, brandishing Kodaks like six-guns and reeking of Coppertone. He didn't like people much. And a lot of people didn't seem to like him.

Even his mother didn't like him much lately. The woman who used to laugh at his childish tricks and bandage his boo-boos had disappeared. She seemed angry with him all the time. His mother didn't hug him anymore either, not that he wanted her to. She'd been out on dates with Mr. Hartwell to see plays and eat at fancy restaurants, leaving Danny to take care of Lucy, because Lucy wasn't old enough to stay at home by herself.

His brother wasn't around much either, but when Jake did show up at the house he acted like a jerk, especially now that he was a real policeman. Jake was always riding Danny about his grades and his attitude, giving little lectures about what Danny should do if he wanted to get ahead in the world. Jake said Danny's friends were misfits and weirdos, that Danny needed to make friends with more normal kids. He wanted Danny to play football and get involved in team sports.

Danny didn't want to play sports. He liked riding his roller board and reading paperback books with guns and half-naked girls on the covers. He liked sitting in a dark theater and watching movies. He liked thinking about things people didn't want him to think about—drugs and religion and sex. Jake said Danny needed to work on his morals. He recommended stupid books like *How to Win Friends and Influence People* by Dale Carnegie, which was the most boring book Danny had ever tried to read, except for *Lolita*, which was supposed to be dirty but was just some old fart talking about himself all the time.

He walked to the back of the observation deck, noticed how the rust on the safety railings had started to wear through the metal. It was quiet in this part of the cave, back where the water pooled into a calm eddy. There was a flat angle of rock at the back of the cave, so big and smooth you could lie down on it. He imagined the actress from the movie last night, lying on the rock in her bathing suit. He imagined himself as the naked creature, rising from the sea to take the woman, dripping wet.

Something moved behind him—a shadow of movement and a hot breath on the back of his neck. The creature was here. He started to turn, but it grabbed him from behind, encircled his neck with a black viselike arm and clamped a hand over his mouth.

"Take it easy, little brother," said a voice in his ear as he struggled against the creature's grip. "Just take it easy. I'm not going to hurt you."

Danny struggled for a moment, then slackened. The creature was too strong to resist. He couldn't escape. It would choke him to death if he didn't relent.

"Okay," he croaked, willing his fear into stillness.

"You'll be quiet, right?" said the creature. "If I let you go?"

"Yes," whispered Danny. It was an easy promise to make. There wasn't anyone around to hear him call for help anyway.

The creature released him. He turned to face his attacker. It wasn't a scaly monster. It was a man, encased from head to ankles in a rubbery black suit. Todd DuBarry, the golden boy. Touchdown Todd. The man everyone said was the *Creeper*. The rubberized suit made Todd seem less intimidating, almost comical, like a wet sea lion perched on a rock

"Are you okay?" Todd asked, sounding contrite. "I didn't hurt you or nothing, did I?"

Danny felt his neck. There was a tenderness just under his chin, but otherwise he felt undamaged. He could breathe. He nodded to affirm his condition.

"You're Jake Stirling's brother, right? Danny?" Todd continued, his voice softer than Danny expected it would be. "What're you doing down here?"

"I work in the shop. I had to open today."

Todd glanced up at the stairs. He was at least six inches taller than Danny, fifty pounds heavier, with bulging muscles under his rubber swimsuit.

"Is anyone else up there?" he asked.

"No," said Danny. "It's just me. I'm supposed to open at nine, but we don't usually get customers until around ten. The owners don't come in until noon today."

"Good. That's good." Todd nodded. He retreated a step, then seated himself on the bottom stairs. He lowered his head and held it with both hands.

"Are you okay?" said Danny.

"I just need to think for a minute."

"What are you doing here?" Danny asked. His fear had abated, replaced by the kindling of an adventurous curiosity. Todd was a man on the run, hiding in a dank cave where bootleggers once plied their business. It was as if one of Danny's pulp novels had come to life. "Why did you grab me like that?"

"I swam in here last night," said Todd, staring at the deck floor. "I dove from my boat and swam in through the rocks. I thought I'd get out through the door in the shop. But it was locked. I figured someone would be here in the morning. I didn't know it would be you. I thought you might yell or something."

Todd lifted his head and gazed over at Danny, his eyes like dark beads of ruin. He looked more defeated than Danny had ever imagined a rich-kid Casanova like Todd DuBarry could be, a wet, shivering dog someone had kicked out on the street.

"I'm glad it's you, Danny," Todd said. "I think you can help me."

"What do you want me to do?" said Danny. The fear drained away. He was now part of some dark conspiracy. The clandestine thrill of it enlivened his mood.

Todd stood and walked over to a hidden part of the deck, just behind the stairs.

"I took some diving equipment from the pier," he said. "A mask and some flippers. I didn't steal them. I borrowed them. I left the Aqua-Lung in Mr. Miller's boat. Call the institute and tell them you found the diving stuff here, okay? Mr. Shapiro will come and pick it all up. Don't tell him you saw me though. Don't tell anyone that you saw me."

"Okay," said Danny. Todd turned his back to Danny and pointed at the zipper running down the back of his wet suit.

"Unzip me," he said. Danny stepped forward, grabbed the zipper handle. and pulled it down from the nape of Todd's neck to the small of his back.

"Thanks," Todd said and started to peel off the suit. Danny

felt uneasy watching him strip, intimidated by Todd's atheli-cism and physical maturity. The jokes and whispers about Todd's fornicating prowess, his seductive appeal to both men and women, suggested a sexual endowment as out of propor-tion as the phallic drawings in Willie's TJ bibles. A dark blue swimsuit appeared around Todd's hips, a pair of trunks so baggy they revealed nothing of what lay underneath. Danny breathed a sigh of relief.

"They sell clothes in the shop, right?" asked Todd, stashing the wetsuit behind the rocks with the other gear. "Something I can wear?"

"There's a rack of Hawaiian shirts," said Danny. "And some sandals. And floppy hats that say La Jolla—The Jewel."

"Good," said Todd. He walked back to the dark spot behind the staircase and returned with a little blue suitcase, which he handed to Danny.

"Give this to your brother," he said. "Tell Jake I gave it to you. He'll know what to do with it. I'm going upstairs. I'm going to borrow some of those clothes. I'll pay you back for them. I promise."

"Okay."

"You stay down here until after I've left the shop."

Todd started up the stairs, then paused and looked back at Danny.

"Don't let anyone else see that case," he said. "Only Jake. Make sure you give it to Jake. He's the only person I trust. You understand?"

Danny nodded. Todd continued up the stairs and entered the shop. Danny felt his blood race with excitement. His dull little life had exploded into a world full of intrigue and danger, like in books or the movies. He sat down on the steps and stared at the blue case Todd had given him, his thoughts racing like a Corvette engine.

Up in the shop, the front door jangled open, then slammed shut with a definitive thud. Todd was gone. Danny flipped the latches on the case and looked inside it, expecting to find precious jewels, a stash of illicit drugs or secret blueprints, but there was only a torn and faded sheet of paper inside, some kind of government form. A police report.

Danny read the report. He got a big grin on his face. Jake would have to wait. This was something he wanted to show to the Perverted Savants Club.

23

Artie Corcoran was livid. Red-faced and about to burst an artery.

"Exactly what are you accusing me of?" he screamed at Captain Lennox and Jake. He was shorter than the two cops, maybe five-foot-six if he stood on his toes, but his outrage had puffed him up like a raging hyena.

"I'm not accusing you of anything, Mr. Corcoran," said Lennox. "I'm merely asking a question. Which you have not yet answered."

The three men stood in the living room of the bungalow that Corcoran shared with Miss Gabor, who'd been dispatched to her boudoir when the two cops showed up. Corcoran narrowed his eyes and hissed.

"What's your grift, copper?" he said. "Who are you working for?"

"The taxpayers of the city of San Diego," said Lennox. Jake admired his boss's steadiness as Corcoran continued his verbal assault.

"I never met a cop yet that didn't have a side grift. Who's

putting up the money? Is it Murchison? Mossello? Maybe the old man himself?"

Lennox crossed his arms and planted his feet a bit wider, bracing himself against the raging squall.

"Officer Stirling," he said, cool as lime sherbet. "Do you have any idea what Mr. Corcoran is talking about?"

"No sir," Jake said.

Corcoran looked over at Jake, then back at the captain. "Get the hell out of here," he said.

"Not yet, Mr. Corcoran," said the captain. "There's still the matter of Mr. Hilton."

Corcoran scowled. "What about him?"

"Miss Gabor says you went looking for Mr. Hilton after her necklace was stolen."

"So what if I did?"

"Nicky Hilton was assaulted later that night. He's still in the hospital."

"That's his problem, not mine."

"You didn't help put him there?"

"No. Of course not."

"Did you see Mr. Hilton that night? Did you talk to him?"

"No. Get lost."

"But you did go out looking for him?"

Corcoran traded his rage for resignation, as easily as switching off a light. "Yes. I went looking for Nicky," he said, his volume reduced. "I checked at his hotel. I looked in a couple of bars."

"Anywhere else?"

Corcoran sighed. "I know a couple of private card games Nicky drops in on when he's in town."

Lennox nodded. He glanced over at Jake, then back to Corcoran.

"We have a witness who saw Mr. Hilton being dragged out of an illicit gambling operation that night. The witness says two men assaulted and abducted Mr. Hilton. Do you know anything about that?"

Corcoran grinned. He leaned in toward the two men.

"I'll tell you something I do know," he said, with a conspiratorial wink. "Nicky Hilton owes a lot of people a lot of money. Some of those people aren't very nice."

"That's all you know?" asked Lennox.

"That's it," said Corcoran. "Now get out of my face."

The corner of Captain Lennox's mouth twitched. He blinked twice, holding back. Corcoran wasn't a lowlife hoodlum. You couldn't slap him around like some punk on the street. Artie Corcoran stayed in expensive hotels and dated movie stars. He had political connections all over the state.

"All right, Mr. Corcoran," said Lennox. "Like I said, we'll let you know if we find the train case. Or make an arrest."

"Yeah, yeah," said Corcoran. "Let me know when you've picked a fall guy."

Lennox turned and walked toward the door. Jake followed, then stopped and looked back at Corcoran.

"Why did you confront Mr. Hoover after the train case was stolen?" he said.

"Who?"

"J. Edgar Hoover. The director of the FBI. He's staying in the bungalow next door. You were observed yelling at him shortly after the necklace went missing. Mr. Hoover said you were asking about the case."

Corcoran rolled his eyes and shook his head. "Do you know who I am, son? Do you have any idea how I make a living?"

"No sir," Jake said. "Not exactly."

"I'm the grease that keeps the gears moving."

"I don't know what that means, sir."

"I bring people together. I make deals. Behind the scenes. That's how this goddam country works. It's not the politicians. They're just driving the car down the highway. The work I do, you don't read about it in the papers. I'm a mechanic. I get under the hood, change the oil, grease the wheels. I keep the car running. Yeah, I scrape my fingers sometimes. I get a little dirt under my fingernails, but I get the job done. Some boy scout in a uniform ain't going to stop me. You get it?"

Jake didn't get it. Corcoran's speech was one big euphemism, as far as he could tell. The man talked in circles.

"What's in the train case?" Jake said, taking a straight line.

"Give it up, son," sighed Corcoran. "You're way out of your league. Just be a good little policeman and find it. That case is my property."

"I thought it was Miss Gabor's case."

"I bought it. It's mine."

"Were you angry at her for losing it?"

"What?"

"Maybe angry enough to hit her?"

Lightning flashed in Corcoran's eyes again. "You little shit," he said. "Fuck you. You're a little fish. A guppy. You're nobody."

Captain Lennox cleared his throat. "I think we're done here," he said, turning away and opening the door. Jake followed.

"Hey kid," shouted Corcoran. Jake stopped and looked back.

"Ask the old man if you really want to know what's in the case," said Corcoran. He glared at Jake with a gambler's confidence, like he knew the cards in everyone's hand. "He's usually in the restaurant with his boyfriend this time of night. Ask that sonofabitch what's in the case. Ask him to explain it."

"Let's go, officer," said Captain Lennox, his voice terse and commanding. Jake followed him outside. Corcoran shut the door behind them with a vacuuming swoosh.

"What the hell was that?" Lennox said as he stomped down the path toward the parking lot.

"Sir?"

"Accusing the guy of slapping his girlfriend? Where the hell did that come from?"

"Miss Gabor had bruises, sir, around her left eye. She used makeup to cover them up."

"How'd you spot that? We barely saw her."

"Last night, sir. I went to see *Bus Stop* at the playhouse. I spoke to Miss Gabor during the intermission. That's when we … I noticed the makeup."

Lennox stopped and turned. He gave Jake the Wade eye.

"Goddammit, Stirling," he said, threatening Jake with his bony forefinger. "When your superior officer says he's done with an interview, it's done. It doesn't mean it's your turn to speak."

"Yes, sir," Jake said. "I'm sorry, sir."

"What'd you think you were going to do, anyway, asking questions like that? You think someone like Corcoran's going to confess to slapping his girlfriend around?"

"No, sir. I guess not. What do you think's in the case?"

"Hell, if I know," said Lennox. He turned and started walking again, following the winding path until they arrived at the pool, where he paused for a moment and surveyed the scene. The lights in the pool shimmered a watery blue. The patio tables were empty. The sky above them was full of stars. Lennox entered the lobby, with Jake lurching after him.

"You wait here," said Lennox, pausing near the registration desk. "I'm going into in the restaurant. The management will get antsy if you barge in there with that sidearm and uniform."

"Yes, sir," Jake said. The captain wasn't in uniform, just a regular suit. He wouldn't stir up the clientele the way an officer in uniform would. Jake would feel awkward and clumsy in the restaurant anyway, out of place. Lennox walked to the other end of the lobby and disappeared into the Jacaranda Room. Jake turned, caught the eye of the registrar at the desk.

"Good evening, officer," said the man at the desk.

"Good evening," Jake said.

"Can I help you with anything?"

"I'm fine," Jake said. He hooked his thumbs under his waistband and paced the floor in a slow ellipse, feeling like a puppy that had been scolded for peeing on the rug. The front door opened. A woman entered the lobby. A man in a tuxedo followed her in. The woman was dressed in a black evening dress with gold trim. Jake stopped in his tracks.

"Mom?" he said. His mother stared at him for a moment, processing her own bewilderment. Then she smiled.

"Jake," she said. "What are you doing here?"

"Working," he said. It felt like a stupid thing to say.

"Oh, dear," said his mother, looking concerned. "Has something happened?"

"What? No," Jake said. Everyone got nervous when the cops showed up. Even his mother, who should have known better. "I'm here with the captain. He's talking to someone in the restaurant."

"Oh, that's a relief," she said. "Um, well, Jake, this is Mr. Hartwell."

Mr. Hartwell stepped forward and offered his hand. "It's a pleasure to meet you, Jake. Your mom's told me a lot about you. She's very proud of you."

"Nice to meet you too, Mr. Hartwell," Jake said, shaking hands.

"Call me Glenn," said the older man.

"Glenn." Jake nodded. A part of his brain detached itself from the rest, bouncing around in a dozen directions, but he managed to stay upright and balanced. He knew that his mother had been dating, but this was the first time he'd seen her with one of the local bachelors. None of them knew what to say next.

"Well," said Grace, breaking the strained silence. "I suppose we should go in."

"Is Danny at home?" Jake said.

"Yes, of course," said his mother. "With Lucy."

"I might stop by later."

"Yes, well," said his mother. A glimpse of irritation flashed in her eyes, that look she used to give when she was about to scold him. "He should be there. Lucy goes to bed at eight-thirty."

The drip of ice in his mother's voice was so faint that only Jake would even notice, but it felt like a reprimand. Perhaps his mother saw his question as moral judgement, a veiled inquiry about what time she'd be home. Millie told Jake he was too hard on people. Maybe he was.

"Well," said Mr. Hartwell, with a gentle touch on Grace's elbow. "Shall we go in? Nice to meet you, Jake."

"Yes, you too, sir." Jake nodded. Mr. Hartwell and Jake's mother disappeared into the Jacaranda Room, leaving Jake by himself, feeling like a jerk. He'd tried to be the man of the house after his father died, supporting the family, defending their name, but he didn't live at home anymore. He was out on his own. Mr. Hartwell seemed like a decent man. People said he had a lot of money. Jake's mother needed to move on. They all needed to move on.

The door to the Jacaranda Room opened. Captain Lennox stomped out. He didn't look happy. He leaned in and glared at Jake from six inches away. Jake prepared himself for the wood-pecker finger.

"He wants to talk to you," said the captain, tapping Jake's chest.

"Who does?" Jake said.

"The director. J Edgar Hoover."

"What about?

"Hell, if I know." The captain started tapping his finger again. "You work for me, Stirling. Is that understood?"

"Yes, sir."

"I will not have my officers running errands for the Feds without my approval. You report back to me no matter what he tells you. Every word of it. You come right back to the station. Is that clear?"

"Yes, sir." Jake nodded his head.

"Well, what are you waiting for?" said Lennox. "Get the hell in there."

Jake stumbled as he took his first step, caught himself, then walked toward the Jacaranda Room. He slowed his steps, making a deliberate effort to calm down. The director of the FBI had asked to speak to him personally. His mother would see him talking to the director. He didn't want to screw up. Lennox shouted across the lobby as Jake reached the doorway.

"Your hat, Stirling. Don't forget to take off your hat in there."

24

J ake felt as if all eyes were on him as he followed the maître d' into the Jacaranda Room. He looked straight ahead, hoping to avoid an encounter with someone else he knew. Candles glowed from inside tinted glass jars on the tables and the jacaranda tree for which the restaurant had been named seemed to grow out of the floor. In a back corner booth sat J. Edgar Hoover and his assistant, Clyde Tolson. Sid Richardson, the Texas oilman, had joined them.

"Have a seat, young man," Hoover said, waving his fork to indicate the empty chair on the open side of the table.

"I'd rather stand, sir, if you don't mind," Jake said, tucking his patrolman's cap under his arm. He wondered if his mother had seen him come in, if she was watching him now, appraising his posture and form.

Hoover narrowed his eyes, set down his utensils, and finished chewing his steak. He jutted out his bulldog jaw.

"What do you think of this young man, Clyde?" he said. Assistant Director Tolson looked up from his plate of chicken, mashed potatoes, and peas.

"Well-mannered and fit," he said. "Considerably more so in both departments than his supervisor."

Hoover nodded. "You ever considered applying for job with the FBI, son?" he said.

"No, sir," Jake said. "I've only been a policeman a year and a half now."

"You go to college?"

"No, sir."

Hoover nodded again. He was filing away information, making notes in his head. That's what Jake figured, anyway.

"Well, that can be got around, if you pass the exam," said Hoover. "What made you want to be a policeman?"

"My father was a detective with the department, sir."

"I see. And what does your father do now?"

"My father is gone, sir," Jake said, hoping the director wouldn't dig any deeper on the topic. He didn't.

"Sounds to me like Artie Corcoran bamboozled your boss," said Hoover.

"I wouldn't put it that way, sir."

"Oh?"

"Mr. Corcoran resisted our enquiries. That's all."

Hoover glanced over at Tolson, who looked up from his dinner plate.

"Your boss," Tolson said. "What kind of man is he?"

"I'm not sure what you mean, sir."

"Do you like him? Do you trust him?"

"He's tough, but fair."

"I don't like the man, myself," Hoover said. "Something slippery about him, too eager to make friends. I wouldn't put much faith in the man if I were you."

Jake didn't say anything. He wouldn't respond to an attack on his boss. It was one thing to air out complaints with his mother or Millie, but quite another to gripe to the director of the FBI. The tone of the conversation made him uncomfortable. Did the FBI have something on Captain Lennox or were they just testing Jake's loyalty? The captain had asked him to report on everything the FBI men said. Jake shifted his weight. He might leave the last part out when he gave his account to the captain.

"What makes you think Corcoran assaulted Miss Gabor?" said Tolson.

"Excuse me, sir?" Jake said. They'd shifted focus. The question took him by surprise.

"It wouldn't be the first time," Hoover said, "that Artie beat one of his whores."

"Edgar," said Tolson, sounding like an annoyed spouse. "Let's stick to the topic at hand."

Hoover scowled but remained silent. Tolson turned back to Jake and lowered his voice.

"What's your evidence for abuse?" he said. "Do you have enough to arrest him?"

"It's conjecture at this point," Jake said. "Based on Miss Gabor's appearance and demeanor. She hasn't filed a complaint, so I can't arrest him."

"Do you think it has something to do with the robbery?"

"I wouldn't know, sir."

"Apparently there was an incident involving Miss Gabor and Nicky Hilton a few nights ago. At another hotel?"

Jake nodded. "Mr. Hilton attacked Miss Gabor outside the La Valencia," he said. "He attempted to take her necklace by force. Mr. Richardson's chauffeur intervened on Miss Gabor's behalf and physically removed Mr. Hilton from the scene."

Tolson and Hoover turned to look at their booth mate, who'd remained silent.

"Sid," said Tolson. "What do you know about this?"

Richardson separated himself from the back of the leather booth and leaned forward into the light.

"Zsa Zsa might've said something to me, I guess." He tapped the ashes from his cigarette into an empty highball glass. "I didn't really understand what she was going on about, but she demanded I give the DuBarry fellow a raise."

Jake saw a chance to ask his own questions. "How long has Todd DuBarry worked for you, Mr. Richardson?" he said.

"My driver? It's been a few weeks now, I guess. Start of the season."

"Do you know how I can get in touch with him?"

"Right now? No idea. I don't have a phone number. He checks in every morning around eight."

"Is this Tarzan you're talking about?" said Hoover. Richardson nodded. Hoover turned back to Jake. "You think the chauffeur knows something?"

Jake shrugged, keeping his cool. "I just wanted to talk to him. About the incident with Mr. Hilton. I knew Todd in high school. We played football together."

"Bosom buddies, eh?" said Hoover, staring intently at Jake.

"We were friends, yes, sir." Jake said. He looked back at Richardson. "If you'd let Todd know, the next time you see him. I'd like him to get in touch with me."

"I'll do that, son," said Richardson. "I'll let him know." He flicked his cigarette again and leaned back into the shadows.

"Thank you," Jake said. "Is there anything else I can help you with?"

The three men exchanged glances but didn't say anything. Jake was preparing to leave when Sid Richardson leaned forward again.

"Do you know anyone at this ocean institute down the street?" he said.

"Scripps?" Jake said.

"Yes," said Richardson. "I've been talking to some of them. About their atomic research. I'm considering throwing some money their way, but my friend Edgar here says the place is crawling with communists."

"I wouldn't know about that, sir," Jake said.

"Any trouble there recently?"

"Mr. Shapiro reported a theft," Jake said, remembering the report he'd read. "Some diving equipment and an Aqua-Lung."

"Aqua-Lung. That's one of them underwater breathing things, right?"

"Yes. I believe so, sir."

Richardson turned to the other men. "Shapiro was one of the people Clint and I met with the other day. He's their chief engineer. Jewish fellow."

"A pointy-head Jew." Hoover snorted. "There's a likely Commie recruit if he isn't one already. What's this fellow's first name?"

"Caleb," Jake said. "He's married. His daughter goes to high school with my brother. They seem like a nice family."

"So did the Rosenbergs," said Hoover. "Julius Rosenberg was an electrical engineer."

The men fell silent again, contemplating the challenges of rooting out traitors and communists. Jake remembered something Danny had told him, about Rachel Shapiro. Hoover stared at Jake like a cat watching a mouse.

"What is it, young man?" he grunted.

"Sir?"

"You've got something on your mind. I can tell. Spill it."

"It's just something I've heard," Jake replied. "It's not important."

"C'mon now, young man. Let's have it."

"At school, Mr. Shapiro's daughter refuses to say 'God' in the pledge of allegiance."

Hoover raised his left eyebrow. It was a note he'd been straining to find.

"You get that, Clyde?" he said. "Caleb Shapiro. Start a file on this fellow. He's an atheist. Likely a commie. Send a couple of agents to talk to him."

"I think they already did," Jake said. Mac had attached a note to the theft report.

"What's that?" said Hoover.

"FBI agents. Mr. Shapiro said two of them came to the institute after the Aqua-Lung went missing."

Hoover looked over at Tolson.

"You know anything about this, Clyde?" he said.

"I'll check with the local office," said Tolson. "It's probably unrelated, but we don't want them getting ahead of us."

"What's this all about?" Jake said. The men glanced at each other. Tolson took the lead again.

"Officer Stirling," he said. "Are you aware that the U.S. Navy conducted an underwater atomic bomb test off the coast of San Diego last year? Operation Wigwam?"

"I remember hearing something about it."

"Did you know that scientists from the Oceanographic Institute took part in the test?"

"Yes, sir. I heard that too."

"Well, as you can imagine, our nation's security would be greatly compromised if any of the people involved in the test turned out to be members of the communist party. They could be passing information to the Soviets. You understand it's the FBI's duty to investigate all possible threats?"

"Yes, sir," Jake said. "I understand. But I don't think ..."

"Yes?"

Jake found it hard to envisage Mr. Shapiro as a Soviet spy. The engineer had been reticent about discussing the theft and apologized for taking up Jake's valuable time when he came into the station to pick up the Aqua-Lung. Shapiro seemed diligent, a man who took painstaking pride in his work. Jake admired that quality in people, whatever their religion or creed.

"Information is power, son," Hoover said, as if reading Jake's thoughts. "It corrupts all men."

"I suppose so," Jake said. He nodded to indicate his assent. The FBI knew more about spies than he did. That was their job. Sid Richardson muttered something under his breath. Hoover glared at the oilman.

"What's that, Sid?" he said. "Something on your mind?"

Richardson smiled, leaned forward, and flicked cigarette ashes into his glass. "I'd like to get back to the robbery. I understand this young officer recovered the necklace. Perhaps he can help us with the train case."

A drop of sweat trickled down Jake's armpit. A request was coming, a solicitation for which there was no good answer, something that might require him to choose between his conscience and his job. Between loyalty to his boss or his country. A moral conundrum, as Danny would say.

"We have a favor to ask you," said Mr. Tolson, his eyes narrowing in concentration. "Concerning the train case, we'd like you to bring us any, and all, information you hear before you report it to anyone else. And by anyone, I mean your boss."

"We don't trust your captain," said Hoover. "He's a blabbermouth."

"What the director means," said Mr. Richardson. "Is that Captain Lennox is too much of a political man for our taste. Ambitious. He lacks the discretion required for something as delicate as this."

"Your country comes first, son," Hoover said, jutting his chin out again. "Remember that."

Jake nodded his head, a slight tilt, the smallest committal he could make. He'd promised the captain a full report on this conversation, but the top men at the FBI were asking him to keep Captain Lennox in the dark. It felt like he'd arrived at a crossroads, that whatever decision he made now would affect the rest of his career. Before he could respond any further, the maître d' returned to the table.

"Excuse me, director," said the maître d'. "I'm sorry to interrupt."

"What is it?" growled Hoover.

"It's Mr. Chandler, sir. He's quite insistent. He wants to speak with the young officer."

"Me?" Jake said.

"Yes. Mr. Chandler's at table seven, across the way."

Jake turned his head, scanned the restaurant. In the dark reaches, he spotted a man in a dark suit raising a glass to him. He turned back to the maître d'.

"Thank you. I'll stop by Mr. Chandler's table after I finish here."

The maître d' nodded and turned to leave.

"Just a minute," said Hoover.

"Yes, sir," said the maître d'.

"Is that the writer you're talking about? Raymond Chandler?"

"Yes, sir."

"Tell him to come over here. Tell him I want to talk to him."

The maître d' grimaced, as if a worm had crawled into his mouth.

"Well, what are you waiting for?" said Hoover. "Go get him."

The maître d' departed, still green in the gills. Hoover turned his attention to Jake again.

"You report back to us, Stirling," he growled. "Before you tell your boss anything. Is that clear?"

"Yes, sir."

Hoover stared at Jake for a moment, then nodded and leaned back in the booth.

"Clyde and I both appreciate this, young man. You're a credit to your family."

The maître d' returned to their table. He looked even more ill.

"What is it, man?" said Hoover. "Where is he?"

"Pardon me, sir. Mr. Chandler has declined your invitation."

"He what?" sputtered Hoover. "What did he say?"

The maître d' cleared his throat. "I would prefer not to repeat it exactly, sir. The gist of his response was that you should visit his table if you wish to talk to him."

"Who does that goddamn bastard think he is?"

"Now, Edgar," said Tolson. "Let's not ruin our dinner. You know how these Hollywood people can be."

"I'll fix that pompous son-of-a-bitch," said Hoover, setting his jaw. "I've got a file on him."

"Yes, yes," Tolson said, as if consoling a child. "Do you have anything more for Officer Stirling, or shall we let him return to his duties?"

Hoover looked up at Jake, his face hard and flushed. "No," he said. "We're done here."

25

Raymond Chandler slumped against the back of his booth in The Jacaranda Room, eyeing Jake through thick-framed glasses. His black suit blended into the dark leather upholstery and the ghostly triangle of his starched white shirt seemed to float up from inside his dinner jacket, supporting the pallid, waxy face that teetered above it. He raised a glass in salute as Jake approached.

"Good evening, Officer Stirling."

"How can I help you, Mr. Chandler?"

"I see you've made friends with the great man."

"Police business, sir. Nothing more."

"Your boss didn't look happy when he stomped out of here."

"I don't know what you're talking about."

Chandler guffawed like a horse clearing its nostrils. "I see. The young man has learned politics, the art of the half-lie," he said. "How did Mr. Hoover take my refusal of his summons to kiss the ring?"

"He was disappointed, I think."

"How about the boyfriend? What did he say?"

Jake stiffened his posture, preparing for another inquisition from Chandler, caught a glimpse of his mother looking at him from two booths over. She caught his glance and looked away. Jake returned his attention to Mr. Chandler.

"Sir, I'm on duty. If I can be of help to you in any way—"

"Did you find my gun yet?" said Chandler.

"No, sir. I haven't looked for your gun. As I told you before, you need to get in touch with our evidence room."

"And as I told you before, I've already done that. You saved my life, Stirling. I'd like to save yours."

"How are you going to do that?"

"By showing you the world as it really is."

Jake sighed. *No good deed goes unpunished.* That was something his father used to say, sitting at the kitchen table, working on his notes and a six-pack of Schlitz. Chandler leaned forward, separating himself from the coffin-like embrace of the leather booth. His eyes became focused, intense.

"You see those men over there?" he said. "The four of them at the table in the middle of the room?"

Jake turned to look. Two of the men at the table barely fit in their chairs. They sat across from each other, looking large and intimidating. Two smaller, older men sat between them, dressed in gray suits. Jake didn't recognize any of them, but he could tell by their manner that they were from out of town. Another state, another country.

"The big palookas are muscle," said Chandler. "Bodyguards for the mafia bosses. Marcello's the one with his back to us. Lansky's the little Jew."

"Meyer Lansky?" Jake said. "I thought he lived in Florida."

"Crooks take vacations too," Chandler said. "They like to go to some neutral ground where they can do business in peace. Carlos Marcello runs the mob in New Orleans."

The writer paused for a moment, took a sip of his lime-green cocktail. "Now, young Stirling," he continued, his voice taking on a steadier, academic tone. "You might want to ask yourself, what does it say about the director of the FBI that he's staying in the same hotel and dining in the same restaurant as two of the biggest gangsters in the country?"

"I don't know," Jake said, disconcerted by the presence of big-time mobsters in his little town. He wondered if Captain Lennox knew they were here.

"Those Texas oilmen who own this place," said Chandler. "Clint Murchison and Sid Richardson. They're the connection. All expenses paid."

"I don't understand."

"Hoover and his boyfriend get comped here every year. So do the mob guys. Joe McCarthy and his wife used to stay here. On the house. Nixon too."

"The vice-president?"

Chandler nodded. "Those Texas boys aren't the rubes people think. They know how to make friends. Word is they pass along tips from the gangsters to their buddy Hoover when he goes to the track. I hear the director has a knack for picking winners."

"Gangsters launder their money through racetracks," Jake said, recalling Mr. Miller's lesson in racetrack finances.

"Score one for the young officer," said Chandler. "Apparently, he's not entirely ignorant in the ways of the world."

"Are you saying Mr. Hoover gets tips from gangsters about races that are fixed?"

"I'm saying that favors are done. Sid Richardson gets a tip from one of Lansky's people. Sid goes to the races with Hoover. Sid expresses his hunch about a certain horse in a certain race. The director has learned to trust Sid's hunches. That's all."

"But that's dishonest," Jake said.

"And illegal," said Chandler. "If you could prove it. Haven't you ever wondered how the mob stays in business? Why the FBI is more concerned with communists than organized crime?"

"Communism is the greatest threat to our freedom," Jake

said. "Besides, everyone knows the mob's lawyers tie up the courts to keep their bosses out of jail."

"Maybe," said Chandler. "Did you know the Feds had a contract with Lansky's people during the war, that he put muscle on the docks and in the shipbuilder's unions?"

"What for?"

"To ward off saboteurs. Or labor strikes. Depends on your point of view."

"That was different," Jake said. "The war was different. We were fighting pure evil."

"That's true. The Nazis were worse than us. The rest of us are just ordinary evil."

"I'm not evil, sir. And I don't think you are either."

Chandler, for once, seemed taken aback. The whole restaurant, for that matter, appeared to be holding its breath and, for a moment, Jake feared they were listening to him. But it wasn't Jake's pronouncement that had sucked the air out of the room. It was the arrival of the movie star Zsa Zsa Gabor and her bungalow mate, Artie Corcoran. As the pair crossed the room to their table, the sleeves on Gabor's powder blue dress fluttered like gossamer wings, nudged by a draft from the ceiling fans. In heels, she was the same height as Corcoran, perhaps even taller. The front of her dress revealed a generous décolletage, highlighted by the sparkle of an opulent diamond necklace. Jake glanced over at his mother. She and her date, Mr. Hartwell, were as entranced as the rest of the room. Gabor and Corcoran took their seats. Everyone else let out their breath. The restaurant returned to its previous thrum.

"Now that's what my Hollywood friends call an entrance," said Chandler. "Can I assume the ostentatious display of rocks decorating the lady's bosom is the item previously reported as stolen?"

"Yes, sir," Jake said, figuring that Chandler already knew, that the old man was testing him again.

"Any arrests yet?" said Chandler.

"No. But we're making progress."

"You just need to tie up a few threads?"

"Yes, sir."

"The devil's in the details, son, like writing crime novels."

"I suppose so."

"Now, young Stirling, about my gun, could you do me a favor?"

"What is it?"

"Stop by that evidence room of yours one day, when you get a chance. Find out if my gun is still there. You don't even have to return it to me. Just make sure it's still there."

"Why wouldn't it be?"

"Just find out for me, would you? Get a good look at the thing, make sure it's mine. British revolver, a Webley MK IV. Can't be many of them around these parts. You'll know it when you see it. You tell me it's there and I'll continue my crusade through official channels. I'll stop worrying over what might have happened to it. Would you do that for me?"

Jake didn't answer immediately. Chandler was a cynical old souse, but the man's riddles and jibes carried with them a kind of bruised dignity.

"I'll have a look," Jake said. "Give me a week."

"I won't be here next week," said Chandler. "I'm moving. This place gives me the heebie-jeebies."

"Are you going back to England?"

"No. To a house on the beach. Not far from my old one. Can't remember the address. Ask our friend Miller. He'll know where to find me."

Jake nodded again. "Have a good evening, sir."

"You too, Stirling. Don't let the bad guys win."

"I'll do my best, sir."

Jake turned and headed toward the exit. His mother caught his eye and waved him over to her table.

"Glenn has a question for you, dear," she said. Jake turned his attention to her date.

"Yes, Mr. Hartwell?" he said, wondering if he'd ever escape from the Jacaranda Room. Hartwell looked somewhat chagrined, as if Jake's mother had insisted on his speaking to Jake.

"That man you were just talking to?" said Hartwell. "Is that Raymond Chandler, the writer?"

"Yes, sir. That's Mr. Chandler."

"I'm a big fan of his books."

Jake gave a thin smile and nodded.

"Have you read any of them?" said Hartwell.

"No, sir. I don't get much time for reading."

"My younger son, Danny, read one of his books, I think," said Grace. "He reads a lot of those kinds of books."

"We'll have to compare notes then, Danny and I," said Mr. Hartwell. He turned back to Jake.

"Do you think Mr. Chandler would mind if I talked to him?"

"Perhaps Jake could introduce you," said Grace, expressing enthusiasm for the idea.

"I need to get back to work, Mom," Jake said.

"Yes, of course," said Hartwell. "I'll go over and introduce myself. I hope it's okay."

Jake looked back at Chandler, the elegant lizard, slumped in his booth.

"I'm sure he'll have something to say to you," he said. "You might not like what it is."

Mr. Hartwell pursed his lips, weighing Jake's remark.

"Have a good evening," Jake said, then continued his trek toward the entrance, hoping he could make his way to the lobby without further interruption. He longed for the familiarity and isolation of his squad car. The maître d' stood at his station, keeping an eye on the diners. He smiled as Jake approached.

"All done for the night, officer?" he said.

"Yes, thank you," Jake said. "Sorry for the intrusion."

"Happy to be of service," said the maître d', as if police

incursions were a regular event. He moved to open the door. Jake took one last look around the room. He thought of Millie working at the diner, wondered what she'd make of this place. He couldn't afford to buy her dinner at a restaurant like this. He nodded to the maître d', re-entered the lobby and headed for the parking lot, then stopped dead in his tracks.

"Can I help you, sir?" said the clerk at the registration desk. Jake shook his head. It was only now that he realized what he'd seen before he left the restaurant. One of the palookas at the mob bosses' table had surrendered his seat to Artie Corcoran.

26

J ake turned his car onto La Jolla Shores Drive, down past the Del Charro Hotel on his way to Shores Beach. It had been three hours since he'd escaped the clutches of the Jacaranda Room and its formidable patrons. He had six hours still left on his shift and looked forward to doing some regular police work, something that would dispel the obsessive churning inside his brain. The radio squawked, asking for confirmation. Two people had called into the station. Both reported the same thing. *Shots fired.* He grabbed the microphone, gave Mac a 10-4 and said he was on his way.

He touched the brakes and turned down toward the beach, then took a right at Kellogg Park, working his way along the mile of open land between the Beach Club and the Ocean Institute. The calls had come in from both places, which suggested the shots must have come from somewhere in between. He rolled down his window and dropped the car's speed to a crawl. The park and the beach were deserted, with no sounds but the roar of the surf and a cry of seagulls. He reached the end of the park and started up the incline toward the Institute. The beach dropped out of sight. He pulled into the Institute's parking lot, made a U-turn, then headed back for a second pass. A man appeared in his headlights, next to the exit. Jake braked to a stop.

"Mr. Shapiro?" he said.

"Yes," said Shapiro, shielding his eyes from the light. "Is that Jake Stirling?"

Jake opened the door and climbed out. "Yes, sir,'" he said. "Did you report gunshots?"

Shapiro nodded. He pointed toward the ocean. "There's a car down there," he said. "On the beach. It looks like it drove off the bluff."

"Show me," Jake said. He pulled his flashlight from his belt and followed Shapiro to the top of the stairs that dropped down to the beach.

"There," said Mr. Shapiro, pointing to his left. Jake swept his flashlight down across the ridge and spotted a black sedan resting awkwardly at the bottom, its front bumper angled into the sand. It was a Cadillac limousine with torpedo bumpers, tire hoods and extravagant rear fins.

"I've seen that car before," said Mr. Shapiro. "At the hotel up the street."

Jake focused his light on the license plate. He felt his skin prickle. He'd seen the car before too. "Texas plates," he said. "I'll go down and have a look. You stay up here."

"I intend to," Shapiro said.

Jake walked down the steps and across the sand toward the Cadillac. He stopped twenty feet from the car, unhooked his holster, and rested his hand on the heel of his gun. His flashlight beam flickered across the tinted windows like a meteor flaring against the night sky.

"Hello?" he called. "Is anyone in there? This is Officer Jake Stirling, San Diego police."

No one answered. A high-pitched yowl cut through the night. Jake swung his flashlight up the ridge, spotted an opossum slinking away through the ice plant. He took a deep breath and returned to the automobile.

"This is the police," he called again, as he edged toward the car. Shots had been heard. He had to be cautious. "If there's someone inside the automobile, please respond if you can."

No one responded. Jake could now hear the low putter of the car's engine over the sound of the surf. It was still running. He drew up next to the passenger door, lifted the handle and pulled. A smell of blood and feces drifted up from the cabin. There was a dead man inside.

The man had slumped forward in death, face down toward the floor. Jake ran his flashlight over the body. A big man, with blond hair. A wet ragged hole in the back of his tropical shirt. He couldn't see the man's face, but there was no doubt in Jake's mind. The dead man was Todd. A physical sensation rolled through his body, a wave of sadness and regret. It was too late to save Todd. Maybe it always had been.

The car engine sputtered and coughed. Jake snapped out of his daze, reached across Todd's body, and switched off the ignition. A wave crashed on the shore. He stepped away from the car. Mr. Shapiro shouted down at him.

"Someone's coming!'"

Jake turned. A blaze of light surrounded Mr. Shapiro, outlining his silhouette at the top of the stairs. A car door opened and shut. Jake heard a voice and a second silhouette appeared behind Mr. Shapiro. Jake placed his hand on the butt of his gun. The second silhouette hailed him.

"Stirling!" shouted Captain Lennox. "What's going on down there?"

Jake released his hand from his pistol and moved toward the staircase. "There's a dead man in the car," he shouted back. "I think it's Todd DuBarry."

"I'm coming down."

Lennox walked down to meet Jake. He was still dressed in his jacket and tie, dark slacks, and shined shoes.

"You sure it's him?"

"I didn't get a good look at his face. But it's him."

"Well, hell. That kid was just asking for an ending like this. Any sign of that train case?"

"No, sir," Jake said. "I haven't looked any further. I didn't want to disturb the scene. I think this is Mr. Richardson's car. From the hotel. Todd was working as Mr. Richardson's chauffeur."

"You mean that oilman who was sitting with Hoover and Tolson?"

Jake nodded. He switched his flashlight back on and pointed it at the body. "It looks like an exit wound in his back. Mr. Shapiro reported gunshots."

Lennox nodded in agreement. "He's gunshot, for sure. Damn, Stirling. You caught two in one week. On the La Jolla beat. That's gotta be some kind of record. You think they're related?"

"Maybe," Jake said. He hadn't yet told the captain about his interview with the call girl in the red dress, Lola. "I think Todd was at the gambling house the night of the shooting."

"You saw him there?"

"Just something I heard," Jake said, protecting Lola. "Someone who knew someone who was there."

Captain Lennox stared at Jake for a moment, then returned his gaze to the dead body. "Well, it wouldn't surprise me if Todd DuBarry tried to do business with those crooks," he said. "Maybe he tried to sell them that diamond necklace."

"I'd recovered the necklace by the time Todd was there," Jake said. "I think it was something to do with the train case."

Lennox nodded. "I wish we could find that damn thing," he said. "How did the car end up down here?"

Jake turned his flashlight onto the ridge above. "There's no guardrail up there. The engine was still running when I got here. He must've lost control of the car after he was shot. Or maybe he panicked and accidentally drove off the ridge and someone shot him down here. I turned off the ignition. I didn't touch anything else."

"Did you call it in yet?"

"No, sir."

"Okay. Get back to your car and call it in. Give me your flashlight and I'll take a look around."

"Yes, sir." Jake handed his flashlight to the captain. "What about Mr. Shapiro?"

"We'll need a statement from him. He can come into the station tomorrow if he doesn't want to do it tonight."

Jake headed back to his car. He was halfway up the stairs when the captain shouted at him.

"Jake?"

"Yes, sir?"

"Bring some gloves with you when you come back. And some evidence bags. I found something."

Jake nodded and continued to the top of the stairs, spoke to Mr. Shapiro, then called in to the station and requested a detective. And a coroner's wagon. He opened the trunk of his car, retrieved his gloves and some evidence bags, then headed back down to the beach. Mr. Shapiro still stood by the top of the stairs, a dark crease in his brow.

"What is it, Mr. Shapiro?" Jake said.

"Those two men were here again today. The FBI agents. They were looking for Todd DuBarry. That's him down there in the car, isn't it?"

"Yes," Jake said. "I'm afraid so. What did the FBI agents want?"

"They asked about the Aqua-Lung that was stolen. Again. They asked about Todd working here. It was all very strange."

"What do you mean?"

Shapiro rubbed his cheek for a moment, then sighed. "I've been interviewed by FBI agents before. More than once. For security clearance related to government work that we do at the institute. They've got a file on me. Jewish. Atheist. United World

Federalist. McCarthy would've had a field day with my records. I'm no fan of Hoover, but his agents, at least the ones I've dealt with, are usually professional, well dressed, and focused. There's a certain air to them, a kind of gentile arrogance. The men I talked to today were vulgar, slovenly, crude."

"Are you sure they were FBI agents?" Jake said. Shapiro's visitors sounded like the same men who'd visited Miss DuBarry a few days ago. Her description matched Mr. Shapiro's.

"They showed me their badges," Shapiro said. He shrugged. "It's been a long day. I need to go home and get some sleep. I'll stop by the station tomorrow and fill out a statement."

"Thank you," Jake said. He started down the stairs.

"Oh, Jake," said Mr. Shapiro. "I almost forgot. Your brother Danny called me this morning. He found the rest of the gear that went missing. The flippers and masks and such. It's all accounted for now. Nothing missing."

"Where did Danny find them?"

"I'm not sure exactly. I picked them up from the Cave Shop where he's working. You might want to talk to him."

"I will."

"What's going on?"

"I couldn't say, sir. We're trying to figure it out."

"Yes. Well, I'll leave you to it. Good night."

Mr. Shapiro walked off into the darkness. Jake continued down the steps to the beach. Captain Lennox stood on the other side of the limousine. He'd opened the driver side door.

"Come take a look at this," he said. Jake circled around the front of the car, then stepped up next to the captain.

"There," Captain Lennox said, pointing down toward the floor. "Next to the gas pedal. You see it? Put your gloves on and bag that for me."

"Shouldn't we secure the scene first?" Jake asked, invoking protocol.

"I'm in charge of the scene, Stirling," the captain said, brushing aside Jake's concern. "Just bag it for me."

Jake slipped on his gloves, squatted down by the door and inspected the cut pile carpet under the steering wheel. A gun lay next to the gas pedal. He reached across Todd's dead feet and lifted it out of the car. It was an old revolver, rusty and loose.

"We could be looking at suicide," said Lennox, standing above him. "I think the kid shot himself. Right through the heart. And the bullet came out through his back."

Jake placed the gun in the paper evidence bag and folded the top of the bag. There were a lot of guns in the world, but he'd only seen one like this before. More than a year ago, in a house by the sea where the old artillery batteries had rusted into ghostly war monuments. Jake had saved a man's life that night. A drunk and disconsolate old writer who'd tried to eat his Webley revolver. It was the same gun.

27

Rachel Shapiro squatted to inspect a piece of eucalyptus bark that lay on the ground, admiring its graceful curl. Pieces of the trees' parchment-like bark littered the mesa above the Institute. Her father liked to tell her about the eucalyptus, how the trees had been brought here from Australia and planted a hundred years ago, how they'd taken root in the dry ground of Southern California and survived. Her father said people from other lands could flourish here, too. They could put down roots and grow families. Her father had told her the story so many times she was tired of hearing it.

Rachel's father had brought her along for his meeting with Uncle Roger this morning. Uncle Roger wasn't Rachel's real uncle. He was her father's boss at the Institute, Dr. Revelle. Rachel's real uncles had died in Germany during the war. Dr. Revelle was loud and enthusiastic, unlike her father, who spoke softly and rarely put more than a couple of sentences together at once. Her father liked to listen to people, ask them questions and point out problems with what they'd said. Uncle Roger was explaining one of his big ideas to her father right now.

"What do you think?" Uncle Roger asked after he'd finished his pitch.

"How big do you need the sign to be?" said Rachel's father, waving a roll of blueprints in the air.

"Like one of those highway billboards," said Uncle Roger, spreading his arms to indicate the size of his vision. "Say, from that tree over there to this one here."

"We're not really set up for printing anything that large," said her father. "I'd need to get bids if we go out of house."

"Talk to Mosher, the architect. He says they can get the printing done at cost. They've worked with the billboard people before. Your end would be mostly construction. I need you to build the frame."

Rachel's dad put his hand on his chin, grunted.

"What do you think, Rachel?" he said. "Come take a look."

She dropped the piece of curled bark and walked over to her father. He handed her one end of the blueprint and rolled it out between them.

"Uncle Roger says we're going to have a university here someday," her father said.

Rachel looked at the drawings—boxes and rectangles cross-hatched with markings for streets. There were labels on all the rectangles. First College. Second College. Ten more rectangles marked three to twelve.

"Wouldn't you like to go to college up here, Rachel?" said Uncle Roger.

Rachel surveyed the eucalyptus grove. "They're going to build it in the trees?" she said.

"That's right," he responded. "The University of California is going to build a campus right here."

"Assuming the voters approve the referendum," her father said.

"Have faith, Caleb," said Uncle Roger. "The public will be on our side. But I need to start my recruiting drive now. Poaching Nobel-Prizers from the ivy halls of Harvard and Yale will get us good press and keep the ball rolling. That's why I need the sign. So they can envision the plan when I bring them up here."

"What about housing?" said Rachel's father. "Some of your professors are bound to be Jewish."

"We'll need to get those covenants off the books," said Uncle Roger, nodding his head in acknowledgement. "If we want to attract the best people."

Rachel's father grunted. She'd heard him talk about the covenants before, the rules that prevented Jewish people from buying houses. Her father and mother talked a lot about being Jewish, about Germany and the war, about parents and relatives who'd died there. Rachel would sometimes find her father sitting in his study at night staring at the books on the shelves, looking as if he'd fallen under a witch's spell. Rachel's mother said not to bother him when he was like that.

The next morning her father would be himself again. He'd ask Rachel how she was doing in school, what she was learning, where she'd been with her friends. He'd ask her about college—what she was thinking, where she might go, telling her college wasn't just where girls went to find a rich husband. Both her parents said a higher education was important for Jews, that a bachelor's degree was a start, but a Master's or PhD would be even better. Her parents talked about being Jewish a lot, but they hardly ever went to the synagogue. Education was their true religion.

A volley of gunshots blasted the morning air, startling her. Target practice had begun at Camp Matthews. The steady crack of rifles was a regular accompaniment to life at the Institute as it echoed down from the mesa. Up here, on top of the mesa, the barrage was louder, more present. Her father glanced up from his blueprints.

"Don't bring your visitors up here when that racket's going on, Roger," he said. "That's all they'll remember about the place."

"No." Uncle Roger chuckled. "We don't want anyone catching a stray bullet, either."

"Stray bullet?" said Rachel. She moved in close to her father.

"He's joking," he said. "Weren't you, Roger?"

"Yes, yes," said Uncle Roger. "No need to be worried, Rachel. Now what do you think of these plans? Would you like to go to college here?

Rachel looked at the blueprints for the university again. "Yes," she said. "It looks nice."

"There, Caleb," said Uncle Roger. "Your daughter approves. We'll build her a university. Rachel can go here after she graduates high school."

"The campus won't be ready that soon."

"Well then, after she earns her BA, she can get her PhD here."

"Perhaps," said her father, distracted by something on the blueprint.

"Can I go look for acorns?" said Rachel. She was bored. There were still some acorn trees left on the mesa, lonely oaks that had survived the onslaught of imported eucalyptus.

"Don't go too far." Her father nodded. "We won't be here much longer."

Rachel left the two men behind and walked further into the trees. She didn't really care about acorns, but she enjoyed looking for the rabbits that grazed on them. Sometimes you could see coyotes out hunting for the rabbits. She and her mother had seen a coyote last Sunday while riding horses. The woods had been quieter then. There was no target practice on Sundays.

The rifles cracked again as she tramped through fallen eucalyptus leaves and crunched her feet on the fallen bark. She stepped in behind a big tree trunk and leaned back against it, out of sight. If her father called for her, she could step out and wave at him, set his mind at ease. He worried about so many things, especially her. Sometimes Rachel felt jealous of her friends, Willie and Danny. Their parents didn't watch them like hawks, wanting to know where they were every minute of their day. She wondered if her father would worry less if she were a boy.

The rifle fire continued, a stuttering roar. Birds in the trees twittered and chirped. Rachel closed her eyes and listened. She could hear her father and Uncle Roger still talking, but she couldn't make out the individual words, only the steady murmur of voices.

She heard a new sound, from another direction, toward the shooting range. A sound of huffing and digging. She opened her eyes and searched through the trees, saw a black flash of movement. A Labrador retriever romped and weaved through the forest. Rachel stepped away from her tree so she could see the dog better. It raised its head and ran over to her.

"Hi, boy," Rachel said, patting the Labrador's head. It barked once, then trotted back toward the spot it had come from, pausing to look at her, imploring her to follow. She glanced back toward her father, then set out after the dog. She entered a clearing where the sunshine poured in. The dog barked again. It lay down next to a pile of leaves on the ground.

"What is it?" said Rachel as she approached. "What is it, boy?"

The dog whimpered as Rachel got closer. She stopped. The pile of leaves had a body underneath them. Rifles volleyed again from the shooting range. Rachel took a step closer.

Someone whistled. The dog raised its head and ran away. Rachel stood, transfixed by the body. A dead woman lay on her back, her eyes open and staring up at the sky. She had no clothes on, except for a scrap of green dress pushed up to her armpits. The woman's legs were splayed open, her skin pale and gray, with patches of dark purple splotches on the inside of her thighs. There was something wrong about the woman's face, something incomplete. A dark blotch of sticky leaves covered a sickening hole where her left eye should be.

The Labrador retriever returned and lay down next to the body. An animal clomped through the woods after it. Rachel looked up from the body. A woman on a horse entered the clearing. It was Mrs. Marechal, who owned the stables where Rachel and her mother had rented their horses last Sunday.

"What'd you find there, Bo?" said Mrs. Marechal, pulling her horse to a stop with the reins. Her eyes grew big. "Holy cow!"

"She's dead, isn't she?" said Rachel, her voice trembling.

Mrs. Marechal climbed down from her horse and tied off the reins.

"Come here, Bo," she clucked. The dog rose and walked over to her. Mrs. Marechal grabbed the dog's collar and petted its head.

"What happened to her?" said Rachel. Mrs. Marechal squatted down next to her dog and stared at the body.

"Rachel, that's your name, right?" she said. "You're the Shapiros' daughter?"

"Yes." Rachel nodded.

"What're you doing up here all by yourself?"

"I was looking for acorns ... for rabbits," said Rachel. "My father brought me up here with Uncle Roger." She searched for her father, but he was blocked by the trees. "I saw your dog and I followed him and ..."

Rachel's voice trailed off. Her throat felt constricted, locked up tight. The air had gone out of her lungs.

"Take it easy now, Rachel," said Mrs. Marechal. "Step back and look somewhere else. Take a deep breath. Try to relax."

"Okay," said Rachel, averting her eyes from the body. She stepped back toward the trees, then stopped and took a deep breath, her heart pounding in her ears. She took another deep breath.

"Better?" said Mrs. Marechal.

"Yes."

"Okay, Rachel," said Mrs. Marechal. "Now listen to me. Does your father have a car? Did you drive up here?"

Rachel nodded. Mrs. Marechal continued.

"Go back to your father and tell him to call the police. Tell him that Mrs. Marechal from the stables found a dead body up here."

"Who is she?" said Rachel.

"I don't know," said Mrs. Marechal. "You just run along now and tell him. I'm going to wait here until the police arrive. Do you understand?"

"Yes," said Rachel, nodding. "I understand."

"Okay, go ahead now. Be careful."

Rachel walked back through the woods, toward her father and Uncle Roger. Rifles cracked on the shooting range. She started to run. Pieces of eucalyptus bark and dry leaves flew up from under her feet. The rifle fire continued. She began to run faster than she'd ever run, a panic rising inside. She couldn't see her father and Uncle Roger, couldn't hear them. Had they gone back to the car? Had they left her up here? The rifles cracked again from behind her, spraying stray bullets all over the mesa. One of those bullets might hit her and make a big hole in her face. She'd lie on the ground with blood pouring out of her eye. This was a horrible place to build a university.

28

Jake sat on a cold metal bench in the San Diego Police department's evidence room downtown, waiting for the clerk to return with the case files he'd requested from the night Raymond Chandler had tried to shoot himself. He wasn't in uniform. He had the day off. No one knew he was there, and the clerk wouldn't care, but Jake needed to prove to himself that the Webley revolver Todd DuBarry had used to put a bullet through his heart wasn't Mr. Chandler's gun. The old man's taunts now seemed like a prophecy.

Some cop needed a plant. They can't find the gun. You tell me it's there, I'll stop worrying over what might have happened to it. Chandler's words lit up Jake's brain like distress flares over the beach. A flotilla of menacing strangers invaded his thoughts, like pieces on an invisible chessboard—mobsters, oilmen, movie stars, G-men, and spies.

The clerk returned to the front counter and waved a manila envelope at Jake.

"Officer Stirling?"

Jake rose from his seat and crossed to the counter.

"These are your files," said the clerk. "Case 19550210—14. Sign here, please."

Jake signed the flap of paper attached to the envelope. The clerk took Jake's badge number and added it to the registration book. Jake signed the book as well, next to his badge number and name. The clerk pushed the manila envelope across the counter.

"There you go," he said.

"That's all there is?" Jake asked, lifting the envelope. It felt almost weightless.

"That's it."

"There's no gun in here," he said.

"We don't keep guns with the files. When a gun comes in as evidence, we take a photo of it, hang a tag on the gun, note the tag number on the photo. We lock all guns in a secure room."

"I need to see the gun," Jake said.

"Sure," said the clerk. He reached below the counter, pulled out another form, and slapped it down in front of Jake.

"Request form 1046. Fill that out and we'll get your weapon for you."

"It's not my weapon," Jake said.

"You'll see a tag attached to the gun in the photo," the clerk said, continuing over Jake's demurral. "There's a number on the tag. Write that number on the form. Any more questions?"

Others had lined up behind Jake, detectives and lawyers in suits. He moved down to the end of the counter and emptied the envelope. His handwritten notes from over a year ago were there, along with his typewritten report. The detective's follow-up report was also included, along with a mugshot of Chandler and a clipping of a story that ran in the newspaper the next day. *Writer Fires Shots in Home.* A small paper bag contained two empty shell casings and slugs the detective had dug out of the bathroom wall. There was a photograph of the Webley revolver, a paper tag tied to the trigger guard.

Jake filled out form 1046, entered the number printed on

the tag in a space labelled *Weapon ID*. He reread his old notes as well as the report he'd typed up the next day. The gun was noted correctly in each document. It was noted in the detective's report as well. He inspected the bottom of the shell cartridges. A capital *K* and a capital *I* were stamped on either side of the rims. He placed all the items back in the envelope and returned to the end of the line, feeling more settled and confident. The cops in his town weren't crooked or incompetent.

The line moved quickly. Jake stepped to the window and handed the clerk the files, along with the completed form 1046. The clerk double-checked the form, then removed the photograph of the gun from inside the envelope and checked the number on the tag. He flipped the photo over and looked at the back.

"Oops," he said.

"What do you mean, oops?" Jake said.

"I thought this gun looked familiar," said the clerk. "It's been RTO'd."

"What's that mean, RTO'd?"

"Returned to Owner."

The clerk placed the photo face down on the counter and pointed at three handwritten letters scrawled on the back —*RTO*. Under the letters was a stamped date. *06-28-56.*

"This gun was returned to its owner. Two weeks ago. June twenty-eight," said the clerk.

"You're saying the owner got it back?" asked Jake.

"That's what I'm saying," said the clerk. "If there's no criminal conviction, folks can reclaim their guns."

"Yes, but ..." Jake said, feeling like he'd been slapped in the face. "The owner asked me to check if his gun was still here. He says he doesn't have it."

The clerk shrugged. "I can't help you there."

Jake stared at the clerk for a moment, sorting through the possibilities. It had been two days since Mr. Chandler had first asked him to check on the gun. Had Chandler's earlier request made its way through the red tape in that time? Or had Chandler, doddering and drunk, misplaced the gun and forgotten he'd ever received it? Perhaps his nurse, Mr. Santry, had confiscated the gun, protecting his employer from self-harm. Or maybe Chandler had lied about the whole thing. He was a writer, after all. He made up stories for a living. The gun in Todd's car could still be Chandler's. He couldn't rule it out.

"Anything else I can help you with, son?" said the clerk. Jake stared at the date stamped on the back of the photograph. June. They were well into July now, and Chandler had only returned from England last week. That's what he'd said, anyway.

"That paper I signed," he said. "The list that's stapled to the envelope. That's all the people who've checked out the files, right?"

"That's correct," said the clerk.

"Can I see it?"

The clerk passed the envelope back. Jake checked the list. The files had only been checked out four times previously. The first three times had been last year, checked out by the detective who worked on the case. The fourth time was last month. June 28. He read the name next to the date and handed the envelope back to the clerk.

"Thanks," he said. "Is there a phone around here I can use?"

The clerk pointed to a phone sitting at the end of the counter. Jake practically ran to the phone, then lifted the receiver and dialed the number he knew like the back of his hand. A familiar voice came on the line.

"San Diego Police. La Jolla Substation. Sergeant McIntyre speaking."

"Mac, it's Jake. Jake Stirling."

"Holy shit, Jake. Where are you? We've been looking all over for you."

"What's up?"

"They found her body up on the mesa, near the firing range."

"Whose body?" Jake said, fear surging through him like an electrical charge. Was Millie dead? His mother? Lucy?

"The floozy who was here the other night, the one that came looking for you."

"Lola?"

"Was that her name? I don't think they have an ID yet. You need to get up here right now. Talk to the detectives. Clear things up."

"What are you talking about?"

There was a pause on the other end of the line as Mac spoke to someone in the office. He returned to the phone and dropped his voice.

"Listen, Jake, I'm sorry. You know how I am with my big mouth. I just blurted it out. They know about you and her."

"What do you mean, me and her?"

"About the other night. When you took her in the patrol car."

"I was interviewing her, about a case."

"Yeah, right, I'm sure it was all above board and all, but it might not look right to some people. You need to talk to the detective, clear things up."

"Okay," Jake said. He sighed. He knew how it looked. He might have been one of the last people to see Lola alive. "I'm downtown. At the evidence room."

"Hang on," Mac said. Jake could hear him addressing someone in the office. Mac came back on the line.

"Just stay put, Jake. Detective Hammond is about to head down that way. He'll look for you there."

"Okay."

"What're you doing down there anyway? Isn't this your day off?"

"Yeah," Jake said, trying to recover his thoughts. He remembered why he'd called in the first place.

"Listen, Mac. I saw your name on a file I was looking at. It looks like you checked the same file out last month."

"What case was this?"

"Mr. Chandler. The writer who tried to shoot himself. A year ago April. I got the call that night. Took his gun away."

"Yeah, I remember that."

"Why'd you check out the file in June?"

"Geez, I don't remember. I'm down there every week, dealing with stuff that comes in. Why are you asking?"

Jake paused for a moment, searching for words that wouldn't sound like an accusation or raise undue suspicion if it got around. Mac had a big mouth.

"They don't have the gun down here," he said. "There's an RTO on the photo. Returned to Owner."

"Yeah, right, now I remember," said Mac. "It was that old British revolver. I brought it back to the station. Someone had filled out the papers. The captain asked me to take care of it."

"So, you returned the gun to Mr. Chandler?"

"I gave it to Wade. He was going to deliver it personally, doing the guy a favor. You know how he likes that, doing favors for the upper crust."

Mac chuckled. Jake winced. He hoped his visit to the evidence room wouldn't ruffle anyone's hair. Mac would tell the captain. Jake had stepped outside the lines of his job again.

"Thanks," he said, trying to sound nonchalant. "I guess that explains it. I'll see you later."

"You make sure to wait there. Detective Hammond, remember?"

"Yeah. I got it. I'll be here."

Jake hung up the phone and collapsed on the bench at the end of the counter. Guilt and suspicion traded punches inside him like heavyweight fighters. He'd never been questioned by a detective before, not the way he would be now, as a person of interest in a homicide case. He remembered his father explaining his work, interviewing suspects and witnesses, how they moved their hands and their eyes, shifted in their chairs or altered their voices whenever they lied. Detective Hammond would scrutinize Jake the same way, looking for signs of deception.

Jake wondered how often his father had been in this room, checking out evidence, reviewing the files. He thought of the notebook his mother had given him, his father's meticulous copy of the official case notes. Those notes were stored in this building, somewhere inside a cardboard box collecting dust in the basement.

He stood up and returned to the end of the line, waited for the two customers ahead of him, then stepped up to the clerk's window.

"You want to see that file again?" said the clerk. "I didn't put it away yet."

"No," Jake said. "I want to see something else. A case file from a few years ago."

"You know the case number?"

"I don't have the number. I'd like to see everything you've got on the *Creeper*."

Danny, Willie, and Rachel sat inside the cool darkness of the concrete bunker below Nautilus Street, preparing to convene a new meeting of The Perverted Savants Club. Danny called them to order and noted the members in attendance.

"Why do you do that?" said Willie. "Call our names?"

"It makes it official," said Danny. "I have to note the attendees."

"It's dumb," said Willie. "It's not like we don't know who's here."

"That's not the point," said Danny.

"Can we just get started?" said Rachel. She had no time for Danny and Willie's childish squabbling. Her father had said he would pick her up outside the high school at three, after he'd gone to the police station and filled out a report.

"What's your hurry?" snarled Danny.

"Nothing. I just don't have time to fool around."

"Okay, okay," said Danny. "What's your offering?"

"I didn't bring anything."

"You're supposed to bring something every week," said Danny. "Not just when you feel like it."

"I brought in two books last week."

"Yeah," said Willie. "That's right. They were kind of science-y, though."

Rachel glared at the two boys. Her eyes turned to the book-shelf, the large hardbound volumes she'd placed there. *Sexual Behavior in the Human Male* and *Sexual Behavior in the Human Female* by Alfred C. Kinsey. She'd borrowed the books from her parents' library at home. Without their permission. Hanging out with Danny and Willie was going to get her in trouble. She crossed to the shelves, grabbed one of the books and put it in her knap-sack. Perversion wasn't a game anymore. She'd seen the real thing.

"What're you doing?" asked Willie.

"I don't want to be in this club," Rachel said, stuffing the second Kinsey book into her knapsack.

"Okay, okay," said Danny. "You don't have to bring some-thing every time."

"Yeah, Rachel," said Willie. "Don't be mad. We were just razzing you."

"This club is stupid," she said, feeling her voice break. "Everything's stupid. It's all horrible."

The boys didn't respond. Maybe they didn't care if she left the club. She imagined them making fun of her after she'd gone, telling themselves they were better off without a stupid girl in the club. She closed the knapsack, tied down the straps, and turned toward the door.

"What's wrong with you?" Danny asked. Rachel stopped and stared at the door hatch, only three steps away. If she left now, she might never return. They might never be friends again.

"I found a dead body this morning," she said.

"Whoa," said Willie. "Was it nasty?"

Rachel continued to stare at the door as she spoke. "It was a woman. She was naked. A man killed her. He'd pulled her dress up."

"Where was this?" said Danny.

"On the mesa above the Institute. In the woods near Camp Matthews."

"Did the guy mess with her?" asked Danny.

Rachel turned to look at the boys' expectant faces, eager to take in her horror story. Her friends were cretins and dopes like all the other kids at the high school. Rachel couldn't wait to graduate and get away from them all.

"Did he rape her?" she said. "Is that what you want to know, Danny?"

Danny shrugged, like it was no big deal. It made Rachel mad. She dropped her knapsack and walked over to him, stood above him with her hands on her hips.

"I don't know, Danny. I don't know if he raped her. She was naked. You could see her pointy little tits. You could see her vagina. Her legs were twisted, and her skin was gray. She had purple and green bruises on her thighs. There was a big bloody hole in her face. There, Danny. How's that? Is that what you wanted to know? Is that perverted enough for you?"

"I'm sorry, Rachel," said Willie. He dropped his head and looked at the ground. "That sounds horrible. I'm sorry you had to see that dead girl."

"Thank you, Willie. What about you, Danny? What do you think?"

Danny continued to stare back at her. He didn't say anything.

"It's like those trashy books you read, isn't it, Danny?" Rachel was furious. At Danny. At herself. At the world. "Was it as much fun to hear me tell you about it as it is to read in those books? Did it give you a boner?"

"Hey!" said Willie.

"I'm leaving," said Rachel. She headed for the door.

"Wait," Danny said. Rachel stopped. She folded her arms across her chest, waiting for an apology.

"I need to show you something," he said. "I don't know what I should do."

Rachel frowned. "What is it?" she said.

Danny opened the straw basket that sat by his feet, a basket he'd borrowed from The Cave Shop's inventory. It had *La Jolla - The Jewel* sewn in bright thread on both sides of it. He pulled something out of the basket—a little blue suitcase.

"Where'd you get that?" said Willie.

"Todd DuBarry gave it to me."

"Oh shit!" cried Willie. He leapt from his chair and caromed around the room, cursing and wailing.

"What's going on?" said Rachel.

"TD stole that from the French lady!" cried Wille. "The policemen thought I took it. They put me in the jail."

"When did this happen?" said Danny.

"I wanted to show you that lady's picture," Willie explained. "I was saving it for our meeting. But the policeman took it. He said I was possessing indecent materials. That man in the hospital. He took the picture. He said he fucked that lady six ways to Sunday."

"Willie!" Rachel yelped in surprise. Willie shrugged apologetically.

"Excuse my mouth, Rachel," he continued. "But that's what he said. It was that same guy we saw, Danny, the one those big guys dragged out of that house. They beat him up pretty bad. The cops tried to blame it on me. Because I'm a colored boy. The cops give colored boys the third degree. Your brother took me to the hospital, but the man said it wasn't me, that I didn't hurt him. Then Jake let me go."

Willie returned to his seat on the milk crate. "I'm sorry, Danny," he continued. "I had to tell Jake. He knows we went to that house. I told him about Todd too. How I saw him with the blue suitcase in that French lady's room. He's the one that stole her necklace."

Rachel ran her hand through her hair, trying to understand what Danny and Willie were talking about. They were so weird sometimes. And immature. But Danny and Willie were nicer to her than a lot of the other boys at the high school, the ones who made fun of her thick glasses, broad shoulders, and dark frizzy hair. The had let Rachel join their club, even if it was a stupid club. They were her friends.

"Todd DuBarry's dead," she said. "My father's at the police station right now."

"Oh, shit," said Willie. "Did they arrest him?"

"Who?"

"Your father."

"No. He's just giving a statement. It was last night. He heard some gunshots near the Institute. Then he saw Todd's car on the beach with his body inside."

They all went quiet, absorbed in their own thoughts. Rachel felt her unwieldy sadness break into shards of relief. The boys knew the burden she carried, her shock and revulsion from seeing the dead girl. She was glad she'd told them. Danny broke the silence.

"Jake's going to kill me," he said.

Rachel and Willie looked over at him. Danny tapped his fingers on top of the little blue case.

"Todd told me to give this to Jake. He made me promise."

Rachel shook her head in disbelief.

"Why didn't you give it to him?" she said.

"There's something inside here, something the Perverted Savants need to see."

"Is it naked pictures of that French lady?" asked Willie.

"No." Danny flipped the latches on the train case and opened the lid. He reached into the train case and brought out a sheet of faded yellow paper. "There's a secret compartment and this was inside it."

"What is it?" said Willie.

"It's an arrest report. From the New Orleans police department. For moral indecency and soliciting a minor."

"What's that mean, soliciting?" said Willie.

"It's offering someone money to have sex with you," said Rachel.

"Like a prostitute?"

"Sort of. If a man offers a girl money for sex, he's soliciting."

"It wasn't a girl," said Danny. "This guy they arrested paid a boy to have sex with him."

"He's a homosexual then," said Rachel. She pointed at the knapsack where she'd stashed her parents' sex books. "Kinsey says that ten percent of all men are homosexuals."

"Whatta men do when they have sex?" said Willie. "It don't seem right, two men doing that stuff. Women, they got that place for their babies ..."

"What—" said Rachel.

"Shut up and let me finish!" said Danny, waving the arrest report at them. "We have to talk about this. It's important. Here." He handed Rachel the report. "Read it yourself."

She read it, then looked back up at Danny.

"Oh my god," she said. "Do you think ... ?"

Willie snatched the paper from Rachel and read it.

"I don't get it," he said. "Who's John E. Hoover?"

30

"You seem distracted today," said Millie. She and Jake had gone walking in Cove Park after her shift at the cafe. They'd taken a seat in one of the palm-thatched palapas overlooking the ocean. "Are you okay?"

"I'm fine," Jake said, but there was a shrouded agony in his eyes, straining against an invisible tide, an anguish she'd never seen before. He'd arrived at the coffee shop just before her shift ended, anxious to see her alone after work. But he'd said almost nothing during their stroll through the park. Something big had built up inside him. Millie feared an ultimatum was at hand, perhaps even a marriage proposal. Jake was the best thing that had happened to her since her divorce; his guileless manner reassuring and kind, but she needed more time to recover from the lingering wounds of her marriage. She wouldn't surrender her independence as easily this time, no matter how handsome and well-mannered her suitor might be. There was a remoteness in Jake that worried her, an anger behind that opaque, lovely smile.

"Millie?" Jake said.

"What is it?" She could tell by the tone of his voice that

whatever came next was important to him. She prepared to explain herself and soften the blow.

"I don't think you should see me anymore," he said.

"What?" The question jumped from her mouth like a startled cat. It wasn't what she'd expected. It hurt.

"I'm sorry," he said.

"You want to break up with me?" Millie said, still stunned.

"No." Jake shook his head. "I like being with you. More than anything."

That was a relief. "What is it, then?" she said.

"There's something going on at work. Something bad."

Jake stood up. He walked to the corner of the palapa and stared out at the ocean. Millie waited. He deserved her patience as much as she deserved his.

"There's this girl," he said. "She's a prostitute."

"Oh, Jake," Millie sighed, feeling stabbed in the heart. Men were lecherous bastards.

"It's not what you think," he said, turning to look at her. "She died. Someone killed her."

"Oh my gosh," said Millie, remembering the news Mr. Miller had brought to the lunch counter earlier in the day. "Is it that girl they found on the mesa?"

"Yes," Jake nodded. "I should have done something. I should have protected her."

Conflicted feelings tumbled around Millie's heart like disturbed acrobats, jumping from disgust to fear to kind-heartedness. She wanted to hug Jake, to hold his body close to hers, absorbing his pain. She didn't move to him, though. She waited. She knew there was more on his mind.

"I tried to talk her into going to a shelter," Jake said. "She wouldn't do it. She wouldn't listen to me."

Millie regretted that for even one moment she'd doubted Jake. She knew how much he cared for his family—his mother and younger siblings—how he tried to protect them. Jake treated everyone with respect, even when they didn't deserve it.

"I was the last person to see her alive," he continued. "That's what the detectives think, anyway. They think I murdered her."

"Oh!" Millie put her hand over her mouth, shocked that anyone could imagine Jake doing something so cruel.

"She was a witness," Jake said. "To a robbery and a murder. She was in my car two nights ago, telling me what she saw. Mac, at the station, saw me leave with her. She wouldn't talk to anyone else, only me. And now she's dead."

They both stared out at the ocean, collecting their thoughts, looking for words that were deep enough, strong and true. Millie found her words first.

"Do you remember the other night," she said. "When we went to the Playhouse, what I said about my divorce and my past, that you could ask me about it anytime?"

"I remember," Jake said.

"I want to tell you," she said. "I want you to know. I got married when I was seventeen, before I left high school. I ran away from home. My parents are very religious. My father disowned me."

"I'm sorry."

"I'd only known my husband a month when I married him. I was young and foolish. He was older than me. He said he loved me, but as soon as we got married, he changed. He started to hit me. I thought it was my fault at first. I didn't have any experience with men. I thought I must have done something wrong. I tried to do what he wanted, to obey him like it says in the wedding vows, but it didn't make any difference. He'd always find some excuse. He wouldn't stop hitting me."

Millie paused. The pain had welled up inside her again, the black fear. The last two years had been a slow crawl toward the surface and now the light seemed within reach. She'd let a new man into her heart. He'd shown her nothing but kindness and decency. She felt naked in front of him now, but not ashamed.

Jake sat down next to her, put his hand on hers. She wished he would take her into his arms and squeeze tight, but that wasn't Jake's way. He was cautious and polite to a fault, but he'd never tried to take advantage of her situation, never looked at her the way other men did—a divorced woman, easy pickings, an old maid alone and desperate for any kind of love she could find.

"Miss Gabor's rich and famous," Jake said. "That guy hit her too."

The remark was so incongruous it brought Millie up short. That was Jake, too, saying odd things at the oddest times, things you couldn't figure out at first, but later made sense. He'd listened to her when she'd told him about Miss Gabor covering her bruises. He'd paid attention. And now, perhaps, he was trying to tell Millie she wasn't alone, that what had happened to her had happened to other women, even a glamorous Hollywood actress.

"I'm not sorry," Millie said. "About getting divorced. I didn't do anything wrong."

"I know you didn't."

"And neither did you, Jake. With that girl in the car. You'll find a way out of this. You didn't do anything wrong."

Jake removed his hand from hers, retreating into his own torment again. "I was stupid," he said. "I could have handled it better."

"Everybody does stupid things sometimes, Jake."

"I guess," Jake said. He dropped his head and stared at the ground. Millie had never seen him so defeated. She reached her arm across his shoulders and leaned her cheek in next to his, felt the sturdy warmth of his body. She felt the unhappiness too, the little boy still buried inside. A tremor pulsed through Jake's body, welling up like a wave of despair.

"It's like there's a cloud over me," he said. "A dark, evil cloud I can't escape."

Millie thought of the dread she'd lived under after she'd filed for divorce, when she'd moved to town on her own to hide from her husband, how she'd feared he would find her and beat her, maybe even kill her. Her days had become sunnier, but the gray clouds still clung.

"I looked at some files today," Jake said. "Down at the evidence department. From the *Creeper* case."

"That was your father's case, wasn't it?" Millie said. She hadn't been in town when it happened, but she'd heard all about the *Creeper* from her customers. One slow afternoon at the diner, Max Miller had regaled her with the whole story. It had helped her understand Jake a little better, about his father, but she'd never brought it up with him and he'd never talked about it. Until now.

"Someone tampered with the files," he said.

"What do you mean?"

"They went through my father's case notes and changed the letters. He'd written two sets of initials in the margins—TD and OWL. Somebody changed the L to E. They added two marks and changed the capital Ls to capital Es. It says O-W-E instead of O-W-L."

"How could you tell?"

"I have my father's personal notebook at home. He made a copy of his official notes every night. He'd sit at the table with a six-pack of beer and copy his notes from one book to the other, word for word. His copy says O-W-L."

"But what do they mean?" said Millie. "The initials?"

"I think TD stands for Todd DuBarry. I don't know what OWL stands for. Or OWE. But whoever changed it must know."

"Maybe Todd knows. Maybe you could ask him."

"Todd's dead."

"Oh gosh!"

"I found his body last night. The captain says it's suicide. He thinks Todd killed himself."

"What do you think?"

"I don't know," Jake said. "But it's all connected. Todd and Miss Gabor's necklace and the girl who was killed. There's this gun, too, that shouldn't have been where it was. I feel like I'm a pawn on some big, invisible chessboard. Other people are moving pieces around, but I'm stuck on my little square. I can't see the rest of the game. I can only move forward. One square at a time."

"And this is why you don't want to see me anymore?"

"I want to see you," Jake said. "But I'm afraid something might happen to you. Because of me. People are dying because of me."

Millie withdrew her arm from Jake's shoulders. She stared across the lawn toward the street, then beyond the street and up the stairs to her little apartment, covered in afternoon shadows. It had become her safe space, that little cubbyhole in the side of the hill in the most beautiful, peaceful little town she'd ever seen, a place from a dream, where a handsome young policeman treated her like a precious flower. Safe and sound. Out of harm's way. Perhaps it had been a dream, after all.

"Who are these people you're talking about?"

"I can't tell you. Not exactly. It's probably better if you don't know."

"But you think they might hurt me?"

"I don't know. Not right now. No. But ... I have to move forward. There's nothing else I can do."

"Isn't there someone you can talk to? Someone that can help?"

Jake raised his head and sat up. He turned and looked her in the eye. "I don't trust anyone right now. Except my family. And you."

Millie reached out her hand and touched Jake on the cheek. A tiny bead of water lay against his skin, in the dark circle below his left eye. She wiped it away. It frightened her to see him so vulnerable, so apprehensive. She leaned in and kissed him on the lips, a soft and lingering kiss, stronger and deeper than any kiss they'd shared before. He stroked her hair. Sparks of desire moved in his fingertips. She brushed her lips across Jake's cheek and whispered in his ear.

"I want you to come home with me, Jake Stirling. I want you to stay with me tonight."

Jake pulled his head back and looked into her eyes and she knew he would stay with her, that nothing could separate them, not now. She giggled at the next thought that crossed her mind.

"What is it?" Jake said.

"I just thought of something," she said. "Something my father taught me. About chess."

"Chess?"

"Yes. You said you felt like a pawn in a chess game, didn't you?"

Jake nodded.

"Well," Millie said. "If a pawn makes it all the way to the other side of the board, it stops being a pawn anymore. It gets exchanged for a stronger piece—a queen, a bishop, a rook. Or a knight. A shining and gallant knight. That's what you can be, Jake. I know it. Because that's what you are to me."

31

Jake knocked on the door of the house on Neptune Place overlooking Windansea Beach. Raymond Chandler had moved out of the Del Charro Hotel and into this house, a mile north of the larger home he'd once shared with his wife. It was just after one in the afternoon. The door opened.

"Hello, Jake," said Mabel Denton.

"Hello, Mrs. Denton," Jake said. "Is Mr. Chandler in? I'd like to talk to him."

"Mr. Chandler hasn't been feeling well," she said. "They said no visitors."

"Who said that?"

"Mrs. Fracasse. She's looking after him now. Mr. Santry has gone back to England."

"Can I speak with Mrs. Fracasse?"

"She's not here. She's running some errands."

"I only need to talk to Mr. Chandler for a couple of minutes. It's important."

Mrs. Denton leaned out of the doorway, took a glance up and down the street.

"He just sat down to lunch," she said, stepping back from the doorway. Jake entered the house, followed her across the foyer and into the dining room. Mr. Chandler sat at the table, contemplating a shallow bowl of tomato soup, with a large white napkin tucked into his shirt.

"Someone to see you, Mr. Chandler," said Mrs. Denton. Chandler looked up from his soup bowl, befuddled and confused.

"Stirling," he said. "You're not in uniform."

"No, sir. I'm off duty until later. This is a personal visit."

Chandler stared at Jake for a moment, then down at his lunch.

"Tomato soup," he said. "That's all they feed me now. Goddamn tomato soup."

"Now, Mr. Chandler," said Mrs. Denton. "You know that's not true. You had oatmeal this morning and baked chicken last night."

Mrs. Denton left the two men alone and went into the kitchen and started scrubbing a pot.

"I like tomato soup," Jake said. Chandler made a sour face at him.

"Did you find my gun?" he asked.

"I'm not sure," Jake said.

"What the hell does that mean?" said Chandler.

Jake pulled a chair out from under the table, took a seat across from Chandler.

"I found the files on the incident," he said. "That night I came to your house, when I took your gun away."

"And?"

"There's no gun in evidence storage. There's a photo of your gun that says RTO on the back."

"What's that mean? RTO?"

"Returned to Owner."

"Balderdash," said Chandler, twisting his lips in disgust,

though Jake wasn't sure if it was the missing gun or the tomato soup that had set off his revulsion.

"I have to ask," Jake said. "I know you've moved a lot lately. Is it possible the gun was returned to you and then got misplaced? Maybe it got stashed in a box with some other items?"

"This is all pish-posh, Stirling," Chandler said. "Get to the point."

He glared at Jake. Jake continued, undeterred. "Could someone have stolen the gun after it was returned to you? Someone at the Del Charro?"

"Like who? My nurse? Santry was a bossy son-of-a-bitch, but he wasn't a thief."

Jake knew from his training that it was better to elicit a name from a witness rather than suggest one and ask for confirmation. But sometimes a memory needed to be jogged. Especially in an old man with a pickled brain.

"Todd DuBarry," he said. "Have you ever heard that name?"

"No." Chandler shook his head. "Who is he?"

"Mr. Richardson's chauffeur. At the Del Charro. Blond guy, a little taller than me."

"I remember seeing someone like that around."

"Mr. Richardson lets hotel guests use his limousine sometimes. Did you ever use it?"

"No."

"Was Todd DuBarry, the chauffeur, ever in your bungalow?"

"Not that I'm aware of. Where are you going with this?"

Jake sighed. He didn't know where he was going. Not exactly. He'd spent the night with Millie, in her bed, making love, both of them completely naked, fused together like they'd never let go. It was the first time he'd been with a woman that way, beyond the clumsy groping of high school dates, grabbing at each other in the backseat. Millie was more passionate and more self-assured than any woman he'd been with before, her bed a warm burrow of erotic dreams.

They'd only managed a couple hours of sleep before they rose at five-thirty so that Millie could get to work. He'd walked her to the waffle shop, not caring if anyone saw them together, even at that time of day. He'd felt new and shiny, as if the false walls of propriety and restraint inside him had crumbled away.

Those bright feelings were forgotten once he'd returned to his apartment and found the door unlocked. Someone had been in his home while he'd been with Mille. They'd gone through his closet and medicine cabinet, rearranged what little furniture he had in the place. It was the same M.O. as the *Creeper*, nothing taken except the inhabitant's sense of security and peace of mind. He'd checked with his neighbors next door, but they hadn't seen or heard anything.

"What did you mean?" he asked Mr. Chandler. "When we talked at the pool. About a plant?"

"What's that?" said Chandler.

"You said some cop might use your gun as a plant. Why did you say that?"

"Why are you asking?"

"Todd DuBarry, the chauffeur, was shot and killed last night. He's dead. There was a gun in his car, an old Webley like yours."

Chandler was silent a moment. He picked up his spoon, blew on his soup, then put the spoon down.

"You want a drink, Stirling?" he said.

"No sir," Jake said. "I don't drink."

"I could use one. Mabel, how 'bout it?"

"You know I can't do that, sir," said Mrs. Denton from the kitchen. "Mrs. Fracasse would fire me for sure."

"To hell with Jean," said Chandler.

"Finish your soup first," said Mrs. Denton, sounding even more resolute. "The doctor says you have to eat."

Chandler growled, looked at his soup, then tasted it. He put the spoon down again.

"Who's this girl I heard about, Stirling?" he asked.

"What girl?"

"The dead one. The hooker. The one you were screwing."

Jake sighed. The rumor and innuendo had already started to spread. He couldn't let it get to him. He wasn't his father. Or Todd DuBarry. He had to keep moving forward. That was all he could do.

"Her name was Lola," he said. "She witnessed a crime and shared that information with me. I tried to protect her. That's all there was to it."

"Lola," said Chandler, rolling the name across his lips with a sneer. "Not her real name, I expect."

"I don't know, sir."

"What did she tell you, about this crime?"

"I'm not at liberty to discuss that," Jake said.

"Did she come to you or just make it up on the spot?"

"She came to the station. She asked for me. She would only discuss the information with me. No one else."

"It didn't by any chance have something to do with the limousine driver, this Todd fellow, did it?"

"As a matter for fact, it did," Jake said. "How did you know?"

Chandler pushed his soup away. He stared out toward the picture window as he drummed the fingers of his left hand on the table, cogitating.

"Red herring," he said, after a moment.

"What's that, sir?" Jake said.

"Hookers don't have hearts of gold, Stirling," said Chandler. "That's a fantasy created by sentimental hacks who never slept with one. A hooker's heart is cash green."

"What's this fish you were talking about?"

Chandler chuckled. "The red herring," he said. "It's an old writer's trick. You show people one thing in order to distract them from what's really going on. Misdirection. Like a magician. I'd bet dollars to donuts someone paid this Lola to tell you that story, whatever it was."

"To make me look in the wrong direction?"

"Exactly."

"Who killed her, then?"

"Could be anybody. She was a hooker. If I were writing a book, it'd be the same guy who paid her to tell you that story. Poor girl can't change her testament now. She can't renege."

Jake rubbed his forehead. He felt lost, abandoned on a deep ocean with sharks all around.

"About your gun—" he said. Chandler interrupted him.

"If it's my gun this fellow had on him, I sure didn't give it to him. That means someone else did. The real question for you is, did they give it to him before or after he died?"

"After? But that would mean—"

"It would mean the chauffeur didn't kill himself. That someone else killed him and tossed the gun in his car to make it look like a suicide. Cops drop guns on dead bodies all the time. It's an old trick they learned from gangsters. If there's someone you want to get rid of, you shoot the guy, then make it look like he drew on you first. No one can prove they didn't. Self-defense rules."

Jake leaned back in his chair. He'd hoped his visit with Mr. Chandler would clear things up, that it would explain how Todd DuBarry had managed to end up with the Webley revolver, but now he felt more confused than ever. Had the captain planted the gun? Or had someone else done it before the captain arrived? Gangsters or FBI men? The old man cleared his throat and moved his bowl of soup back in front of him.

"Forget about my gun, Stirling," he said. "It's too late for that. Look for the guy who tells you a story, who explains everything and tries to wrap it up with a bow. That's the guy you need to watch out for."

Jake felt a heaviness descend on his shoulders. The fog hadn't lifted. It had only grown thicker. Lola and the gambling boss were both dead. Todd was dead too and Miss Gabor's train case was still missing. Men far above Jake were searching for it, powerful men who pulled strings and pushed people around, playing a violent game for high stakes. Jake was a lowly patrol-man, not even a detective. A pawn. He could only move forward one square at a time and try to get to the other side of the board.

"Thank you, Mr. Chandler," he said, rising from his chair. "Enjoy your lunch."

Chandler looked tired and pale, utterly defeated by his bowl of soup. He said nothing.

"I'll walk you out," said Mabel Denton, coming in from the kitchen and drying her hands on a dish towel.

"That's okay," Jake said. "I can find my way out."

She walked to the door with him anyway.

"I didn't thank you yet," she said.

"For what?" Jake said.

"For helping Willy get out of jail. I'll bake you a cake."

"I'm glad I could help. Willie didn't do anything wrong. Nothing criminal, anyway."

"That boy will be the death of me. He's too inquisitive, always sticking his nose into things."

"Hanging around with my brother doesn't help any," Jake said. "I don't think Willie and Danny are good for each other."

"No," said Mabel, smoothing out her apron. "I don't suppose so. Your mother has her hands full too."

They stood in the foyer for a moment, as if hoping they might find a solution to their intertwined familial concerns. Jake turned toward the door.

"He's sick, Jake," said Mrs. Denton. "Mr. Chandler, I mean. The doctors don't know what to do. It's the alcohol. They say he'll die soon if he doesn't stop drinking. Mrs. Fracasse says he has only a year, maybe two. She's doing her best to help him. They're going to get married."

"Married?"

Mabel nodded. "He's a soft touch, you know, under all that bluster and bile. Like with Mrs. Fracasse's daughter. He's so

gentle and sweet to her. You wouldn't believe it's the same man.
It's the drinking that ruins him."

"It ruins a lot of people," Jake said. "It ruined my father."

"Your father was a good man, too, Jake. I just wanted you to
know about Mr. Chandler's condition. Don't take too long if you
want to talk to him again. He likes you."

"He does?"

"He says you're the only cop he's ever met whose badge
doesn't tarnish."

"I guess that's a good thing," Jake said. "Thanks, Mrs.
Denton."

"I'll bake you that cake sometime," she called after him as
he walked down the street. "Just let me know what kind you
like."

Jake crossed the street and headed back to his apartment.
He thought of Millie again, her soft lips and strong legs, the
sturdiness in her heart and the grace in her smile. Their love
wouldn't tarnish either.

32

I t was dark in the closet, and it smelled like old coats, but Lucy Stirling tried to be brave. Danny had told her not to come out until he returned. He'd promised to bring her a box of red licorice if she stayed in the closet and didn't tell anyone he'd left her all by herself. Lucy didn't like being in the house all alone. Danny was a blockhead.

Mother had made macaroni and cheese for dinner, but a policeman had come by the house and Mother had gone away with him in his car. She'd told Danny to look after Lucy but after she'd left, two men as fat as walruses came by and knocked on the front door. Danny pretended no one was home. The men walked around the to the side of the house. They jiggled the windows and doors, but couldn't get in.

After the men went away, Danny called someone on the phone. He told Lucy to hide in the closet with Veronica, her plush toy Octopus. Lucy didn't like being stuck in the closet. Veronica didn't like being there either.

"I want to go play in the tidepools," Veronica said. She didn't speak, but Lucy could hear what Veronica was thinking.

"We have to be quiet," Lucy whispered. "Danny's going to bring us some red vines if we're good."

"I love red vines," Veronica said. "They make my eyelashes shiny."

"You have pretty eyelashes," said Lucy. Real octopuses didn't have eyelashes, not like Veronica's. Lucy had seen a real octopus, one day at the beach when a man in a diving mask and big flippers walked out of the ocean with an octopus wrapped around his arm. Kids on the beach went over to look at the octopus, but Lucy stared at it longer than any of them, until Danny grabbed her by the arm and tried to drag her away. Danny didn't like the man with the octopus. Danny called the man names.

Lucy had seen an octopus in a movie once, too, a giant octopus that attacked San Francisco. *It Came from Beneath the Sea.* That was the name of the movie Lucy had seen at the Cove Theater, along with Danny and his friends, Willie and Rachel. A giant octopus grabbed a submarine underwater. It tore down a bridge and climbed onto a clock tower. The people said it was an atomic bomb that made the octopus so big, that *ray-day-shun* had mutated it. Lucy wondered if Veronica the Octopus would get that big if she got the ray-day-shun.

There was a noise outside the closet, the kitchen door opening. Danny might have come home. Or Mommy. Or the walrus men had found their way in.

"Shh," she said, whispering to Veronica and placing her index finger against her lips. "We have to be quiet."

She sat in the dark, listening. You could hear things better when it was dark. You could hear the wind and the trees bending outside. You could hear insects crawling across the wood floor, the rustle of Mommy's dress and the saw-like whoosh of the corduroy pants that Danny wore to work.

"Hello?" a voice said. There was a man in the house. "Is anyone home?"

She heard the man's footsteps clump across the floor. She

pictured him moving from one room to the other. There was something familiar about the man's voice, but Danny had told Lucy to stay quiet. He might be testing her. If she gave herself away, Danny wouldn't give her any red vines.

The man passed by the closet. The shadows from his shoes danced along the crack of light at bottom of the door. He passed by again, then stopped in front of the closet. Lucy closed her eyes and buried her face in Veronica's tentacles, holding her breath, not making a peep. The door opened and light came tumbling in.

"Lucy?" a voice said. "What're you doing in there?"

Lucy lifted her head and looked up at her older brother. Jake the policeman. Wearing his uniform. All the fear went away.

"I'm playing," she said, holding up her plush toy. "With Veronica."

"Where is everyone?" Jake said.

Lucy shrugged.

"C'mon out of there now," Jake said, reaching down with one hand. Lucy grabbed his hand, and he lifted her out of the closet. He reached down and grabbed Veronica, who was trying to hide.

"I remember this toy," Jake said. "I gave you this, didn't I?"

Lucy nodded and blinked. The light hurt her eyes. "That's Veronica," she said. "She's an octopus. Like the one we saw at the beach, when Danny called your friend a pervert."

Jake stared at Lucy a moment, then sighed. "Where is Danny, anyway?"

"He went to the clubhouse, I think."

"The clubhouse? Where's that?"

Lucy shrugged again. "I dunno," she said. "He goes there sometimes with his friends. With Willie and Rachel. It's a secret club. For perverts."

Jake pressed his lips into a thin line and sighed again. "I don't like the sound of that much. Where's Mommy?"

"A policeman took her away."

"What?" Jake frowned. He looked angry.

"Are you mad at me?" Lucy asked.

"No, no," Jake said. "I'm not mad at you, Lucy. Here, let's go in the kitchen. Are you hungry? We'll have some milk and cookies."

Lucy followed Jake into the kitchen. She seated herself at the table while Jake poured two glasses of milk from the refrigerator. He opened the cabinet and retrieved a half-finished package of Oreos. He placed it on the table with the glasses of milk. Lucy took one of the cookies, dipped it in her milk and started to chew.

"There," Jake said. "That's good, huh?"

Lucy nodded. Her brother looked tired and sad.

"Okay," he said. "Tell me what happened, just before Mommy went away."

Lucy finished chewing and swallowed. Her brother sounded so serious. His face looked flat and gray like a concrete wall.

"A policeman came to the back door," she said. "He wasn't a policeman like you, though. He didn't have a police car."

"What kind of car did he have?"

"Just a regular car."

"Okay. Do you remember what he said to Mommy?"

Lucy shook her head.

"Did he say his name?"

Lucy frowned, trying to think of the man's name. "Mommy told Danny she was going with Wade."

"Wade? That was the policeman's name?"

"I think so. Mommy told Danny to stay here and babysit me. That she was going with Wade."

"Did Mommy say why she was going with him?"

Lucy stroked Veronica's soft tentacles. "No. Mommy didn't say anything. Danny said you were in trouble."

"Danny told you that?"

"Yeah."

Jake picked up the phone on the counter and brought it back to the table. "Did Danny say why I was in trouble?" he asked.

Lucy shook her head again.

"Danny's a blockhead," she said.

"Yeah, I know," Jake said. He lifted the receiver and started to dial.

"Some men tried to get in the house," Lucy said. "That's why I hid in the closet."

Jake put the receiver back down. "What kind of men?" he said.

"Fat men," said Lucy. "They looked like walruses in big coats. They went around to all the windows and doors."

"Did they get in?"

"No. They went away. Then Danny called Willie, but Willie wasn't home, and Danny said he had to go to their clubhouse. He told me to get my toy animals and hide in the closet, that he'd bring me some red vines if I was good."

Jake said a cuss word under his breath. The phone rang. They both flinched. The phone rang again. Jake picked up the receiver.

"Hello," he said. "No, she isn't here right now ... this is Jake ... hello Mr. Shapiro ... no I don't know when she'll be back ... my brother ... yes, you can talk to me."

Jake glanced over at Lucy as he listened to Mr. Shapiro on the other end of the line. She took another Oreo from the pack and offered it to Veronica, but Veronica didn't like cookies. She only liked M&Ms and red vines. Lucy dipped the Oreo in her milk.

"I just heard about this club myself," Jake said, talking to Mr. Shapiro. "I don't like the sound of it either. I'll talk to Danny. Your daughter ... Rachel, yes. There was nothing physical, was there? Just the magazines and books?"

Lucy could hear Mr. Shapiro's voice on the line, but it was

only a buzzing sound. She couldn't understand any of the words. Mr. Shapiro sounded angry. Adults were always angry about something. Sometimes they were sad. Mommy looked so pale when she went with Wade.

"Uh-huh," Jake said. "Yes, I'd like to talk to her ... Hello, Rachel. This is Jake Stirling, Danny's older brother ... the policeman, yes. Now don't be afraid. You're not in any trouble. Just tell me what you told your father, why you think Danny's in trouble."

Lucy finished her cookie and reached for a third one. Mommy would only let her have two. She never brought the whole package to the table like Jake did. Jake watched Lucy take another cookie. He didn't say anything. He was too busy listening to Danny's friend Rachel on the phone.

"Okay," Jake said. "All you did was look at stuff together. That's why you took the books from your father's library. Danny brought some books, too and ... what's that?"

Jake jerked upright in his seat. He almost knocked over his glass of milk. "Tell me about the case, Rachel," he said. "Describe it to me."

Lucy froze, holding the third Oreo above her glass of milk. Jake's eyes got so big it frightened her. He looked like a cartoon policeman. His knuckles turned white as they tightened around the receiver.

"Don't cry now, Rachel ... you did the right thing," he said to the phone. "I'm going to find Danny now and get the case from him. Where is this clubhouse? Where by the school? Yes, I remember that day. Yes. I know where you're talking about. Thank you. Goodbye."

Jake hung up the phone. He picked up the milk bottle and Oreos.

"Danny's in trouble. I have to go find him," he said, stashing the milk and cookies in the refrigerator. Oreos weren't supposed to go in the refrigerator. They went on the shelf.

"Do I have to hide in the closet again?" said Lucy.

Jake went to the kitchen counter and grabbed a pencil. He wrote something on the notepad, the one their mother used to write down her grocery lists.

"I'm writing a note for Mommy," he said. "So she knows you're with me. Bring your animals. We're going for a ride in my police car."

33

Danny Stirling sat in the back seat of a 1955 Buick Roadmaster, squashed into the corner by the bulky man sitting next to him. His roller board was gone, abandoned somewhere near the intersection of Bonair and Draper. He hadn't noticed the car parked on the street. Its front door had opened as he swooped by, separating him from his sled and leaving him sprawled on the pavement. Before he could recover, he'd been snatched from the street and shoved into the car. The man in back pinned Danny against the seat with one arm as the man in front put the car into gear, pulled out and drove toward Nautilus Street. The driver flashed a badge in the rear-view mirror.

"FBI," he said. "You Danny Stirling?"

"Yeah, that's me," Danny said, rubbing the side of his face where it had caught the upper edge of the car door. He glanced up at the man who restrained him. He didn't look like an FBI agent, not the kind you saw on TV or at the movies. FBI men had square jaws, flat stomachs and smooth faces that probably smelled of Burma Shave. The man in the back of the car smelled like old garlic pizza. His face was stubbled and fat. The man in front didn't fit the mold either.

"Your friend here says you have something of ours," said the driver.

Danny realized there was another person in the car, on the other side of the man pressing him into the seat. He leaned his head forward and peered around the man's belly. Willie Denton peered back.

"I'm sorry, Danny," Willie said. He looked scared. Danny felt scared too.

"Shut up," said the back seat man, extending his arms to press Willie and Danny back into their seats.

"Where are we going?" said Danny.

"Thought we'd take a look around your little clubhouse," the driver said. "I understand you boys have been dealing in contraband and pornography."

"You're not allowed to do that," said Danny. "Not without a warrant."

The man in back chuckled. "You think you're real smart, don't you, kid?"

"I bet I'm smarter than you."

They turned onto Nautilus and started up the hill.

"Is that it?" said the driver, pointing up the ravine toward the bunker. "Is that your little clubhouse?"

"Show me your warrant," said Danny. The man in the back seat grabbed Danny's ear and twisted it.

"Oww!" cried Danny.

"Yeah, that's it," said Willie. "That's the clubhouse."

The big man released Danny's ear.

"Don't be a smartass, kid," he said. "Just answer the man's questions. We'll get this over quick, and you can go back to riding your roller board thing."

"Willie here says you built that thing yourself," said the driver.

"That's right," said Danny, rubbing his ear.

"Whattya call it?" asked the driver.

Danny shrugged. "Don't call it anything."

"You looked pretty smooth riding that thing, like you were on ice skates or something. You should call it a skateboard. Sure, that's it. A skateboard. You should take out a patent. I bet you could make a lot of money selling those things. Don't you think, Jerry?"

"Yeah. Sure. That's a real good idea, Lou."

They passed the high school. Danny saw a police car parked in the lot. The man in back noticed it too.

"You see that cop car?" he said to the driver.

"Yeah, I saw it. He's doing something at the school. Keep an eye out, though."

As they continued up the canyon, the bunker disappeared below the street.

"Don't look like we can drive down there," said the man in the front. "Guess we'll walk."

He spun a U-turn in the middle of the street, parked and killed the engine, then turned to address the boys in the back seat.

"Now boys, when you take us down there, just be cool and let us look around the place. That's all we want. Understand?"

"Yessir," said Willie. Danny nodded.

"No funny stuff," said the man in back. Jerry. "You boys are in enough trouble as it is. Pornography is a federal crime."

The driver climbed out, opened the passenger door, and curled one finger at Danny.

"Out," he said. As Danny climbed out, the man grabbed his neck from behind with a rough, sand-paper grip. On the other side of the car, Willie stepped out and got the same treatment from Jerry.

"Down we go," said the front seat man, Lou, pushing Danny toward the edge. Their feet slipped on the ice plant as they made their way down the slope, but no one fell. They reached the bottom of the ravine, walked around the bunker, and stopped in front of the door.

"How do you open it?" said the man holding Danny.

"Where's your warrant?" said Danny. The man squeezed his neck so hard that it hurt.

"We don't need no warrant, son."

"You're not a real FBI agent," said Danny. The next thing he knew he was doubled up on the ground, gasping for air. The man had punched him in the stomach. Danny rolled on the ground, unable to breathe.

"Okay, Buckwheat," Jerry said, addressing Willie. "It's your turn. Open the door."

Danny heard feet shuffling, then the creak of the metal door.

"It's this rope here, see," said Willie. "You pull on the rope."

Willie led Jerry into the bunker. The other man grabbed Danny by his pants belt and hauled him through the hatch door. It clanged shut after them.

"Oops," Willie said.

"What?" said the driver.

"The rope."

"What about it?"

"We left it outside. We can't get out now."

"What?"

"The handle's busted. You gotta use the rope."

"You dumb shit kid," said Jerry. "Why didn't you tell us that?"

"I was scared," Willie said. "You shouldn't have hit Danny like that."

Jerry shoved Willie to the ground next to Danny.

"You're some smartass little punks, you know that?"

"Relax," Lou said. "We'll figure it out. Let's look around first. You got that flashlight?"

"I thought you had the flashlight."

"Shit. What're we going to do now?"

"Sir?" said Willie.

"What is it, kid?"

"There's a clip light over there, above the desk."

"I found it," said Jerry. He flipped the switch, then chuckled. "Take a look at this, Lou."

The driver stepped over to the desk.

"Hey, that's good," he said. "Did one of you draw this?"

"I did," said Willie.

"It's that Hungarian dame, isn't it? Look at those ta-tas. You got some real talent, kid. Let's see what else is here."

Lou flipped through Willie's sketchbook. He whistled.

"You got a dirty mind, kid. You are some kind of freak."

Jerry knelt down by the bookshelf and picked through it with fat stubby fingers.

"What do we have here?" he said. "Some dirty picture books. I'll take those ... hey, I know this book. Lou, you ever read this? The Killer Inside Me? That is one sick fuck of a cop."

"I don't read shit like that," said Lou. "I read fairytales to my kids. Bring that stuff over here. Let's have a look."

Jerry swept up the items from the bookshelf and deposited them on the desk.

"Any sign of the case?" said Lou.

"I didn't see nothing."

Lou turned back to the boys.

"Okay, where is it?" he said. "Where's the train case?"

Something moved in the shadows on the other side of the room. A blue train case arced through the air and tumbled across the dirt floor.

"Take it," a voice said. A man emerged from the dark.

"Who the hell are you?" said Lou.

"Officer Jake Stirling," the man said, pointing his revolver at the two men. "San Diego Police Department. Keep your hands up where I can see them."

"Take it easy, officer," Lou said, raising his hands. Jerry

stepped in close behind him and raised his hands as well. "We're FBI."

"Show me your identification," Jake said.

"I can't do that," said Lou.

"Why not?"

"I got my hands up."

Jake took a step closer.

"You're hoodlums," he said. "I saw you having dinner with those mobsters, Marcello and Lansky."

"He's onto us, Lou," Jerry said. "Guess we better come clean. About the hoodlum thing."

"Yeah," said Lou. "Our cover is blown." He glanced back at Jerry, then down at the boys on the floor, then over at Jake again. "Okay. Take us in. We'll call the old man, let him know you blew our cover."

"What're you talking about?" Jake said.

Lou sighed. "Hey, kid," he said, looking back down at Danny. "Come over here. Reach in my right jacket pocket and take out my badge."

Danny glanced over at Jake, who nodded his permission. Danny stood up, reached inside Lou's jacket and pulled out a leather wallet, then brought it over to Jake.

"Open it," Jake said, keeping his eye on the thugs. "What's it say?"

"Federal Bureau of Investigation," said Danny. There was a photograph of the man on the card, a copper badge pinned inside the wallet as well. "Louis T. Ellenstein."

"Let me see," Jake said. Danny turned out the wallet so his brother could see it.

"We're undercover," said Jerry. "The FBI's got a sting operation in place."

"You're both FBI agents?" Jake said.

"Well," said Lou. "I am. Technically Jerry works for Marcello, but we got his nuts in the wringer so he's working for us. He's screwed now."

"Screwed like a Miami whore," Jerry said.

"I'm sorry," Jake said. "I didn't know."

"It's not your fault, kid," said Lou. "You're just doing your job."

"What do you want?" Jake said. "What's so important about that train case?"

Lou turned and looked back at Jerry, who shrugged. Lou turned back to Jake.

"That's classified," he said. "Top-secret stuff. Listen, son, there's still a way we can make this work."

"How?"

"You let us go right now. We take the case with us, get in our car and drive away. You'll never see us again."

Jake stared at the two men for a moment.

"I'm supposed to give the case to Director Hoover," he said. "He asked me to show it to him before anyone else."

"This'd be the same thing. We'll make sure he knows it was you that found the thing. You'll get your boy scout badge."

Jake looked at Danny, then over at Willie. He turned back to the FBI men.

"Pick it up," he said, indicating the case on the floor. "We'll talk about this outside ..."

The FBI men lowered their hands. Jerry leaned down and retrieved the train case. Danny handed the wallet back to Lou, who slid it into his pocket.

"Now how do we get out of here?" asked Lou.

"I got it," Willie said, lifting himself from the floor. He walked to the desk, reached behind it, and removed a wire hanger that had been squashed and reshaped into a gaffing hook. He crossed to the door, slid open the spy window and extended the hook out the door. He fiddled around for a bit, then hauled in the rope, gave it a tug, and opened the door.

Lou chuckled as he crossed the floor toward the exit. "That was a good one, kid," he said. "You really had me going there about the door being locked."

Willie smiled with a kind of pride as the men passed him and stepped through the hatch. Jake followed behind them. He still had his gun out.

"Shut the door, Willie," Jake whispered as he passed. "Stay here and lock it up tight."

34

Jake heard the latch drop on the metal door behind him. Danny and Wille would be safe inside the bunker. Safer, at any rate. He kept his gun pointed at the two thugs.

"Stop right there," he said. The FBI men looked at him like he was nuts.

"What's going on?" said the smaller one, Lou.

"You're not with the FBI," Jake said.

"I showed you my ID, didn't I?" said Lou.

"You're not working undercover. An FBI agent wouldn't carry a badge on him when he's working undercover. Not when he's dealing with mobsters. That's stupid."

Lou twisted his lips to one side and narrowed his eyes at Jake.

"You really need to let us go, officer. Jerry here is going to be very unhappy if his snitch act gets blown."

"Very unhappy," said Jerry, edging away from Lou. "Very dead."

"Don't move," Jake said, turning his gun on Jerry. Lou took a step away from them both.

"You either," Jake said, moving his gun back to Lou, then back and forth between them.

"Holster that weapon, officer," said Lou. "Put it down."

"Not until you've answered a couple of questions."

"Make it quick."

Jake ran through all the confusion in his head, "Two nights ago, did you assault Nicky Hilton?"

"Who?" Lou asked.

"Nicky Hilton. Two men beat him up and dropped him in a trash can behind the Little Pig Barbecue."

"We didn't do nothing like that," said Lou.

"I have witnesses," Jake said. He pointed toward their car parked on the street. "They reported two large men, driving a Buick, who dragged Nicky Hilton out of a private gambling house in Pacific Beach."

"Oh, that guy," said Jerry, smirking. "What a weasel."

"He may be a weasel," Jake said. "But I can charge you with assault and battery. Who told you to go after Hilton? How'd you find him?"

Lou grimaced and looked down at his shoes, then took another step away from Jerry.

"This is where it gets complicated, you see," he said. "This undercover stuff. The boss tells me to roust a guy for him. I have to do what the boss says, or he gets suspicious. Next thing you know, my cover is blown. I let Jerry do most of the dirty work. He's going to jail, anyway."

"Fuck you, Lou," said Jerry, drifting away from his partner.

"Stop it!" yelled Jake, feeling he'd lost control of the situation. "Keep your hands up and stop moving!"

The two men froze in position.

"Take it easy, son," Lou said.

Jake felt his hand tremble, wondered if the men noticed. "Was it Lansky?" he asked. "Or Marcello? Who told you to do it?"

"Don't try to be a hero, kid," said Lou.

"What?"

"I know where you're going with this. You wanna make a big score, get your name in the newspaper. It don't work that way. Not for someone like you. Let the professionals handle this. You're in over your head."

"What about Lola?" Jake said. "Did you kill her? Or the gambling house boss?"

Lou looked over at Jerry, who shook his head and shrugged. Lou turned back to Jake.

"No idea who you're talking about, kid. All zeros to me."

"You killed Todd DuBarry, though, didn't you?" Jake said. Todd hadn't committed suicide. Someone had murdered him. Lou and Jerry looked at each other. They both shrugged.

"That's crazy, kid," said Lou. "I don't know where you get that idea."

"The train case," Jake said. "That's why you went after Nicky Hilton. Everyone thought he'd stolen the necklace. Then you went looking for Todd. You went to his mother's house."

"You mean that wacky dame in the glass house?"

Jake nodded.

"We just wanted to talk to the guy," said Jerry. "The chauffeur. We heard he was popular with the ladies, some kind of a hustler. Had a history of lifting jewelry from his lady friends."

"Who told you that?" Jake said.

Lou shrugged. "We hear things. Heard your boyfriend swung from the other side of the plate too. If the price was right."

"What does that mean?" Jake said.

Jerry snarled. "Christ you're dumb, kid. Who are you, Ricky Nelson or something?"

"Shut up," Jake said. "I'm warning you."

Jake kept his gun on Jerry. The man didn't move. He didn't even look like he cared. It probably wasn't the first time he'd had a gun pointed at him.

"What're you gonna do, shoot me?" Jerry said. "Everyone

knew the kid was a hustler. Plenty of action for someone like him at that hotel. Both sides of the street."

"Watch what you say, Jerry," said Lou.

"Fuck you, G-man."

Out of the corner of his eye, Jake saw Lou edge farther away. He swung the gun back toward Lou.

"Look, kid," said Lou. "We just want to take the train case back to the boss. Then we're done. We'll get out of your hair and leave town."

"We'll take it to him together," Jake said. "To Director Hoover."

"Can't work it that way, kid," said Lou. "There's other considerations."

"Who killed Todd DuBarry? Who wanted him dead?"

"Could have been any of 'em," said Jerry. "That Hungarian bitch and her little friend. The oil man. They'd all have a reason. Maybe Hoover or his boyfriend had something to hide."

"Cut it out, Jerry," said Lou. "You're screwing your deal."

"Fuck the deal," said Jerry. "I'm done with this shit."

Jerry dropped his hands and headed for the Buick. Another car pulled in on the street above, blocking the gangsters' car from below. A man climbed out of the car. He drew his gun and pointed it at Jerry.

"Hold it right there, friend," said Captain Lennox. Jerry stopped.

"Shit," said Lou. Jake turned his gun back to Lou. Captain Lennox called down to him.

"What the hell's going on here, Stirling? Looks like you might need some help."

"These men have the train case."

"I see it there. Are they under arrest?"

"They claim to be FBI agents."

"Did you check their IDs?"

"Yes, sir."

"And?"

"This one down here checked out. He showed me his badge."

"Then what're you holding them for? You know the director wants that case."

"Something's wrong, sir. Something just isn't right."

"Did you check for guns? Are they carrying?"

"No. Not yet, sir." Captain Lennox had managed to make Jake feel stupid again.

"Well, let's clear for guns," said Lennox. "Then we'll sort this out. You take the guy down there. I'll handle this one."

"Yes, sir," Jake said. He moved in toward Lou. "On your knees. Hands behind your head."

"You're making a big mistake, kid," said Lou.

"On your knees."

Lou placed the train case on the ground and sank to his knees, then clasped his hands behind his head. Jake moved in close, felt for weapons inside the man's coat.

"Hey, kid," whispered Lou. "You're getting screwed."

"Shut up," Jake said. He finished patting the right side of Lou's coat, found nothing. Lou whispered again.

"That's the guy," he said. "He's the one told us about your friend."

"What?"

"The captain there. He told us."

Jake finished checking Lou's coat. There were no weapons. He moved around in front of Lou, with his back to Lennox and Jerry.

"You're lying," he said.

"I'm telling the truth, kid. You want to find out who killed your friend? Maybe you should look a little closer to home."

"I don't think—" Jake said. Someone yelled. He turned to see Captain Lennox lying on the ground and Jerry escaping up the hill.

"Shoot him, Jake!" yelled the captain. "He's got my gun."

Jake braced himself in firing position, aiming at Jerry as he crested the hill.

"Shoot him!" screamed Lennox. Jake pulled the trigger. Jerry stalled and took a stuttering step to his left. Jake fired again. The big man dropped to his knees, like a weightlifter who'd blown out a knee, then tilted to the right and rolled down the slope. Jake ran toward him, keeping his gun at the ready. Captain Lennox rescued his own gun from the ice plant, then turned it toward Jake.

"Drop!" he yelled. Jake ducked and rolled. Two shots rang out. Jake raised his head, saw the captain fire a third shot, aiming over him. He looked back toward Lou. The FBI agent took a wavering step, a patch of dark blood blooming below his left shoulder. His left hand grabbed at a bloody hole just above his left hip and his right hand extended in front of his face, the palm flattened outward like a traffic cop signaling a stop. Half of the ring finger on his right hand was missing. The FBI man keeled over, face first in the dirt.

Jake rose, checked his gun, and advanced on the Lou's body.

"He had a gun, Jake," said Lennox, behind him. "Find his gun."

Jake scanned the ground as he approached the dead man, looking for a weapon, wondering how he'd managed to miss it.

"You see anything?" said Lennox, behind him, but closer now.

"No, sir. Not yet." Jake said, his eyes intent on the body. "I searched him pretty well."

"I know you did, son. You must've missed something. Look out!"

Something exploded behind Jake. A bright screaming pain shot through his shoulder and sluiced up into his brain. He pitched forward, tasted dirt in his mouth as his face hit the ground. A coppery tang entered his nostrils, a smell like metallic rain. A dark haze descended, and a voice called to him from the end of a long tunnel. It was Danny's voice. Danny was screaming Jake's name.

35

Jake knew he'd been in the hospital for several days—the same room, the same bed. He'd seen doctors and nurses. It had been dark, sometimes alternating with light. There had been visitors when it was light. His mother. And Millie. But he couldn't remember how long they'd been there or what they'd said to him. He could only remember their disembodied faces floating over his bed, their voices calling like seagulls through a narcotic fog.

Everything seemed brighter now, more focused. He could see the needle stuck in his arm, connected to a length of rubber tubing that ran up to a bottle of clear liquid hanging from a steel hook above his bed. There was another bed in the room, but no one was in it. He was alone in his clarity.

The door opened. Captain Lennox walked in. Jake tried to wave, but his arms didn't move. It was almost as if someone had strapped them to the bed, tied him down with restraints. Lennox nodded and pulled up a chair.

"They told me you were awake," he said. "Glad to see it. It was touch and go there for a while."

"How long have I been here?" asked Jake.

"Three days. I wanted to let you know, you're in for a medal. I've started the paperwork."

"What happened?"

"You don't remember?"

"There were two men. We were outside. They had the train case."

Captain Lennox twitched his jaw, then stared at the floor. "This is a hard thing to say, kid. I screwed up. I thought he was going for his gun. You got in the way."

Jake stared at the ceiling, straining to remember, but it was all noise and smoke.

"You shot me?" he said.

Lennox sighed. "It's all my fault, kid," he said. "I'm going to do everything I can to help you out, take care of the family. We started a fund at the station."

Memories flooded back into Jake's brain. The memories sparked a panic.

"Is Danny okay?" he said. "What about Lucy?"

"Everyone's fine," Lennox said. "They're home with your mother. They're safe. We got the bad guys. We recovered the train case. It's over."

"He had a badge," Jake said. "An FBI badge. He said they were working undercover. But I'd seen them before with those mobsters. Marcello and Lansky."

"Those guys were bent," said Lennox. "One way or the other. The FBI's taken over the case. We'll let them sort it out. I need some answers from you."

"About what?"

Captain Lennox cleared his throat. "Why didn't you tell me what you had on Todd DuBarry?"

"What I had?"

"Goddammit, Stirling. Don't give me that innocent act. That colored kid, Denton, told you about seeing DuBarry in Miss Gabor's room. With the train case. Your brother says Todd DuBarry gave him the case to give it to you. Detective

Hammond thinks you and Todd might've been working together."

"No," Jake said. "Let me talk to the detective. I can explain."

"Better explain to me first."

Jake leaned his head back against the pillow. He felt exhausted. Confused. He tried to rub his forehead.

"I can't move my arm," he said.

Lennox's mouth twitched. "The doctor says it could be that way for a while. It's temporary. Probably. Either way, you've got a long road ahead of you. The doctor can explain better than me. But I need you to tell me everything, right now."

Jake closed his eyes and searched through the lingering fog in his brain. He found his starting point, the night of the robbery, and ran through all that had happened since then. He told the captain everything he could remember. Some parts he wasn't sure about, parts that seemed like a dream. Lennox listened, then tilted his head and stared at the floor, rubbing his chin.

"I'll talk to Hammond," he said. "See what I can do."

"Thank you, sir."

"I'm not sure he'll buy it, though," said Lennox. "Detectives don't like coincidences."

"What do you mean?"

"Think about it. You found the dead guy in the gambling house. You met with that hooker two days before she turns up dead. Then there's Todd DuBarry, dead in the limousine. You're by yourself every time. I warned you this Lone Ranger stuff would get you in trouble."

"Yes, sir." Jake nodded. He understood how it might look to a detective.

"Last but not least there's the gun that went missing," Lennox continued. "The one you were asking about at the evidence room. That old Webley."

"What about it?"

"You confiscated a Webley from Mr. Chandler a year and a

half ago, when you went to his house. Not many of those around. Mac says you called him at the station, that you were looking for it."

Jake stared at the ceiling. He didn't like the way this looked either. But he hadn't done anything wrong.

"The gun was RTO'd," he said. "About a month ago. Mac signed for it. That's why I called him. Mac said he gave it to you. He said you were going to return it to Mr. Chandler personally."

"That's about half right," said Lennox. "Chandler was supposed to come into the office to pick it up. He never did. I was keeping it under my hat about the gun. Somebody stole it from the office. Mac's on my list. And now so are you."

"Does Detective Hammond know about this?"

"Not yet. I was hoping to deal with it in house."

"Mr. Chandler asked me to find the gun for him," Jake said. "Ask him."

"Doesn't mean you didn't steal it."

"But why would I look for the gun in the evidence room if I'd already stolen it?" Jake said. "That wouldn't make sense."

"It would be the smart move," Lennox said. "A head fake. Look, kid, I'm just telling you how this might look to the detective. You tell me the truth and we can figure something out. All those folks had it coming, one way or the other."

Jake leaned his head back against the pillow and stared at the ceiling. He knew how detectives worked. First, they'd string together a set of coincidences. Then they'd look for a reason they coincided.

"What's my motive?" he said. "Why did I do it?"

"Hammond thinks it was a burglary racket," said Lennox. "You and Todd DuBarry were working together. Then something went wrong, maybe he tried to cheat you out of your share. That's the idea, anyway. Let's face it. You and TD had some history together."

Jake dropped his head back onto the pillow. The *Creeper*

case had come back to claim him, like his father, like Todd. They'd all told the truth, but they couldn't escape it. The door opened. Someone entered the room. Lennox cleared his throat, then rose from his seat and doffed his hat.

"Your boy's a tough one, Grace. I think he's going to make it."

Grace Stirling appeared at the foot of Jake's bed, a pale angel who hadn't had enough sleep.

"Hi, Mom," Jake said.

"Am I interrupting?" she said.

"Not at all," said Lennox. "I was just heading out."

Grace gave a wan smile and nodded. "Thank you, Wade. I'm so grateful you were there."

"Not at all, ma'am," said Lennox. He stepped away from the chair. "Jake's a hero in my book. Would have made his dad proud. Here, take my chair."

Captain Lennox held out the chair and Grace took a seat.

"Thank you," she said.

"You take care of yourself, Jake," said Lennox. "We'll talk again later."

Grace watched Lennox depart, then turned back to Jake.

"How are you feeling?" she said.

"I'm scared," Jake said. "I can't move my arms."

Grace put her hand to her mouth. Her eyes filled with tears. She reached out and stroked Jake's forehead.

"It's okay, Mom," Jake said. It wasn't okay. Everything had gone wrong, everything he could imagine. He had no center anymore. There was only a great hole inside him, a dark empty pit. His mother's hand felt cool on his brow, reassuring, but it wasn't enough. Everything had changed.

"She's a nice girl, Jake," said his mother. "Millie. That's her name, isn't it?"

Jake nodded. "She was here, wasn't she?" he said. "She's seen me like this."

Grace lifted her hand from Jake's forehead and stared at the wall.

"We're all praying, Jake. Millie too. The doctors say time will tell."

Jake felt his mother's sadness envelop him. She'd been carrying so much pain for so long. He'd worked hard to make up for it, to do his part and relieve her of the burden, but he'd only added to it. He was worse than Danny.

"Is Danny okay?" Jake said.

"He's fine," said Grace. "He's outside. He wants to talk to you."

"What about?"

"He's your brother, Jake. He wants to apologize. He thinks it was his fault you got shot."

"It was," Jake said.

"Don't say that. Even if it's true. He wants to make things right."

"Danny never does the right thing, Mom. Why does he have to make trouble all the time?"

"I don't know, dear." She paused. "I don't know."

Jake shook his head. A dark cloud of anger and resentment descended on him. "I can't talk to Danny right now, Mom. I just can't."

His mother nodded. "I understand. What should I tell Millie?"

"Is she out there too?"

"No. No. I just thought you might want me to tell her something. I could give her a message."

Jake rested his head against the pillow. He wanted to see Millie, but not like this. Not in the condition he was in, unable to move. He felt weak, vulnerable to dark emotions. Despair.

"Tell Millie I'm better," he said. "I'll see her soon."

"Yes, dear. You're going to get better. We're going to take care of you, no matter what happens."

Jake turned his head away from his mother. He didn't want her to take care of him the rest of his life. He didn't want Millie to, either. He'd find a way to take care of himself, just like he always had.

"Oh," said his mother. "I almost forgot. Lucy made you a card."

She opened her purse, pulled out a piece of paper, and unfolded it. It was a piece of construction paper, like kids used in school projects. Grace turned the paper around, showed it to Jake. There were gold stars across the top of the page, a drawing of a man dressed in blue beneath them.

"Is that supposed to be me?" Jake said.

"Yes, that's you," said Grace.

"What's that big thing I'm shooting at?"

"I asked Lucy about that. She says it's a giant octopus. It's from some movie she saw. You see those little people behind you? That's us. Me and Danny and Lucy. You're protecting us from the big octopus."

"I shouldn't have taken her with me," Jake said. He'd left Lucy with her plush toys in the back seat of his patrol car. "She could've been hurt. I didn't know what else to do."

His mother pulled out a tissue. "Lucy's fine, Jake. She loves you," she said, dabbing her eyes. "We all do."

Jake set his jaw, resisting his own tears. He needed to be strong, for himself, for the family, for Millie. His mother rose, folded Lucy's drawing in half, then stood it on the tray table next to Jake's bed. She hesitated, then reached in her purse again, pulled out an envelope and placed it on the table next to Lucy's card.

"What's that?" asked Jake.

"It's from Danny," she said. "He asked me to give it to you. Read it later. When you feel stronger."

Jake felt the resentment surging inside him again. He wanted his mother to leave. "Tell Lucy thank you for the card," he said.

His mother leaned down and kissed Jake on the forehead,

then started to leave. She stopped halfway to the door and turned back.

"What did Wade want?" she asked.

"It was just official business. Clearing up some things."

"He came by that day. That's why I was out. He asked me some questions about you. I didn't want Danny or Lucy to hear any of it. That's why I went with him."

"I know," Jake said. "I understand."

His mother glanced off toward the window, at the sun streaming in. "Is it true?" she asked. "Were you the last person to see that poor girl? The one who was killed?"

Jake felt a twist in his gut, a hardening anger in his thoughts. "No," he said. "The last one to see her was the person who killed her. It wasn't me."

36

Danny Stirling stood on the corner of Nautilus Street and La Jolla Scenic Drive near the top of Mount Soledad. Jake would be home from the hospital soon. In a wheelchair. No one had said it, but Danny knew everyone blamed him for what had happened. They thought it was his fault that Jake was a cripple.

No one had interviewed him or asked him what had happened the day of the shooting. The newspaper stories only listed him as one of two "unidentified minors" who happened to be at the scene. No one would have believed the real story anyway, not if it came from Danny. He was a juvenile delinquent, a troublemaker who'd do anything to get attention, a twisted bit of rope headed for the penitentiary if he didn't shape up by the time he got through high school. People felt sorry for Danny's mother, the things she had to deal with. They said Danny had inherited the dark side of his father's personality, and Jake all the light. Jake was a hero.

They'd made a big deal about it, how John Stirling's eldest son had saved the town from the Mob, how Jake and Captain Lennox had stopped organized crime in its tracks, kept it from gaining a foothold in paradise. It was in all the newspapers, an atonement story of the disgraced detective's son ambushed by two armed and dangerous thugs, how he'd shot and killed them and now carried a bullet so close to his spine that he might never walk again. Even J. Edgar Hoover had weighed in, commending the young man for his service and the sacrifice he'd made for his country. Hoover was full of shit. Hoover was a dirty old man. Danny knew it. Jake would know it now, too, if he'd read the document inside the envelope Danny had sent him. If he hadn't just thrown it away.

Danny placed his roller board on the ground, held it in place with one foot and stared down the hill. It had all started going wrong that first day of summer, when he'd crashed his roller board and asked Willie to hide him from Jake. The bunker was sealed up now, its hatch door welded shut in the name of public safety. The Perverted Savants Club had been disbanded, its little library of smut confiscated and incinerated by the police. That's what Captain Lennox had told Danny's mother, anyway. And Rachel's parents, and Willie's.

Lennox had invited all the parents to a meeting at the station. He'd shown them the filth their children were hoarding and expressed his concerns about their upbringing. He told Grace and the other parents that he wouldn't file charges, that the offending materials would be destroyed and information about the children's vile hobbies kept from the public. The children were minors, after all, and had the right to remain anonymous. Captain Lennox expressed his opinions on the causes of juvenile delinquency and suggested the parents keep a tighter rein on their progeny. The parents thanked the captain for his discretion and concern. They discussed the situation among themselves and agreed that their children were a bad influence on each other. Danny and Rachel and Willie were all grounded, banned from seeing or speaking to one another at least through the end of the summer.

Danny gazed down the hill, planning his roller board ride.

He'd almost made it that day. If it hadn't been for the car headed the other way up the street, he could've taken a better line through the long second curve. His stunt would have been legendary. The kids at school would whisper in awe when they passed him in the halls, embellishing the legend of Daredevil Danny, future test pilot or race car driver. A tough son-of-a-bitch with nerves of steel. The boys would admire his pluck. The girls would desire him. Adults might cluck at his reckless-ness, but they'd secretly marvel at his audacity. Everyone would have said Danny Stirling was fearless. Even Jake might have been secretly impressed.

But it hadn't turned out that way. Danny had failed his own test, like he failed everything. He cheated the other kids out of their money, ran away and hid from them in defeat. They'd call him Dirtbag Danny now—an imposter, a coward, a cheat. And a pervert.

He'd tried to tell people what he'd seen the day Jake was shot, but the words never came out right. No one seemed to understand. His mother said they had to move on, as if nothing had happened, as if Jake living in a wheelchair for the rest of his life was something they'd planned all along. Jake was coming home tomorrow. The family would have to take care of him, help him get dressed and go to the bathroom. Everything would be changed.

Today was a test, a covenant Danny had made with himself. If he made it all the way to the bottom of the hill, he'd go straight. He'd try harder to get along at home and at school. He'd follow the rules. He'd listen to the advice adults gave him and stop making fun of his teachers. And he'd try to believe that hard work and good citizenship were what it took to get ahead in the world.

Most of all, he'd try to forget that powerful men carried dark secrets, that they could be hypocritical perverts and that there was nothing you could do about it. He'd try to forget how he'd screamed like a girl when Captain Lennox shot Jake in the back. The official story said it was an accident. He'd try to believe that what he'd seen with his own eyes wasn't true.

Officer Jake Stirling, while rushing to save two unidentified minors, had been caught in the crossfire between his captain and the crooks. That was the story that appeared in the papers. The captain had expressed his remorse. He'd raised money to pay off Jake's bills. Maybe it was for the best, to forget all the bad things and push them away. Their father had done something terrible once. Something that made him commit suicide. Danny had been Lucy's age then, unaware of the falseness and corruption adults carry with them each day. Their father had deserted them. Disappeared into thin air. John Stirling was officially dead now. Grace Stirling had filed the paperwork. She'd signed and sealed his disposal, burying her husband in the hall of records. She was dating George Hartwell. People said the two of them were well matched.

A car rumbled down the road from above, rousing Danny from his thoughts. The driver turned onto Nautilus Street, tapped his brakes, and pulled over to the sidewalk. He opened the front door, stepped out, and looked back up at Danny.

"Hey, kid," he said. "What're you doing there?"

"Nothing," said Danny.

"What's that thing under your foot?"

"This?" Danny said. "I call it a roller board."

"You're not thinking of going down this hill on it, are you?"

"Down there?" Danny scoffed. "That would be crazy."

"I almost killed a kid, maybe a month ago, when I was driving up this hill. He was riding one of those things. Was that you?"

Danny shrugged. "No. Like I said. That would be crazy."

"Yeah. I woulda' had to scrape his nuts off my window if I'd hit him."

Danny didn't respond. The man looked him over, then shook his head.

"Crazy kid," he said. "I hope he made it."

The man climbed back into his car and set off. Danny waited until the car had passed out of sight, then placed his roller board on the asphalt surface and pointed it down the hill. He seated himself as far back on the board as he could, bracing himself with both feet on the street. He adjusted his position, lined up the angle and pulled his feet onto the front of the board. He lifted his hands off the asphalt and the sled started to roll, picking up speed.

37

J ake sat in a wheelchair in the garden at Scripps Hospital, absorbing the rays of the afternoon sun. He wriggled his fingers. He could move both his arms now. The doctors said his progress was encouraging. They'd prescribed sunlight and fresh air as additional therapy. The nurse who'd brought him down had excused herself to attend to another patient, but she'd be back before long to wheel him back up to his room. There was no one else in the garden. He felt free, for the moment, untethered from the hospital's medical apparatus and oversight.

He'd be leaving tomorrow, going home to recuperate with his family. There'd be no doctors or nurses there, only his mother and Danny and Lucy. They'd have to wheel him around, get him in and out of the chair, change his clothes and help him go to the bathroom. He reached into his robe pocket and pulled out the envelope his mother had left him, the card from Danny. He still hadn't opened it. If he and Danny were going to live in the same house, they'd have to make some kind of peace. They'd both have to listen to what the other one wanted to say. He slid his finger under the seal and tore open the flap.

"There you are," said a voice from the doorway. Jake jammed the envelope back into his robe pocket. Millie walked up beside him, leaned down and kissed him on the forehead. She smelled of honeysuckle and malted waffles. Another fragrance, more florid, tickled his nostrils as well.

"I brought a friend of yours," Millie said.

Miss Gabor appeared on the other side of Jake. She was dressed plainly, in a white blouse, tan skirt and delicate pearl earrings.

"Hello dahling," she said.

Jake stared at Miss Gabor for a moment, then swiveled back to Millie. He didn't know what to say.

"She came by the diner," said Millie. "She wanted to see you. I hope it's okay."

"I don't ..." Jake began, then nodded, acquiescing. "Sit, please."

The two women seated themselves at the table. Miss Gabor seemed less formidable than usual, almost demure, as if she'd cast off her show business airs.

"I'm headed back to Los Angeles," she said. "With Desi and Lucy."

She paused for a moment and played with the rings on her fingers.

"Artie left town. Vamoosed without paying the hotel bill. Mr. Richardson was kind enough to take care of it for me."

"Artie's a rat," Millie said.

"Yes," said Miss Gabor. "I never thought it would turn out like this. Something scared him. I didn't really understand until they returned the train case."

"They gave the case back to you?" Jake said.

"What was left of it." Miss Gabor nodded. "Someone had torn out the bottom and slashed the inside. I think they were looking for something."

Jake closed his eyes. He remembered opening the train case in the bunker before the goons had arrived with Willie and Danny. The case had been empty but unblemished. The damage must have come afterwards, after the FBI got a hold of it.

"Who returned the case to you?" he asked.

"Mr. Tolson. Compliments of the director. That's what he said. Artie answered the door. I've never seen a person look so ... bereft. As if he'd lost all hope. Artie, I mean. After he looked in the case."

"Did he say anything?"

"That it was his meal ticket. That's what Artie said. 'That was my fucking meal ticket.' Pardon my French. Those were his words."

Jake stared at his hands. He wiggled his fingers. The doctors had told him to wiggle his hands whenever he could. Artie Corcoran's meal ticket had been three other people's death warrant. Todd and Lola and the gambling house boss. Five deaths if you included the thugs. Jake had recovered Miss Gabor's necklace the night before Todd met with the gambling boss. If Todd was fencing stolen property, it had to be something else he'd found in the case, something of value to gangsters and G-men and spies. He gave a short laugh.

The two women looked at him like he was crazy. It was the world that was crazy, he thought. The world around him had gone completely insane.

"Miss Gabor," he said. "Are you a Russian spy?"

"Jake!" exclaimed Millie. She looked ready to brain him. Miss Gabor answered the question serenely and plainly, without the exotic embellishments of their earlier conversations.

"A spy? Who's been telling you that? My sisters, my mother and I came to this country during the war. We escaped Hungary while it was under the Nazis. Now it's under the Soviet thumb. I won't go back there. I'm an American now, through and through. This country gave us a new life. It gave us freedom. I'm an actress, not a spy. I detest communism just as much as J. Edgar Hoover."

Jake thought about the director's accusations, the crude remarks Hoover had made about Miss Gabor and her friends. He remembered the photograph Willie Denton had found.

"Has someone tried to blackmail you?" he said.

"With what?"

"Nicky Hilton had ... an intimate photo of you."

Miss Gabor rolled her eyes. "Oh god," she said. "Is he still passing that around? Half of Hollywood's seen that photo by now. The male half, at least. I don't care anymore. I probably got cast in a couple of movies because of it. Men are all wolves at heart."

"Not all of them," Millie said. She reached over and grabbed Jake's hand. "Some are teddy bears."

Jake wasn't sure he liked being called a teddy bear, at least not in company, but he liked the touch of Millie's hand on his. It gave him hope. A reason to move forward.

"Did Mr. Corcoran hit you?" he said.

Miss Gabor fidgeted with her rings again. "Yes," she said. "Artie was angry. He blamed me for losing the train case."

"It wasn't your fault it was stolen."

"Men like that don't need excuses," Millie said.

"Perhaps," said Miss Gabor. "I'd never seen that side of Artie before. It was my fault, in a way. I suspected the chauffeur, right from the start."

"Todd?"

Miss Gabor sighed. "Yes. Todd. You remember how Nicky tried to take the necklace away from me and Todd intervened? That's how it started. Afterwards, on the way home, in the car, I explained the whole situation to him, to Todd. I was still very upset. I said I'd be better off without the damn thing, that it had been nothing but a collar around my neck since the day Nicky gave it to me. The chauffeur, Todd, asked me if I had the necklace insured, which I had. He said he could take care of it, if I was interested."

"Were you?"

"I didn't say yes. But I didn't say no. I was angry. I wasn't thinking clearly. That young man was so considerate and obliging. A gentleman. It was his idea to escort me back to my room, to make sure I was safe. He offered to drive my friends and me to the races the next day in Mr. Richardson's limousine. When I got back from the races and found the case missing, I knew what had happened. I knew it was him."

"Did you ask him to steal the necklace? Did you give him permission?"

"No, but ... I can see now how he might have misinterpreted my response."

"Why didn't you tell me this earlier?" Jake said.

Miss Gabor shrugged. "He'd done me a favor, really. I'd get the insurance money. Diamonds are sweet, but money is meat, as my mother used to say. I had no idea there'd be such a hullabaloo. Artie didn't want me to tell anyone. He said he'd take care of things. But I had to call the police, you see. The insurance people always need to see a police report. I was still angry with Nicky for attacking me in public and causing a scene. That's why I fingered him."

Jake weighed Miss Gabor's confession. It didn't really change anything. He'd suspected Todd since the day Willie Denton had told him about seeing Todd in Miss Gabor's room. Lola had seen Todd in the back room with her boss, a known fence. Todd must have found something else in the train case, something else he'd been trying to sell. It explained a lot, but it didn't explain why so many people were dead. It didn't explain the Webley revolver either, how it had made its way from the evidence room downtown to the floor of Sid Richardson's limousine.

"What else was in the train case?" he asked.

"I have no idea," she said. "Artie wouldn't tell me."

They were silent a moment. Miss Gabor might be guilty of withholding information, but Todd had taken the case without her explicit consent. That was on him. Miss Gabor's confession cleared up some details, but it didn't explain everything. Jake might have been knocked off the board, but he had a feeling the game wasn't over.

"I saw Mr. Corcoran talking to some gangsters," he said. "Meyer Lansky and Carlos Marcello. At the Jacaranda Room. One of their goons surrendered his seat to Mr. Corcoran."

"Oh yes," said Gabor. "I remember. The goon, as you call him, came over and sat with me."

"Did he say anything to you?"

Miss Gabor shook her head. "He wasn't much of a conversationalist. He just stared at my chest."

"Did Mr. Corcoran say anything to you, after he came back to the table? Did he say what they talked about?"

"No. I never asked about Artie's business."

"Did you know those men were gangsters?"

"Well, I knew they weren't Boy Scouts. Artie did business with lots of people, including some disreputable types. I think this whole trip was just business for him. It certainly wasn't about us. I thought perhaps he was getting serious when he invited me to come down here. But it was business, through and through, right from the start. I was window dressing, a distraction, a boutonnière on his lapel. He met with all sorts of people at the hotel. It was almost as if he'd planned the whole thing. I think they ... oh, I don't know."

The nurse reappeared, determined to take Jake back up to his room. She undid the brake and pulled Jake away from the table. The two women rose from their chairs.

"Wait," Jake said, raising his hand. The nurse paused.

"What were you going to say Miss Gabor?" he asked.

"I don't really know anything," she said, clearing her throat. "It's just a feeling I got. A woman's intuition."

"What was it?"

Miss Gabor shrugged. "I think those men were all bidding on something."

"Thank you." Jake nodded. "And thank you for coming to see me."

"No, dahling," said Miss Gabor reclaiming her actress voice. "It's I who should thank you. I'll never forget what a brave young policeman from La Jolla once tried to do for me."

Her jewelry clinked as she leaned down and kissed him on the forehead, the florid scent of her perfume filling Jake's nostrils. Gabor stood up and looked over at Millie.

"You take care of this young man, my dear. He's special."

Mille leaned down and kissed Jake as well, on the lips. She lingered there a moment, their faces close, their breath intermingling. It wasn't a goodbye kiss Millie had given him. It was a promise.

"Your mom asked me to dinner tomorrow, after you get home," she whispered. "Do you want me there?"

Jake nodded. He wanted it more than anything. Millie rose, wiped her eyes, and glanced at Miss Gabor.

"We'd better get going," she said. Miss Gabor nodded. The two women left. The nurse took Jake up the elevator and got him settled in bed again. One more day.

After the nurse had gone, he remembered the card in his robe pocket. Danny's card. He retrieved the envelope, opened it, and pulled out the piece of paper inside. It wasn't the get-well card he'd expected. It wasn't a hollow apology note from his brother, either.

It was a thirty-year-old arrest report from the New Orleans Police Department. The police had arrested a man for moral indecency and soliciting a minor. Jake read the name, then read it again. John E. Hoover. He remembered Chandler's tawdry assertions about the FBI director. Was this the proof? Was this what Artie Corcoran had been selling—a powerful man's reputation, a secret so damning its exposure would ruin the man's career and rattle the halls of the White House and Congress?

Corcoran had put his "meal ticket" up for bid, pitting Hoover against the mobsters to drive up the price. But the plan had gone sideways when Todd DuBarry stole the train case. That was why five people had died. Jake put the report back in the envelope, the envelope back in his pocket. He stared at the sunlight streaking in through the window. The world was corruption and the light, at this angle, illuminated the dust and the grime that floated in the invisible air.

38

Jake sat at the dining table in his parents' house, eyeing the stacks of cardboard boxes that filled the room. It was his house now. And Millie's. They'd been married for a month, but she'd only moved in yesterday. His mother had left them a hamburger casserole to celebrate the occasion, along with a bottle of champagne. The champagne had been Mr. Hartwell's idea. Jake had allowed himself one glass to please Millie. To celebrate.

Mrs. Denton had dropped by earlier in the morning with the chocolate cake she'd been threatening to bake for him all summer. She'd offered to come by again and help clean, because Millie still had to work at the diner and Jake had saved Willie from gangsters. Everyone in town treated Jake like a hero. He had a medal to prove it. He didn't feel like a hero though, sitting by himself at the dining room table. He felt defeated by the cardboard boxes crammed in around him. The house felt haunted without anyone there.

His mother had given them her old dining room furniture, the last vestige of Jake's childhood still in the house, stained and scratched with half-remembered clues to its history. Everything else had been thrown away or packed up and transported to Mr. Hartwell's new house on the other side of Mount Soledad. Their lives had transitioned swiftly and with little ceremony, as if each couple felt they had no time to waste. Jake and Millie would begin their marriage on the frame of his parents' old one. They'd buy new furniture and apply a fresh coat of paint to the place. Perhaps that would chase away the lingering ghosts.

One of those apparitions sat on the dining room table directly in front of him—his father's duplicate case notebook. Jake had started unpacking things this morning after Millie left for work, hoping to make himself useful, when he'd come across the notebook in one of the boxes packed up from his old apartment. He hadn't looked at the notebook since before he'd been shot. It lay open on the dining room table, displaying the pages where John Stirling had drawn a rectangular chart, a timeline of break-ins and reports related to the *Creeper* case. Jake stared at the initials in the margins, raking his memory. Something impossible had happened since the last time he'd looked at the chart.

The initials in the margins had changed.

The TDs were still there, but the letters O-W-L now read O-W-E, like the official notes he'd found in the *Creeper* case files at the evidence room. He felt sure his father's private notebook used to have O-W-L written in the margins, not O-W-E. Unless it was the notebook down at the evidence room that said O-W-L. He searched his memory, baffled and confused. The gun battle, the bullet in his back, the doctors and drugs had weakened his powers of recall. His mind felt clearer now than it had in a month, but sometimes he'd fall into a stupor, only to wake up and find Millie's worried face looking at him, asking if he was feeling okay. Millie was patient and generous, but Jake feared she'd grow tired of his awkward moodiness, exasperated by his ongoing absentmindedness. He'd lost focus. He wasn't himself.

O-W-L. He was sure it had been written that way. The letters in the two notebooks had been different but now they matched. O-W-E. The doorbell rang.

"It's open," he called. The door was unlocked during the day. There were deliveries coming, furniture and wedding gifts. Family and friends who'd check in. Jake didn't want to push himself to the door every time someone showed up. The bell rang again.

"It's open." Jake swiveled his wheelchair and raised his voice. "Come in."

The door opened. Captain Lennox entered the foyer.

"Over here, captain," Jake said. Lennox advanced across the floor, doffed his hat.

"I'm on my way to the station," he said. "Thought I'd stop by and see how you were getting along."

"Still unpacking," Jake said, waving his hand at the boxes.

"Yeah, I can see."

"You want some coffee?" Jake said. "Millie put some in a thermos for me."

"No thanks," said the captain. "I just had a meeting with Detective Hammond. It's good news. He says you're in the clear."

Jake felt a wave of relief roll over his body. The part of his body he could feel, anyway.

"What happened?" he said. "What changed his mind?"

"Your buddy, Mr. Chandler. Sounds like he came through for you."

"What do you mean?"

Captain Lennox leaned over the table. "What's that?" he said, indicating the notebook.

"It's my dad's old casebook. From the *Creeper* case. He kept a second one. Copied his notes to it every night. Just in case something happened to the original."

Lennox clucked. "I thought it looked like a casebook," he

said. "Your father was a hell of a detective. One of the best. You find anything interesting?"

"There used to be ..." Jake paused. It might be better if he kept some things to himself. He closed the notebook and pushed it away. "Never mind. It's nothing important. What happened with Mr. Chandler? What did he say?"

Lennox pulled a chair out from the table and took a seat. He stared at his hat while he spoke, turning it in his hands.

"Todd DuBarry stole Chandler's gun. We're sure of it now. Mac found the receipt slip, with Chandler's signature at the bottom. It was misfiled. Detective Hammond interviewed Mr. Chandler, showed him the receipt. That jogged his memory, I guess. Hammond asked Chandler about you, told him what kind of trouble you were in. The old man changed his story, said he was sober now, not drinking. He said he remembered leaving the gun in the back seat of that limo, claimed he was blotto at the time, forgot all about it."

"Well, that's a relief," Jake said, leaning back in his chair. Detective Hammond had connected Todd to the gun, providing corroboration for Lola's story. And that left Jake in the clear.

"Here's how I think it went down," said Captain Lennox. "Todd DuBarry made friends with that actress, Miss Gabor. Flirted and sweet-talked her into trusting him like he did with some of the local ladies. That's his M.O. Once he's on Miss Gabor's good side, he looks for a time when he knows she won't be around and makes off with the necklace."

"And the train case," Jake said. "He took the train case."

"Exactly," said Lennox. "Except he doesn't know about this other thing Corcoran had in the case, whatever it was that Director Hoover was looking for. Those goons went looking for it too. That's why they beat up Nicky Hilton. Todd hears about what happened to Hilton and figures he's next in line. He finds Chandler's gun in the back seat, decides to keep it for protection. He knows the necklace is hot, so he hides it in his mother's house, waiting for things to blow over. You with me so far?"

Jake nodded. It fit with Miss Gabor's confession, her suspicions about Todd.

"Okay," said the captain. "This is where you come in, Stirling. You hear about Todd from Willie Denton and follow a hunch about where Todd might have stashed the necklace at his mother's house. You find it. You confiscate it. Now Todd's in real trouble. Maybe he's got debts, maybe he owes money to the gambling house boss. The necklace was going to pay it all off, but now it's gone. In the meantime, he's found something else in the train case, figures it might be worth something, but he's not sure. He takes it in for appraisal, to see if the gambling boss will take it as payment. Something goes wrong and he ends up shooting the guy."

"What went wrong?" Jake said.

"Who knows?" said Lennox. "Maybe the guy threatened Todd. Demanded his money back. Maybe the stuff in the train case was too hot to handle. Maybe it looked like a set-up and the gambling boss told Todd to get the hell out. It doesn't matter. The girl saw Todd with the case and the gun, right?"

"Yes," Jake said. "That's what she told me."

"I think Todd killed her too."

"Why?"

"Had to. She was a witness."

"Todd wasn't like that. I mean, he might have shot the guy in the gambling house in self-defense, but I can't believe he'd kill that girl. Not like that. Not in cold blood."

"Unless she was shaking him down."

"Blackmailing him?"

"She was a hooker, son. Not Florence Nightingale."

Jake nodded. Lola had said she needed money. The captain had years of experience dealing with criminals both petty and bold.

"I think Todd reached the end of his rope," the captain said. "He knew he'd gone too far, even for him. His rich friends weren't going to save him this time. That's why he killed himself."

"I guess," Jake said.

"It's more than a guess, son. Detectives recovered slugs from each scene. They look like they're from that same gun. That Webley revolver."

Jake stared at a dark spot on the table, a stain that had been there for as long as he could remember. Lennox cleared his throat.

"Detective Hammond's on board with this story," he said. "The rest of the case will take care of itself."

The story made sense. Jake couldn't deny it. The dead had all played on the wrong side of the law—a hooker, a fence, and a gigolo thief. They'd gotten what was coming to them. That's how the justice system would see it. There'd be no arrests, no courtroom testimony, no cops on the stand, and no one going to jail. The case would be closed and forgotten. All the evidence, including Jake's notes, would go into manila envelopes stashed in file boxes placed on a shelf in the evidence room downtown.

"How about you?" asked the captain. "You got anything else you want to add to the story? Did you ever find out why everyone wanted that train case?"

Jake stared at the table a moment. Hoover's arrest report was stashed at the bottom of a shoebox along with the rest of his get-well cards from the hospital, a faint paper echo of Chandler's tawdry assertions. The slip of paper was powerful, like an atom bomb, and Jake knew he had to be cautious with it. Trust no one. That was the new game he'd learned to play.

"No sir," he said. "I have no idea."

Lennox nodded. "There's something else I wanted to ask you," he said. "How would you feel about taking over Mac's job?"

"What's Mac going to do?"

"He's getting promoted. To East County division."

"I'd be the new desk sergeant?"

"That's right. It's the one job I can think of where that wheelchair won't be a problem. You can stay in La Jolla. And you'd be working for me. Not much of a change, really."

Jake looked around the room, at the bare walls. Millie's salary and tips would keep food on the table but not much else. Mr. Hartwell had promised Grace that he'd help the new bride and her crippled husband if they needed it, but Jake didn't want his stepfather's charity. Desk sergeant wasn't the kind of job he'd imagined for himself back in the police academy, but he could still be a cop. He'd make a decent salary. Maybe enough that he and Millie could raise children. One kid, at least.

"Thank you, captain," he said. "I'd like to talk to Millie first."

"Of course," said Lennox. "Run it by the old ball and chain."

Jake scowled. He'd never think of Millie that way. Their marriage wasn't a prison. It was a release, a liberation from the past. He'd never behave like his father, withdrawing from his marriage bonds a little bit at a time until even his physical body had disappeared. Jake would take care of Millie and their kids. If they were able to have children. Nothing would get in their way.

Captain Lennox rose from the table, placed his hat back on his head. "I'm just glad Hammond got that statement from Chandler before he left town. That was lucky for you."

"What's that?"

"Chandler moved back to England."

"Again?"

The captain shrugged. "He's one of those restless types, I guess. Never happy. Can't make up his mind about anything. He's a drunk."

"He's lonely, I think," Jake said. "He's a writer."

"To drink or not to drink, that is the question." Lennox smiled. "Didn't some writer say that?"

"Not exactly," Jake said. He hadn't paid much attention in his high school English classes, but he remembered that line from Shakespeare. The teacher, Mr. Crosby, had read the whole speech out loud in class one day. The words stuck in Jake's head. *To be or not to be.* Later he'd imagined his father asking himself that question over and over again, then answering it by drowning himself in the ocean. Choosing not to be.

"You think Mr. Chandler was telling the truth?" he asked. "About leaving the gun in the limousine?"

Captain Lennox cleared his throat. "Let's put it this way," he said. "I think Mr. Chandler owes you for saving his life."

"I suppose," Jake replied.

"Todd DuBarry's dead and gone, Jake. He won't be missed."

"Except by his mother."

"Well, sure. The parents. But they weren't close, at least from what I heard. I don't think TD had any real friends."

"Except me," Jake said, feeling another weight on his conscience. "He trusted me. He tried to give me that train case."

"I'd sure like to know what was in that damn thing," said the captain, still nudging, angling for a confession or clue.

"Me too," Jake said, refusing the bait.

"Well then, Officer Jake Stirling," the captain said, pulling up anchor. "Let me know if you want to be Desk Sergeant Stirling. I can't leave the position vacant for long."

"Thanks, captain," Jake said. "I'll talk it over with Millie tonight."

Captain Lennox turned on his heel and left. Jake settled his gaze on his father's notebook and thought about the initials written inside. O-W-E. Maybe the O stood for Officer. Officer Jake Stirling would be OJS. Jake didn't know any patrolmen whose name started with W and E. Not off the top of his head. He'd check the rosters when he got back to work. The original marks hadn't been O-W-E, though. They'd been O-W-L. And the officers on patrol would have been different back when John Stirling scratched out the initials in the notebook's margins.

Look for the guy who tells you a story. That's what Mr. Chandler had said. The words bounced around in Jake's head and dragged his thoughts into dark waters, like Lucy's movie octopus reaching its tentacles into his brain. Most of the patrolmen from his father's time on the force would have moved on to other assignments by now, cross-promoted to other districts or up the ladder of command. Captain Lennox had been one of those patrolmen. Officer Wade Lennox. O-W-L. Chandler's assertion rose to the surface again.

Look for the guy who tells you a story, who explains everything and wraps it up with a bow. That's the guy you need to watch out for.

The captain's story had been perfect. Wrapped up with a bow. The previous chess game may have ended, but another one had begun, a game Jake's father had played; a dangerous contest John Stirling forfeited in death. Lennox and the *Creeper* were connected somehow. Jake would need to dig deep into his father's notes, uncover evidence and check every angle before he made his next move. He'd be careful, discreet. This time he knew who his opponent would be.

39

Jake jolted in his wheelchair seat as Max Miller pushed him across the lawn at Mount Hope Cemetery, a mile east of downtown San Diego. They headed towards the burial party that had gathered around an open grave.

"I thought there'd be more people here," Jake said. "Wasn't he famous?"

"Ray didn't make a lot of friends," Miller said, as he pushed Jake's chair toward the funeral gathering. "He didn't have much else in his life, not to speak of anyway, not after Cissy was gone."

"I never read any of his books. I guess I should."

"He didn't sell that many, you know. Not like Erle Gardner."

"Who's that?"

"Perry Mason."

"Oh yeah," Jake said. "Millie and I watch that show on the TV. It's pretty good, except the police always get things wrong. I didn't know there were books."

"Isn't that our new chief of police over there?" Miller asked as they continued down towards the funeral party. Jake looked over at the crowd, felt a stony shadow pass over his heart.

"Yeah, that's him," he muttered. Officer Wade Lennox had come a long way since he'd started out on the La Jolla beat, from patrol cop to sergeant to captain to precinct chief in only five years, appointed by the mayor two months ago to be interim chief of police. It was Lennox who'd made the arrest in the *Creeper* case, who'd detained Todd DuBarry late that fateful night more than five years ago, the only patrolman on duty each night the *Creeper* had struck, the remarkable coincidence of it charted out in John Stirling's private notebook.

Jake knew more now than he had two years ago, but he had no real evidence to support his suspicions, nothing that detectives at Internal Affairs would take seriously, not enough to convince them to reopen the *Creeper* case, let alone support an investigation of their new chief. He'd learned some things from the old duty logs and reports, but the overall picture was still opaque, out of focus. An essential piece of information seemed to be missing. He didn't know where he would find it, where to look next.

Chief Lennox spotted Jake and Mr. Miller and walked over to greet them. Mr. Miller halted the wheelchair. The chief extended his hand.

"Good to see you again, Sergeant Stirling," he said. "Mr. Miller."

"You too, chief," Jake said, shaking hands. It was part of the game.

"How's everything at my old substation?" asked Lennox.

"About the same."

"All quiet on the western front?"

"Yes, sir."

"And the wife? Any ankle biters yet?"

"One on the way, sir."

"Congratulations, Stirling. Glad to hear it."

The minister who stood by the grave raised his hand and cleared his throat.

"I think they're getting started," said Miller. They rejoined the group. Miller angled Jake's wheelchair into a spot at the end of the front row, giving them a view of the mourners as well as the minister. Jake spotted Mabel Denton in the group, and Mr. Morgan, the newspaper reporter. He didn't recognize anyone else.

The minister intoned his opening prayer and Jake's thoughts drifted back to the night he'd found Mr. Chandler in the bathtub, cradling his old service revolver. Something had changed in his life that night. Some indefinable line had been crossed. His good deed had led to a wreckage of dreams.

Mr. Chandler was dead. Jake and Millie were going to have a baby, though his mother had beaten them to it. To their own middle-aged surprise, Grace and Mr. Hartwell had managed to bring a baby girl into the world the previous year. Lucy had the sister she'd always wanted, though the difference in years wouldn't allow much time together before Lucy moved out on her own. She'd be a teenager this year.

Danny was gone. No one knew where. He'd enrolled at the state college after high school but dropped out three weeks into his first semester. He called home to ask for money a couple of times early on and sent Lucy a postcard once a month. He claimed to be living on the road, picking up work where he could and writing the great American novel. He never left a phone number or an address. Danny's friends from high school, Rachel and Willie, had gone off to college, Willie to art school in L.A. and Rachel to UC Berkeley. Jake assumed Danny had lost touch with them. People changed after high school, usually for the better. In Danny's case, it was hard to say.

In truth, Jake didn't think much about his brother anymore. He had a wife now, and soon a new baby to keep him occupied. He had a job, forty hours a week behind the desk at the La Jolla police station. He was getting physical therapy twice a week and the doctors said he might still climb out of his wheelchair. He hoped to get back on the beat someday, become a real policeman again. Being a desk sergeant was dull business, but it paid well enough that Millie had left waitressing three months ago when her pregnancy started to show.

The minister finished his brief eulogy. The casket was lowered into the ground. Mrs. Denton dabbed at her eyes with a handkerchief, but the rest of the group were dry-eyed and stoic. The casket settled into the grave. Two women stepped forward and dropped roses into the trench. The mourners began to disperse. A man broke off from the group and approached Mr. Miller. It was the newspaperman, Mr. Morgan, the youngest of the four writers Jake had met at the Whaling Bar that fateful summer two years ago.

Miller and Morgan greeted each other warmly then moved away to discuss some business between them. Chief Lennox walked over to Jake. He had something tucked in his armpit that Jake hadn't noticed before, a cloth bag. Lennox pulled the bag from under his arm and placed it on Jake's lap.

"What's this?" asked Jake.

"Something I pulled from the evidence room. Have a look."

Jake opened the bag. There was a gun inside, an old revolver.

"I saw in the paper about Mr. Chandler," Lennox said. "He asked you to return it to him, didn't he? I thought you'd want to honor the man's request. RTO it for good."

"I don't think I should do that, sir," Jake said. "I'd be tampering with evidence."

"Don't play Boy Scout with me, Stirling. Those cases are officially closed. It's time to move on. We know what happened."

Jake stared at the gun in his lap, remembering all the trouble it had brought him, the death it had dealt, changing men from a light to a lump with a squeeze of the trigger. That's how Chandler had described killing German soldiers in the first war. Some guns never got fired in anger or fear, never killed anyone, but this gun had done more than its share. It had killed Todd DuBarry. And Lola. The gambling boss. It had almost killed Mr. Chandler. The gun might be old and falling apart, but it was still evil, a wickedness that couldn't be buried, forgotten. Any practical evidence the gun might provide had long since been wiped clean. He lifted the bag from his lap, held it out for the chief.

"I don't think Mr. Chandler would want me to, sir."

"Chandler's dead, son. He was a drunk."

"He was my friend."

Lennox glared at Jake the way he used to, giving him the Wade eye. Jake glowered back, resolute. The left side of Lennox's mouth twitched. He stepped forward, grabbed the bag, tossed it into the burial pit then turned back to Jake.

"Don't forget who your real friends are, Sergeant Stirling," he said, fixing his eyes on something above and behind Jake. "I'm the chief of police. I can do things for you. You understand that don't you? I can do anything."

Jake didn't respond. Lennox walked past him. Jake stared at the dark hole that held Chandler's casket. His face felt flushed and hot. He turned his wheelchair away from the tomb and back toward the living. Chief Lennox had joined Mr. Morgan and Mr. Miller in conversation. A car pulled up in the distance behind Mr. Miller's wood-paneled Chrysler.

Mabel Denton stepped in front of him, blocking his view. "Hello, Jake," she said. "I hoped you'd be here. Mr. Chandler asked me to give you this."

She held out a book. Jake took it, looked at the cover. It was new, with a solid black dust jacket and *Playback* printed in red letters at the top. *Raymond Chandler* in white below. The back cover had a full-sized photographic portrait of Chandler, looking more sober than Jake remembered him—an old man, thin lipped, with the same bowtie and black-framed glasses he often wore. A pinprick of light needled out from Chandler's left eye like a last burning ember of contempt.

"He signed a copy for me too," Mabel said. "It takes place in La Jolla."

"Excuse me?" Jake said, trying to look past her to see who'd climbed out of the car.

"His other books are set in Los Angeles," Mabel said. "This one's in La Jolla. He calls it Esmeralda. He wrote something inside. Something for you."

Jake's eyes returned to the book. He opened the cover, found a note inscribed on the title page.

"To Sergeant Jake Stirling," he said, reading the inscription. "The man who took a bullet for fair Esmeralda and got this damned scribbler to put an honest cop in one of his books. Yours truly, Raymond Chandler."

"He liked you, Jake," Mabel said. "He was really upset when he read in the papers about what happened, after you got shot. I told him you saved Willie. He said you got in over your head."

"Yeah," Jake said. "He warned me. He was right."

The meeting of Miller, Morgan and Chief Lennox broke up. Morgan and Lennox headed back to their cars. Miller headed for Jake. His countenance looked pale, graver than the one he'd put on for the funeral. Something had happened. Something serious.

"What's going on?" Jake asked when Miller arrived. Miller avoided his question and turned to Mrs. Denton. A man climbed out of the car in the distance.

"It's so sad about Mr. Chandler," said Mrs. Denton.

"Yes. I think Ray was ready, though," said Miller. "Don't you?"

"I wish he could've been buried with Mrs. Chandler."

"Yeah. Me too. I don't know what happened there. Religion, I guess."

"They'll be together now. In heaven."

"I'm sure Cissy made it. I'm not sure about Ray."

"You're terrible, Mr. Miller."

"I know. How's Willie doing?"

"Just fine. He's got an internship. Drawing cartoons for some TV people."

Miller laughed. "Good for him. There's plenty of jobs in TV. They pay well too, better than the book trade, anyway. Jake, you ready to leave?"

Jake nodded. They said goodbye to Mrs. Denton. Mr. Miller stepped in behind Jake and took control of the chair.

"What's going on?" Jake asked. "What were you talking about to Captain Lennox?"

"Something's come up," Miller said, pushing Jake across the lawn. "I'll explain when we get to the car. I see you've got a copy of Ray's last book there."

"He wrote something in it for me," Jake said, watching the man on the road.

"Well, how 'bout that? I guess you'll finally have to read one of his books."

"I guess so."

"It's not his best," said Miller.

"You've read it?"

"Sure. There's a police officer in it who reminds me of you."

They arrived at the road. Mr. Miller halted the wheelchair.

"What are you doing here?" Jake asked the man standing beside Miller's car.

"Good to see you too, brother," Danny replied. He was wearing a white T-shirt, blue jeans, and a leather jacket. He looked like he hadn't had a haircut in months. His eyes were dark and direct, more self-assured. His body looked taut and muscular. Jake's little brother wasn't a kid anymore.

"I'm sorry," Jake said, realizing he'd sounded angry. He was glad to see his brother, but he wasn't ready to trust him. "When did you get home?"

"Last night. I decided to come home for a visit. I promised Mom that I'd find you this morning. I can take him from here, Mr. Miller."

"Sure," Miller said. Some sort of silent communication passed between Miller and Danny, a look in their eyes.

"What's going on?" Jake asked, frustrated by the men's elusiveness.

"Your mother's down at the morgue, Jake," said Miller. "You need to go to her."

A surge of panic unzipped Jake from his neck to his waist. "Did something happen to Mr. Hartwell?" he said. "Did something happen to Millie? To Lucy?"

"Lucy's fine," Danny said. "They're all fine."

"Morgan just told me, Jake," Miller said, taking over. "They found a body. A man's body. Up on the mesa. Near Camp Matthews. They were breaking ground for the new university. Early this morning. The body had been there a while."

"Millie told me you were here," Danny said. "Mom asked me to come get you. We need to be there with her. It's …"

Danny paused. Something inside of him broke and his eyes swelled with tears. Jake knew why his mother had asked Danny to find him. It was there in Danny's voice, in his eyes. The story they'd told themselves for the last five years was a lie.

"The body they found," Danny said, his voice breaking. "They think it's our father. Detective John Stirling. Dad didn't drown himself."

"He didn't abandon us, Danny, not like they told us he did," Jake said. "He never wanted to leave."

He lifted one arm and beckoned. Danny leaned in. They embraced and clung to each other like brothers should. Jake whispered in his brother's ear. "Dad loved us. We both knew it, somewhere inside."

They broke their embrace. Danny wheeled Jake down to his car and Jake arranged himself in the passenger seat while Danny packed the chair in the trunk. A black and white police cruiser pulled up beside them. Chief Lennox stared through the open window at Jake. The look on his face was disdainful, almost a sneer. Pain slashed through Jake's body, as if the bullet buried inside him had new velocity. The bullet Lennox had put there. The chief drove off. Danny climbed into the driver's seat and looked over at Jake.

"What is it?" he asked. Jake felt steel forming inside him.

"We're going to find out what happened, Danny," he said. "Wherever it leads. You and me."

Danny nodded and started the engine.

"I'm with you, brother," he said. "Wherever it leads."

HISTORICAL NOTES

The events depicted in this book are strictly fictional, a speculative work that imagines the interactions between some of the historical figures who passed through or lived in La Jolla, CA during the 1950s. Here's a brief guide:

Raymond Chandler (1888 – 1959) was a famed American-British crime novelist and screen writer. He had an immense influence on American literature and his novels, including *Farewell, My Lovely* and *The Long Goodbye* redefined private eye fiction.

Max Miller (1899-1967) was a reporter for the San Diego Sun. His collection of short vignettes, *I Cover the Waterfront*, became a nationwide best-seller in 1932, inspiring a Hollywood film and hit song of the same name.

Zsa Zsa Gabor (1917-2016) was a Hungarian-American film actress and celebrity, best known for her many marriages and extravagant lifestyle.

J. Edgar Hoover (1895-1972) was the first, and longest-tenured, director of the Federal Bureau of Investigation. His success in bringing Depression-era gangsters such as John Dillinger to justice was overshadowed by his later reticence to pursue organized crime figures as well as his persecution of US citizens for their sexuality and political beliefs. Based on his longtime personal relationship with the FBI's associate director, **Clyde Tolson** (1900-1975), many believe Hoover was a closeted homosexual.

Roger Revelle (1909-1991) is considered by many as the father of modern climate science. A National Medal of Science award winner he was instrumental in establishing the Scripps Institution of Oceanography and the University of California, San Diego.

Clint Murchison (1895-1969) was one of the richest men in the USA, with an estate estimated at $500 million dollars at the time of his death. **Sid Richardson** (1891-1959), his partner in the Del Charro Hotel also made his fortune in the oil business and became a leading philanthropist in the Dallas/Ft Worth area. Both men were early supporters of Dwight Eisenhower's presidential campaign. Murchison was married twice. Richardson never married.

Nicky Hilton (1926-1969) was the playboy son of hotel magnate Conrad Hilton and married briefly to Elizabeth Taylor. His stepmother, Zsa Zsa Gabor, later claimed to have had an affair with him while she was married to his father.

Ted Geisel (1904-1991) is better known as Dr. Seuss, the world-renowned author of many of the most popular children's books of all time, including *The Cat in the Hat, How the Grinch Stole Christmas* and *The Lorax*.

Meyer Lansky (1902-1983) was a Russian American gangster known as the "Mob's Accountant". He developed a gambling empire that stretched from London to Las Vegas to Cuba. **Carlos Marcello** (1910-1993) was an Italian American crime boss based in New Orleans. Some have claimed Marcello was a co-conspirator in the assassination of U.S. President John F. Kennedy.

Lee Marvin (1924-1987) was an Academy-award winning American film star, best known for his roles in *The Dirty Dozen*, *Point Blank* and *Cat Ballou*. He appeared in the 1956 summer stock production of *Bus Stop* at the La Jolla Playhouse, along-side Hollywood character actors **Fred Clark** & **Benay Venuta**.

Neil Morgan (1925-2014) was a reporter, columnist and editor at the San Diego Union-Tribune and a long-time civic activist in San Diego. He co-wrote (with his wife **Judith Morgan**) *Dr. Seuss and Mr. Geisel: A Biography*.

Lucille Ball and **Desi Arnaz** produced and starred in one of the most popular television series of the 1950s, *I Love Lucy*. They founded and co-owned *Desilu* productions, one of the largest independent television production companies of its time.

Allan Witwer (dates unknown) was a hotel and restaurant manager, which included his time in charge of the Del Charro Hotel.

Artie Corcoran is a fictional character who combines two historical figures—**Arthur Samish** (1897-1974), an influential lobbyist in the California legislature and **Jimmy Corcoran** (dates unknown), an FBI agent who claimed to have helped hush up sex charges against a youthful Hoover involving a young man in New Orleans. Corcoran died in a plane crash while traveling to a Caribbean island owned by Clint Murchison.

Evelyn Marechal and her husband, **James,** converted their La Jolla stables into the original Hotel Del Charro before selling it to Clint Murchison in 1951.

All the rest of the characters in *The Esmeralda Goodbye* are fictional.

ACKNOWLEDGMENTS

To Cornelia Feye at Konstellation Press for continuing to support my writing efforts. She is a pleasure to work with. To my editor Lisa Mathews for her detailed critiques and kind blessings. To my copyeditor Martin Roy Hill for curbing my comma abuse and making sure I got the gun stuff right.

Additional thanks to those who assisted in my research for this book—Edie and Milton Kodmur, Terrie Leigh Relf, Matt Coyle, my sisters Ann and Kate Colby, my brother Fred Colby, Dr. Herb McCoy, and especially to Dana Hicks, Deputy Director and Collections Manager at the La Jolla Historical Society for going through the archives and pulling files for me.

To my beta readers, who braved plot holes, lapses of logic and inconsistent characters to give me an early take on where this book was going and might go. Thanks for your feedback—Fred Andersen, Linda Castro, Ann Colby, Fred Colby, CY Davis, Tom Flowers, Barbara Haines, Judy Johnson, Tom Leach, Rena Lewis, Terrie Leigh-Relf, Tam Sesto, Penn Wallace, and Sandra Yeaman.

And to my wife, Maria, whose support and critical input makes every book better, before any of these other folks even get a look at it.

ABOUT THE AUTHOR

Corey Lynn Fayman was born in La Jolla, CA in the same hospital where Raymond Chandler died. He holds a B.A. in English, with a specialization in creative writing and poetry from UCLA, and an M.A. in Educational Technology from San Diego State University. His creative career includes work as a musician, songwriter, sound designer, educational technologist, multimedia developer and college professor. He is the author of six mystery novels, including the San Diego Book Awards Geisel award winner *Ballast Point Breakdown*.

"As an independently published author, I rely on the recommendations of enthusiastic readers to help spread the word. If you enjoyed this book, please consider posting a review on Amazon or Goodreads. A couple of sentences and a good rating are much appreciated!"

Sign up on my website or follow me on Facebook for news, giveaways and special offers.

Website: www.coreylynnfayman.com
Facebook: www.facebook.com/coreylynnfayman

Made in the USA
Coppell, TX
11 July 2024

34520188R00174